KILL ZONE

KILL ZONE

LOREN D. ESTLEMAN

THE MYSTERIOUS PRESS · NEW YORK

Book design by John W. White

Library of Congress Catalogue Number: 83-63041
    ISBN: 0-89296-065-5 Trade Edition

FIRST EDITION

To Leo and Sue Kuschel, who know why.

CHAPTER I

IN THE END THEY VOTED TO NAME THEM-
selves after the eight notes in the scale.

The decision capped four weeks of planning.
Early on, someone had suggested that they address one another
by code names to keep the pigs guessing about their identities;
just what those names should be had sparked as many arguments
and consumed as much time as anything else in their strategy.
One of the women pitched the months of the year and the signs of
the zodiac, but the others voted that down because it was trite and
left four names unused, which ran counter to their ideal of
precision in every detail. The days of the week were considered
and abandoned because there were only seven, and the gods of
Olympus and Asgard were dismissed because someone snickered
every time someone else was hailed as "Zeus" or "Balder."

After that it got to be a game, with the eight sitting around
whatever room they were meeting in that day, brainstorming
names as a way of winding down from more intense things like
stations and timing. Even when they weren't gathered, one of

1

them might call up another in the middle of the night and bark out his idea in place of "Hello," and the two who played handball could be overheard on the YMCA court grunting names of Walt Disney and Sesame Street characters between serves.

But as their deadline loomed and the minor point became one of the few still unresolved, then the last, then at last the jokes stopped. Two of the men almost came to blows when one called the other's idea "fucking stupid." They were restrained, but it had become obvious that the success of the entire undertaking was in danger for lack of popular aliases.

Appropriately, it was the key figure in their plan, the black musician who would later be called Mike, who supplied the solution. They were arguing after midnight in the rented house in Hamtramck where the thing had started, and Mike, sitting on one hip on the piano bench supporting his head in one hand, was plink-plunking on the keyboard with one finger of the other. The leader, a tall, ruddy blond with a sleekly drooping moustache— they would call him Don—swiveled his head and shouted at him to stop the racket. But he broke off in mid-shout, and as the others' voices died they heard Mike running up and down the scale over and over.

Don liked it because there was precision in music, because it went well with Siegfried, the name they had chosen for the group, and because the names of the notes adapted easily into common Christian names they could all remember. Whatever Don liked Larry liked, and because Larry liked it Doris liked it too, and with Mike they had a majority, since Sol never voted. The eight notes it would be.

Don had fought in the siege of Khe Sanh, been wounded twice, and recommended for a DSC, although the recommendation was withdrawn because of certain psychological data in his medical file that later led to his discharge. He had an X-shaped scar on his right cheek where a piece of shrapnel had been removed. It figured prominently under SCARS AND MARKS in his FBI file. He was 36, the oldest in the group.

Ray, 28, held a degree in demolitions from a small California trade college. A small, thin man with a sharp face and incurable acne, he had served fourteen months in San Quentin for manslaughter after a charge he had planted on location in Malibu went off prematurely, killing a fellow MGM special effects man.

Mike had played bass fiddle for the house orchestras of a number of hit television series until he was arrested for selling narcotics to an undercover police officer. At 30, this wide-set black man was supporting a $150-a-day heroin habit. He was here for the money.

Fay was 24, a native of Detroit who had kept her hair cropped close to her skull since her first battle with lice at the age of six. Her lover, a Black Panther chief later slain in an FBI raid on his Mt. Elliott Street safe house, had drilled her in the operation and maintenance of automatic weapons. She in turn served as instructor for the group. Don was the only white person she trusted. She felt no kinship with Mike, whom she accused of demeaning their race by performing for the hoojies, but at present he was her only covenient source of cocaine.

Sol killed for a living. Somewhere in his twenties, from somewhere back East, this slender man with a tight cap of platinum hair was an independent contract murderer, an expert with blade and gun whom Ray had met through a former fellow inmate from San Quentin. Of all of them, Sol alone was on salary. Don was paying him out of the proceeds of the fencing operation he ran out of his pawn shop on Gratiot.

Larry was there because he worshiped Don. He had been a small boy when his brother was killed in combat and Don sent Larry's family a letter reporting the circumstances, but Don had been a frequent visitor to their home since his return from Vietnam and was like an uncle. The group had been drilling weekends on a private island in Lake Superior belonging to Larry's parents, who were vacationing in Europe. He was 18, the youngest in the group. With his delicate features and black hair worn over his ears, he looked a little to Doris like Lord Byron.

Teddy was a captain in the Michigan National Guard. The crewcut 32-year-old, having blamed politics for denying him his last chance to make youngest major in the command, had forged requisitions to arm the group with M-16s, .45 caliber semiautomatic pistols, ammunition, and some gelatin explosives. The Guard had a warrant out for his arrest.

Doris at 19 was a few months older than Larry, but they had been living together in his family home in Grosse Pointe in his parents' absence. Although the fine-boned blonde also came from wealthy people, she dressed in sweatshirts and jeans and sandals and always looked as if she had just come in from the rain. She thought she was in love with Larry. Since Larry was close to Don, the others tolerated her, but Fay had given up on teaching her how to fire an M-16 and had settled for letting her just hold it.

"Do, re, mi, fa, sol, la, ti, do," sang Don, in one of his rare mischievous moods. "People come and people go."

They picked the second Friday in August. That was far enough into the season, yet far enough away from its close to insure against having too many people on their hands. Even then they waited to see what kind of night it would be, because too much moonlight made them targets from outside and not enough made for poor pickings. If it rained they would scrub the whole thing. It sprinkled that morning, but by the time the sun went down a moon worn a little on one edge showed behind racing clouds. The air was cool and still damp. They separated the pluses from the minuses and voted to go.

CHAPTER 2

THE LARGEST PASSENGER-CARRYING steamboat in the world rocked infinitesimally on the wrinkled surface of the Detroit River, its eighty-year-old hull pale in the lights from the dock. Excursion employees referred to it and its slightly smaller sister vessel as the "ice cream boats," and their triple-decked configuration and many coats of white paint trimmed in blue and red did invite comparison to the dishes banana splits were served in. The champing of the engine was a soft moist sound at this remove, exhaling invisible black oil-smoke into the night sky above the broad three-toned stack towering over the pilot house.

Captain Edward Macomb Fielding—"Cap'n Eddie" to the men who sailed under him—bounded down the gangplank sucking a cold pipe and drawing a black leather windbreaker on over his white uniform shirt. Coming on 65, with a hearing aid in the bow of his steel-rimmed eyeglasses, he walked with a forward list and a slight stoop that concealed his startling height of six-foot-five until he was standing next to someone of lesser stature and looking down on the top of his head. His sunburned flesh was cross-hatched all over and his neck and wrists looked frail, but his handshake was bone-crushing and when he smiled— a thing he rarely did—he showed a double row of tobacco-stained teeth that had obviously grown in his mouth. He was in his eighteenth year of command on the river. Before that he had skippered ore carriers from the Detroit docks to the Keweenau Peninsula and back for twelve years.

Two security men in white uniforms stood at the gate of the cyclone fence, halfheartedly scrutinizing the well-dressed crowd lining up on the other side. The guards were window-dressing, there mainly to discourage riffraff, which on the moonlight cruise meant men without neckties and women in slacks. They had no authority to conduct searches or make arrests even if there were incentive to smuggle contraband aboard. Unlike the daytime excursions, this one didn't dock at Boblo Island on the Canadian side, just steamed up and down the river for four hours and tied up back here.

Cap'n Eddie nodded to his first mate, Phil Holliday, lit his pipe, and the two stood surveying their prospective cargo. Once or twice the captain caught sight of a familiar face from a previous trip and tilted his head in greeting, touching two fingers to his visor. Other tour captains, he knew, preferred to remain aloof on the bridge like some exiled Ahab, but for all his stern looks Fielding enjoyed people and always liked to see what kind of passengers he was carrying this trip. No two loads were exactly the same.

"More youngsters than usual," he commented. "I wonder how many of them know the old steps."

Holliday grunted. He had freckles at 40 and a sandy handlebar moustache he fussed over for an hour each morning. "Gigolos mostly, judging by all the stags."

"Just so they don't start doing the Twist to 'In the Mood' or something like that."

The first mate smiled but said nothing. He had sailed with Cap'n Eddie four seasons and still was not always sure when the old man was joking.

Don saw the two sailors watching the crowd and turned his

head as if to cough, looking confidence back at Larry, fidgeting ten places behind with Doris on his arm. Larry was aware of the scrutiny. He hoped it wasn't that they'd been recognized. They had all made the trip before, usually during the daytime run when most of the personnel were different, never more than two to a cruise, and never the same person twice. But the two men in command of the vessel had no replacements and had seen them all before.

More than likely, though, their curiosity had to do with so many young faces among these mostly middle-aged revelers eagerly awaiting their chance to step out to their favorite tunes from the thirties and forties played by an old-time dance band. These sailors, Larry told himself, saw thousands of people every day. Don and Larry were just two more, even if Don was the only one with an X branding his cheek.

In fact, First Mate Holliday recognized the tall young blond man with the gunfighter's moustache and the strange scar, but thought little of his presence tonight. Many tourists and natives made the same trip several times during the season. Boblo was a local institution, there was nothing quite like it in the country.

It was a long line and getting longer. Despite the slack period before the Labor Day rush and the cool weather, there were going to be more people to have to keep an eye on than anyone in the group had hoped. They were strung out through the line, Fay alone because Mike was gone and an interracial couple drew more attention than an unescorted black woman. They were all dressed better than usual, in keeping with the restrictions for the moonlight cruise; even Doris had climbed out of her teenage chic and into a white summerweight dress with small black polka-dots, a light blue sweater buttoned at her throat and worn over her bare shoulders like a cape. Larry had on the gray tailormade suit his parents had given him when he graduated from high school. Fay was wearing a simple green frock and the rest of the men wore sportcoats and ties. Ray's coat was large for his slight frame, but there was a reason for that.

Mike missing was a good sign. That meant he had succeeded in boarding with the band as arranged. That was the pivot their plan swung on. Mike had been rehearsing with the band for a couple of days now. Don had told him he had found and bribed the regular bass player to walk while Mike took his place. In fact, the regular bass player was lying in the Wayne County Morgue with a bullet in his brain and his body burned beyond hope of identification. Sol was earning his salary.

On board, Mike, broad as a barn in the band's uniform of scarlet blazer and white slacks, took his time selecting a cigarette from his pack and hunting up a match to cover the delay in opening his instrument case. The others were already assembling their horns and woodwinds and casting preliminary toots out over the empty dance deck. It had looked for a while as if he wouldn't get this far. When he'd showed up for his first rehearsal, the bandleader, a small thin man in his fifties with a bumpy brown toupee and the sour look of someone past his era, had glanced at Mike's union card and said, "Where the hell were you at rehearsal this afternoon, when I was on the horn all over trying to round up a bass man?"

Mike improvised. "Jack left a message on my answering machine before he went away on that emergency. I only got home and heard it an hour ago."

"Well, you can just go back home and listen to some more messages. I've done without a bass before."

Ordinarily Mike might have panicked at this point. But he'd shot up just before leaving the house and the calm was opening like an umbrella in his chest. He hiked the big case back under his arm. "Do what feels good, man. Personally I think a band without rhythm's like a bike without wheels. Catch you." He'd started to turn.

"Oh, sit down," said the bandleader. "You got music?"

Now, smoking, with one corny saddleshoe propped on the seat of his chair, he had second thoughts about the whole thing. What if the bandleader had found a replacement? If Don hadn't anticipated an unscheduled rehearsal, you had to wonder how many other things he hadn't anticipated. For the first time in a long time the musician felt the itch in his veins twice in one evening.

CHAPTER 3

THE GATE WAS OPENED FINALLY AND THE chattering line shuffled through and onto the gangplank while a deckhand took tickets and the eyes of the security guards prowled the excursionists' clothes for suspicious bulges. Don smiled as he passed them and said something Larry didn't hear. When it came his turn he felt Doris' grip tighten on his arm but let the deckhand's calloused fingers take the tickets from his hand and moved forward, feeling the damp cold under his arms. The guards were big men, the older of the two steely-haired and sour-looking with a hard paunch pushing over his gun belt. But the pair barely glanced at the teenaged couple before turning their attention to the next people in line. Larry and Doris glided past the curious looks of the captain and first mate standing next to the gangplank, and then they were on board. Larry let out his breath.

The deckhand, a tall black man with a long jaw, smiled at Fay, who ignored him except to hand him her ticket. She had a complexion like antique gold and her short hair accentuated her

Egyptian profile. On Sherman her lithe figure with its lean hips and small but firm breasts had made her popular with the Johns, but her refusal to go to bed with a white man had earned her the nickname of Princess among her less particular colleagues.

Clean-cut Teddy received the same cursory examination from the guards as had Larry and Doris, and if they saw Sol at all their attitude didn't reflect it. His build and features were deadly commonplace, as forgettable as last week's lunch. They reserved their closest attention for Ray, whose narrow hunted look and scrawny build under his voluminous sportcoat had drawn official suspicion all his life. They looked him up and down on his way through the gate and looked him up and down again when his back was to them. Nothing showed. But something unspoken passed between the security men when their glances met afterward. No one else in the very long line sparked that reaction.

The boards of the dance deck knocked hollowly under the passengers' feet, a broad varnished area between the bandstand and rows of folding wooden chairs for the wallflowers and those who preferred to watch the dancers and listen to the mellow music. The interior smelled heavily of fresh paint. The boat wore so many coats that a thumbnail left a clear half-moon on the blue-painted steel railing. Whispers brushed the slightly soggy air under the rafters.

There was a long wait while the people who were still boarding mounted the deck and climbed stairs to the other levels. The guards stepped aboard, followed by Cap'n Eddie and First Mate Holliday, who continued up to the pilot house fifty feet above the waterline. Then the burbling of the engine stepped up, tingling underfoot. The gangplank was drawn in, the windlass turned with a stuttering clank. The deckhand who had taken tickets uncoiled all lines from the piles, tossed them to mates on board, and leaped four feet onto the deck.

As the boat pulled away from the dock, loudspeakers in the bow and stern whistled and released a broadcast-trained voice throbbing with masculinity.

"Welcome to the Boblo boat. For the next four hours you'll be cruising on one of the world's busiest waterways that serves as the longest unprotected and freest border in the world between two great nations, Canada and the United States."

Don, standing near the staircase that led to the second deck, took a last look around under the overhead lights to be sure everyone was in position. Ray loitered near the railing, his back to the older security guard, who was watching him. Mike was with the band. Fay and Sol were in the middle of the deck, almost empty now while most of the passengers were at the rail looking out. Larry and Doris were pretending interest in the lights on the Windsor side of the river. Don waited until they had all seen him, then started up the stairs.

"The ship you are on was built in nineteen-oh-two by the Detroit Shipbuilding Company," the voice announced.

Ray reached into his inside breast pocket. The movement stiffened the guard, who relaxed slightly when Ray produced a pack of cigarettes and tapped one out.

"It has a capacity of twenty-five hundred passengers. It is two hundred and fifteen feet long and is moved by a two-thousand-horsepower engine. The captain is Edward Macomb Fielding, a seventeen-year veteran of the Boblo tours."

Ray strolled away from the railing, the guard's eyes following him as he put a match to his cigarette. The guard was thus looking away from Mike while he unlatched the case that usually contained a bass fiddle.

"Everything possible is done to insure the comfort and safety of our passengers on this traditional moonlight cruise."

There was a stiff breeze on the crown deck, where the younger guard approached Don as he was closing the gate marked AUTHORIZED PERSONNEL ONLY on his way to the ladder that led to the bridge. They were in the middle of the river now, with the ghostlit, spidery expanse of the Ambassador Bridge connecting the United States and Canada looming over the bow.

"Sorry, sir. Passengers aren't allowed on this level while the boat is in motion."

"I was just looking for a men's room," said Don, his easy embarrassed smile spreading behind his moustache.

The guard smiled back. He was giving directions to the head on the bottom deck when Don tugged the converted Luger out of the waistband of his pants and sank the muzzle in the guard's stomach.

"Get the hands up and turn around slowly."

The voice continued to throb from the loudspeakers. "All of us at Boblo want you to enjoy your evening. For your dancing pleasure, we are proud to present the music of Chester Crane and his Whoopers. And don't forget our daytime cruises to Boblo Island, the only international amusement park in the world." The tape-recorded Boblo theme came on under his last words and swelled to fill the boat, the singers' voices echoing tinnily off the river's surface.

The music was the cue to move. Mike flung open the big case, hauled out one of the three M-16 rifles and threw it to Sol, who caught it on the fly and wheeled on the older security guard. The guard, just then turning away from Ray, jerked his right hand spasmodically toward the gun on his hip, then threw both hands in the air as Sol flipped off the safety catch with a sharp snick.

"Over the side with it." The killer's tone was dead.

The guard hesitated. But the greasegun-shaped rifle was a rock in the hands of the bland-looking man. The guard lowered his right hand slowly and fingered the gun from his holster and dropped it over the railing. It splashed into the boat's wash.

Most of the passengers were still at the rail. The few who had seen what was happening looked blank. Don had counted on that brief moment of assimilation and had drilled the others to take advantage of it. Mike threw another automatic rifle to Fay and the last to Doris, who almost dropped it, clapping it against her stomach in both arms. They had discussed arming her instead with something she could handle, but she was even more inept with handguns and Fay had argued that she might as well *look* dangerous. The pistols came next; Ray, Teddy, and Larry got one apiece and Mike jacked a shell into the chamber of his and stuck it in his belt under his loose blazer. Next came the portable transmitters, which went to Fay, Teddy, and Larry, with a fourth for Larry to pass up to Don. He slung one over each shoulder by its elastic strap. All this was accomplished in just under ten seconds.

Then a woman passenger screamed, but by then Ray, Larry,

Doris, and Teddy were on their way up the stairs carrying their weapons and transmitters. Ray and Teddy hit the second deck running and took up posts at the bow and stern, their .45s drawing gasps and squeals from the couples gathered there. Larry and Doris took the third. The wicked-looking rifle in the girl's hands started a stampede toward the other end that actually tilted the great boat for a moment.

In the pilot house, Don had his Luger on the guard, the captain, the first mate, and the young man who served as lookout, while the helmsman stood rigid with his back to the gunman and his hands on the wheel. The guard's .38 was stuck in Don's waistband and his free hand held the microphone to the public-address system.

"You are all political prisoners of Siegfried." His words rang tonelessly from the speakers. "Stay away from the rail, do what you're told, and maybe we'll all survive this cruise."

On the second deck, Ray opened his coat and unwound a webbed belt bulging with gelatin explosives from around his waist.

On the dance deck, Chester Crane, his face going angry red under the toupee, said, "Those guns aren't real."

Up close the M-16s, made entirely from plastic and stamped metal, did look like toys. Don had anticipated that reaction and given Sol his orders. The killer swung the squat muzzle on Mike and pressed the trigger.

Mike had time to grin and say, "Shit, man," and then a short, coughing burst spun him into the rail. He sagged sideways, leaving a glistening smear along the painted steel.

The tape recording was still playing in the pilot house. In the pause before the first scream, the professional chorus sang, "Take someone you love to Boblo I-hi-land."

CHAPTER 4

KIND OF EARLY FOR YOU, ISN'T IT, Red?'' asked Bill Chilson.

Randall Burlingame, director of the Detroit office of the Federal Bureau of Investigation, rose from behind his battleship gray desk to grip Chilson's outstretched hand, a weary smile tugging out the corners of his lips.

"I'm used to it," he said. "It's been a long time since I stayed up past two playing stud with drunken Secret Service agents."

The FBI man was tall and broad-shouldered but running to fat around the middle, the soft rolls drawing a large V-shaped crease in his charcoal vest. His once-flaming hair was a bled-out pink these days, and the only people who still called him Red were those who had known him a long time. His bony face, classic in youth, had taken on a granite cast over the years of bickering with Hoover. He owed this long-overdue promotion to the Chief's death and the resultant backlash in Washington.

"You know I'm a grandfather now," he said.

"No kidding. Which one, Randy?"

"Phyllis."

Chilson's brows slid up. "Little Phyllis? Last time I saw her she was catching hell for squirting your shaving cream on the dog."

They howled about that and sat down on opposite sides of the desk. Lounging the old way, on his long spine with the back of his bald head resting on the crown of the chair, Chilson didn't look much different. He had lost all his hair in his twenties and was still wearing amber-tinted glasses to protect his weak eyes, and give or take a line and some loose flesh under his chin he could still pass for 35 with the light behind him. He sure hadn't gained any weight.

Burlingame stuffed a pipe from the leather pouch he had carried since World War II. "You've been briefed?"

"Only up to about midnight last night," Chilson said.

"Then you know as much as we do. We haven't heard from them since then. They're either not receiving our radio calls or ignoring them. By now they must be well into Lake Erie. Coast Guard has helicopters out, but it's a big lake and there's a fog rolling in from Canada."

"How many hostages?"

"They claim eight hundred. No way of verifying that. Boblo doesn't keep passenger manifests. But sources here say that's about right for this time of year. They have, or claim to have, automatic and semi-automatic weapons and enough plastic explosives to blow the old tub to toothpicks. We ran a computer check to find out what's missing from the various armories in this area and came up with several possibles. I've got field men looking into those." He got the tobacco going finally and flipped the match into a brass ashtray doing double duty as a paperweight. "They've given the Governor seventy-two hours to release ten prisoners from the Southern Michigan Penitentiary at Jackson. If this isn't done by midnight Monday—quoting here—we'll be 'skimming blood and powdered meat off Lake Erie for six weeks.' "

"Graphic."

"That kind never lacks for color."

"Think they'll blow it up with themselves aboard?"

"They call themselves Siegfried. Has a doomsday quality, don't you think?"

"These ten prisoners they want sprung," Chilson said. "Any ten in particular, or a random choice?"

"Here's the list they radioed to the Boblo dock."

Chilson skimmed the hasty handwriting on the sheet of notepaper and handed it back. "I recognize some of those names. Are the rest of them killers too?"

"The kind we park behind bars and hope they'll die there because there's no capital punishment in this state and rehabilitation is a joke. Rape-murderers, parricides—two of them stuck up a Stop 'n' Go in Ypsilanti, herded the employees into the back room, and shot them all in the head. They made off with forty-two dollars and change."

"Connection?"

"The computer says no. From the gut?" Chilson nodded. "They don't want us to give in. They chose a demand they know we'll never meet so they can commit mass suicide on the six o'clock news and take along as many of the rotten fucking pig bourgeoisie vacationers as they can."

"Sounds farfetched."

"Five years ago it would have been. Jonesville changed all the rules. This bunch wasted one of their own just by way of demonstration."

"Who are they?"

"The honcho calls himself Don, but go feed that into your Apple and see what comes out. It's probably phony anyway. Anonymity may be the best weapon they have." Burlingame made a face and set the pipe in the ashtray. "What's the Secret Service want with this, anyway? Isn't protecting the President enough any more?"

Chilson scratched his chin, then drew himself upright in his chair.

"This will have to be C and D, Red. Strictly need-to-know."

"Bill, we've called each other by our first names how long now?"

"Long enough that if the squirts up top found out, they'd

have us playing checkers in the park by payday." The Secret Service man grinned quickly. "Okay. Clarence Turnbull. Know the name?"

"Something in government."

"And you a federal man. Well, they had to prod me too when I heard about it. Turnbull's the Secretary of Health, Education, and Welfare. He has a daughter named Carol attending the University of Michigan. She's engaged to marry an intern at the hospital there."

Burlingame said, "I hope this conversation isn't heading where I know damn well it's heading."

"She called her father in Washington Thursday and mentioned that one of the things she was planning to do over the weekend was go on the Boblo moonlight cruise with her future intended. Now, it isn't definite that she's on that boat. But her father tried to reach her at her apartment after this thing broke and there was no answer."

"Broke how? First thing I did was throw wraps on this."

"He has a brother-in-law in the Bureau. The brother-in-law knew about Turnbull's conversation with his daughter and called him at home. When your boss found out he canned the brother-in-law for breach of security."

"Well, we won't be able to sit on it much longer anyway." The FBI man played with his smoldering pipe. "Siegfried doesn't know about the daughter or they'd have mentioned it. If they find out what they've got, and we'll assume they've got her until we hear different, there's no telling what direction they'll go. Makes the whole thing more delicate, but I don't see where it changes—"

The intercom on the desk razzed. He flipped the switch. "This damn well better be an emergency."

"That's up to you." The feminine voice coming from the speaker was cool. "A Howard Klegg to see you. He says it's about the Boblo boat."

"Second." Burlingame turned off the intercom. "This freedom of speech thing is getting out of hand."

"Who's Howard Klegg?" asked Chilson.

"Well, he's not a cabinet member. He's Michael Boniface's lawyer."

"The gangster? I thought he was in prison."

"He is." He hit the switch again. "All right."

Klegg was a frail-looking 70 with thick white hair combed straight back from a high brow and cut off square at his collar. His skin had a bluish cast and was stretched to the point of translucence over high cheekbones and a patrician nose. He was very thin and his brown pinstriped suit, beautifully cut, made him look emaciated. He carried a shiny brown leather briefcase with a gold clasp.

"Mr. Burlingame." He extended a spidery hand at the end of a bony wrist, which the FBI man clasped briefly and released. "And this would be Mr. Chilson of the Secret Service."

The bald man recovered himself in time to shake the old hand, which was strung with wire. Klegg uncovered perfect dentures in a self-deprecating smile. "The people I represent haven't the imagination for code names and ciphers and counter-signs, but their intelligence compares favorably with that of you gentlemen in law enforcement."

They sat down, Klegg drawing up a chair upholstered in blue leather and placing his briefcase on his knees.

"What is it, Klegg?" Burlingame demanded. "I haven't seen you since your client's trial for narcotics smuggling. That was what, two years ago?"

"Eighteen and a half months. Mr. Boniface has counted every day, I can assure you." The lawyer glanced pointedly at the pipe in the ashtray, whose smoke was worming past his nose. Burlingame left it where it was.

Klegg shrugged and waved away the smoke. "I'll make this brief. My client and his people are aware of the situation, of the demand made by the terrorists, and of their threat in the event it isn't carried out by midnight Monday. We know also that Carol Turnbull is aboard, and we know who her father is, naturally."

"We don't know that much," Chilson said. "That she's aboard, I mean. Is this new intelligence?"

"It's an assumption based on information available to us."

"I'd be interested in knowing who made it available."

Klegg's dentures shone. "Ethics, Mr. Chilson."

"I heard something about being brief," grumped Burlingame.

"Just so. Getting to the heart of the matter, Mr. Boniface is prepared to place his not inconsiderable resources at the service of the authorities in expediting this situation."

The FBI man said, "Again. In English."

"I believe it's standard practice in these cases to attempt to trace the criminals involved through underworld contacts. I submit that my client is in a position to do this with results more satisfactory."

"In return for which," said Burlingame, "what?"

"Early parole."

"You know that's out of my hands even if I agreed."

"I also know that a recommendation for leniency from the man who convicted my client can influence the parole board. Mind you," Klegg added, "I'm not requesting a full pardon. Only the opportunity for Mr. Boniface to return to society and begin picking up the pieces of his life."

"Your client is scum, counselor. I spent a good part of my career putting him where he is and I'll need a lot more than a foggy promise of cooperation before turning him loose."

The lawyer's paper-thin eyelids drooped. "And if I said we could identify one of the terrorists?"

Burlingame laughed nastily.

"Let's hear what he has to say," said Chilson.

"He's blowing smoke."

"You can check this out," said Klegg. "Last week, the Detroit police pulled a charred corpse out of a car found torched in an empty lot off Eight Mile Road twenty hours after the car was reported stolen. The dead man had been shot in the head."

The FBI man nodded. "I read about it. He's a John Doe."

"The car answered a witness' description of the vehicle in which a man claiming to be with the musicians' union picked up Jack DeGrew, who played bass viol with Chester Crane and his Whoopers, the previous afternoon. Something about a performance DeGrew had played for below union scale, according to the witness. Crane's band is on the captured boat, I believe."

He coughed delicately. Burlingame moved the ashtray containing his fuming pipe to the other side of the desk.

"The bullet to the head wasn't unique," Klegg continued. "The burned body was. Organization contract killers like to have their victims identified as an object lesson. Independents without protection prefer to cover their tracks. There aren't many independent professionals in this area, and there is only one who fits the description our witness provided."

"Who is. . . ?" the FBI man prompted.

The lawyer sat back, displaying his dentures.

Burlingame knocked out his pipe. "I'm not saying I buy any of this. In any case, reciprocation on my part would depend on results. Are you offering me the killer's name?"

"I think we agree that that alone wouldn't free my client. I'm just confirming his ability to aid in this matter. We—that is, my client—would of course provide the personnel."

"You want me to grant official status to a criminal body?"

"No deputizing or anything like that. We're offering competent civilian service in return for what we request."

"No wildcatting? Your people would work closely with ours?"

Klegg fingered the knot in his silk tie. "'Wildcatting,' as you term it, is what gives us our special advantage. I'm hardly suggesting something without precedent, Mr. Burlingame; consider the late Messrs. Luciano and Giancana." He rose, lifting his briefcase. "I'll be outside admiring your attractive secretary while you gentlemen discuss the proposition. Without meaning to rush things, I'll just point out that you have but sixty-three and one-half hours left." He went out.

After three minutes they called him back in.

The Visitors' Room at the Milan Federal Correctional Facility was bland but not unpleasant, with beige walls, freshly waxed linoleum, and a printed list of rules posted within view of the bare table in the center with a chair on either side. A guard opened the door for a middle-aged man whose startlingly black hair and denims made him look years older than he was, then closed it behind him, the guard remaining outside but watching through the gridded glass in the door. Howard Klegg was seated at the table, looking as he had earlier that morning in Randall Burlingame's office.

"It's on, Michael," he said.

Michael Boniface nodded, lowering his bulk into the other chair. "Get me Macklin."

CHAPTER 5

PETER MACKLIN HATED SMALL towns.

They weren't as bad as they once were. Strange faces no longer drew much attention now that people were moving every few years. But the old posse-consciousness still lingered in these tight communities, and you could never predict what a bystander was going to do when you made your move. That crowd-fear factor he relied upon in the cities was an empty equation once the population dipped below twenty thousand.

It didn't help that he had had to do most of the groundwork on this one, letting his face and figure become familiar to the residents of this farming village forty miles west of Detroit while he nailed down his subject's routine. The advance man they had sent had made perhaps two trips, staying a couple of hours each time, and evidently decided that because the subject did roughly the same things at roughly the same time both days, the rest of his

23

week was identical. Three pages into the briefing packet, Macklin had broken out his walking boots.

Which was nothing new. He had two telephone lines running into his Southfield home, one of which was unlisted, and every time that one rang—never more than once a month, and it was often silent for six—he knew he was in for more work than he had been the time before. The professionals were getting scarce in his end of a business so caught up in corporate image and the Dow Jones average that the people in the front offices liked to forget they sometimes needed men like him. When they made contact, it was with a kind of repugnant awe that assumed he was an evil sorcerer who neither required nor welcomed outside help. They knew nothing of the role teamwork played in committing a successful murder.

Macklin was a killer. Not a mechanic or a heavyweight or a terminator or a lifetaker or any of the other euphemisms affected by the young ivy leaguers with their icy eyes and laser gunsights. He had sunk garottes into fat necks in moving cars and heard arteries popping like corn in an oven when he applied pressure; felt first the stiff, corded resistance, then the soft slick give when his blade penetrated major organs in filthy alleys and hot blood boiled over his hand; burned his nostrils with spent cordite and biological stench when his bullets slammed through his victims' skulls in family restaurants and their sphincters let go. None of those other antiseptic names fit what he did for a living.

He was an even six feet and a hundred and eighty pounds, with jagged features under a quilting of flesh and the kind of eyes that were considered sleepy and dangerous-looking in his youth but now just looked tired. His hair was retreating in twin horns along his widow's peak, which had started to go from brown to gray and then stopped, leaving it the color of house dust. He was in good condition but growing thick through the middle, and no amount of exercise and diet had made a difference in the hard roll over his belt. He was 39—"Jack Benny's age," he reported, in his lighter moments—and there were times when he felt 90.

But not now. As always when working, he was running an adrenaline high. Having eaten nothing since the night before (a custom he had kept since his first high school football game), he felt the stuff pumping pure and heady as strong wine through his veins.

He was sitting behind the wheel of a stolen car in the parking lot of a small supermarket just off the main four corners, watching a large silver refrigerator truck backing up to the entrance of a low building labeled ZACHARY'S FINE MEATS on the other side of the intersection. Every Tuesday and Thursday between two and three in the afternoon, Zachary delivered beefs and hams from his Detroit slaughterhouse to his market here, climbing into the trailer and sliding the laden meathooks along the overhead runners for his two assistants to unhook and carry across the sidewalk to the runners inside the building. Once the truck was in place, the assistants took four to five minutes clearing the walk-in freezer and oiling the inside runners while Zachary shoved the great slabs of meat up to the truck's open doors. For that four to five minutes he was alone in the truck. In the two weeks Macklin had been following him around, that was the only time he was alone all day except at home, which according to the old tradition was off limits.

Macklin didn't know what Zachary had done that had brought him to his attention. He wasn't told such things and he never asked. But he knew the pattern: money borrowed to bolster a sagging enterprise, failure to repay when things were better, threats from one side, taunts from the other, an example to be made. In any case, Macklin was thinking of the what, not the why.

When the truck shut down—he could hear the engine dying from where he was—Macklin left the car and started across the street. There were a few pedestrians in sight, but the automobile traffic was slackening with the close of the lunch hour. He loitered on the flashing pedestrian signal while Zachary's men went inside, then when they were out of sight he hustled across on the red, trouser cuffs flapping in the slipstream from a car sweeping past behind him. On the sidewalk he climbed out of the light jacket he'd had on over a pair of blue coveralls like the kind Zachary and his assistants wore. He draped the jacket over a municipal mailbox and hoisted himself up into the dim flesh-smelling dankness of the trailer and drew the doors shut behind him.

Zachary had his back to the intruder when the trailer darkened. He was a short, broad cylinder of a man with sloping shoulders and a shaved head, an animated fire hydrant. He turned to face the man in blue coveralls like his own and said, "Hey, what the hell—" and then the muzzle of Macklin's gun flashed and three-quarters of an ounce of lead pushed in the butcher's face. The report battered the insulated walls and slammed back on itself, inaudible outside the truck.

Macklin favored .38 revolvers. Twenty-twos were in vogue, but the heavy caliber rendered the *coup de grâce* unnecessary and its intimidating bark kept witnesses in their place. No one on the street was looking at the truck when he let himself out, closing the door again to keep the smoke inside. He retrieved his jacket, ditched the rough-taped and untraceable gun in the mailbox, and recrossed the street. He took the plugs out of his ears and put them in a pocket. Zachary's men were just ambling out of the building when he got back in the car and started the engine.

Driving under the limit and stopping for signals and school buses, he reached Detroit seventy-two minutes later, parked the car legally, fed the meter, and hiked eleven blocks before hailing a cab for Southfield and home.

This circuitous drudgery, combined with the familiar emotional letdown of an assignment's completion, made his arms and legs heavy. Yawning bitterly, he unlocked the front door of his little two-story house on Evergreen and headed for the stairs.

He stopped to glance into the living room. Donna was sprawled snoring in the green Lay-Z-Boy in front of the television set. She was barefoot and wearing her quilted purple bathrobe. An empty shot glass and a half-empty beer bottle stood on the end table next to the chair. Her mass of thick hair, dyed blonde to cover the gray, was tangled and the cigarette between the first and second fingers of her left hand had burned down almost to the flesh. Gently, Macklin removed it and stubbed it out in the rounded-over ashtray on the table.

She had burned holes in three chairs that same way and set

one afire. If Roger, who had been 13 then, hadn't come home from school and awakened her, she'd have burned to death. Now Roger was 16 and had no school to come home from, and Lord knew whose home he was going to these days. Macklin had seen his son three times in the past month. The first two times, Roger had stopped in just long enough to change clothes before going out again. The third time he had been high on something and Macklin had told him to leave. The boy had evidently taken it as a permanent eviction.

Macklin carried the shot glass and the bottle into the kitchen and washed the glass and poured the stale beer into the sink. The kitchen was filthy. The whole house was filthy except for his study and the bedroom he shared with Donna, which he cleaned himself. She hardly ever slept there any more, spending most of her time drinking and sleeping in that chair in the living room, those moments when she wasn't sniping at him. He found it hard to believe that it was that acid tongue that had attracted him to her when they were both 22.

He had considered hiring a housekeeper, but he hardly looked forward to explaining Donna to a stranger and didn't want another pair of eyes and ears around the house anyway. He went back and got the ashtray and emptied it into the kitchen wastebasket and climbed the stairs and took off his shoes and stretched out fully clothed on top of the bedspread.

He was almost asleep when his private line rang in the study down the hall.

CHAPTER 6

A SLAB OF FOG TWO FEET THICK LAY LIKE A silver ingot on the lawn of the big half-timbered Elizabethan house in Grosse Pointe, undisturbed by a slight breeze smelling of metal from Lake St. Clair. Sunlight filtered filmy gray through the overcast. Macklin teased his nickel-colored Cougar up the inclined composition driveway and braked in front of a big man in a black suit standing on the flagstone path, who got bigger as Macklin climbed out and dropped the keys into a cupped palm the size of a canoe paddle.

" 'Morning, Mr. Macklin."

The big man's voice was a surprising tenor, and butter-soft. "Gordy."

Gordy's eyes glittered black in deep slits under a carapace of scar tissue, considering the Cougar's bright metallic finish. "You ought to think about getting some kind of car that don't stick out like a bad rash," he said.

"Reverse psychology," Macklin explained. "Police never suspect someone who drives a neon sign."

"Aw, that 'Purloined Letter' stuff don't work in the real world." The big man wedged himself in behind the wheel, ground the starter, and drove the car around behind the house out of sight of the Treasury men photographing license plates from the back of the delivery van parked across the street.

Macklin walked up the flagstones and stabbed a mother-of-pearl button set in a brass socket next to the door. While he was waiting he snugged up the knot of his necktie and frowned at his reflection in the diamond-shaped window.

"Good to see you, Mac."

The killer hesitated. He could never get used to Charles Maggiore answering his own door. Then he shook the hand that was offered him. "It's been a while."

"Too many Senate committee hearings on organized crime. All my profits go into hiring buffers. Come in."

He complied, and Maggiore closed the door behind him. He was not a small man, but he was shorter than Macklin, and after Gordy everyone looked tiny until you got your proportions back into order. Maggiore was one of those white Sicilians who owe their blond hair and blue eyes to Scandinavian island-hoppers from previous centuries, and several lifts and many hours spent in conference with sun lamps had given him the smooth golden look of an aging surfer. Smart tailoring and a practiced list to starboard made the congenital hump on his right shoulder almost unnoticeable. He was wearing a youthful plaid sportcoat, tan corduroy pants, and cordovan half-boots. Macklin felt overdressed.

"How's work?" Maggiore asked.

"Work's fine."

That meant Zachary was dead. The Sicilian uncovered capped teeth in a boyish grin and made as if to slap him on the arm, though his hand never got that far. Macklin moved in a world of half-gestures and incomplete intimacies. He was used to being feared.

He accompanied his superior down a short carpeted hallway hung with original modern oils in steel frames and through a door into the room Maggiore called the library, although it contained no books. Red leather chairs and a scimitar-shaped desk with a clear glass top and no drawers stood in front of a wall that was all window, made of the same tough plastic that telephone receivers are made of, that repels bullets. Gray sunlight made a tall rectangle where the green floor-length drapes came within eight inches of meeting. The killer had been in the room only once before, the day Maggiore had called him in to introduce himself as Michael Boniface's surrogate while the latter was serving his prison sentence. Since then all Maggiore's orders to Macklin had come through subordinates. The personal call to his private line had been a surprise.

"You've met Howard Klegg."

"Briefly." Macklin took the hand of the man who had risen from one of the chairs, and stopped feeling overdressed. The older man's pinstriped suit hung on his wiry frame like the drapery on a statue of a Roman senator. A diamond winked on the ring finger of his long bony left hand.

"I've given the servants the day off like the last time." Maggiore waved both his visitors into seats and cocked a leg over one corner of the desk. "Two of them are undercover cops. I'm not sure about the cook."

"Why don't you get rid of them?" The leather chair Macklin was sitting in gripped his thighs like a doughy hand.

"I would. But they're so damn good at their jobs I hate to see them go. Drink?" He cocked his head toward a portable bar laden with bottles and decanters in the corner.

"Not on an empty stomach."

"I forgot. Howard?"

Klegg shook his head. He hadn't said a word since Macklin's entrance.

"We'll do this without fanfare, then. Howard has made a deal with the authorities. A new parole hearing for Mike Boniface in return for his assistance with a hostage problem, without official interference in the proceedings. It's a compromise, but a good one. It practically amounts to a promise of a release."

"The Boblo boat?" suggested Macklin.

Maggiore's carefully plucked eyebrows slid up. "Where'd you hear it?"

"On the car radio coming over. Just a short bulletin. They

said terrorists took the boat last night and were steaming toward Lake Erie with eight hundred hostages."

"They say anything about Clarence Turnbull's daughter?"

"Who's he?"

"Later," said Maggiore. "Well, this saves us some time. How soon can you be ready to go?"

"Go where?"

Maggiore glanced at Klegg. At last the lawyer opened his mouth.

"Mr. Boniface asked for you specifically," he said. "Take as many men as you need. Name your transportation, boat or car. Helicopter, if you want it and if the fog lifts. You have sixty-one hours before the boat blows with all aboard."

"To do what?"

"Whatever you have to do to fulfill our part of the bargain with the authorities, preferably without killing any innocents. The method is up to you."

"I wouldn't know what to do with a boat or a helicopter," Macklin said. "I wouldn't know what to do with a car. I'm not Errol Flynn or Roger Moore. I'm just a killer."

Maggiore said, "You're being overly modest, Mac, and there's no time for it. If a killer was all we wanted we could cruise down John R or Erskine and hire ten to a block. This job calls for a cool head and a cake of ice for a heart. Mike knows that and that's why he chose you."

"I'm flattered. I'm also passing this one."

"Can the crap." The Sicilian colored under his tan. "I'm not running a union shop."

"I didn't know that you were running anything without Mr. Boniface's say-so."

"You take your orders from me just as you would from him."

Macklin rose, looking down at Maggiore. "My work is killing. I'm not into boarding ships this week. Call me when you get something I'm good at."

"I'll have you hit!"

"You'll try." One of Macklin's rare wolfish grins cracked the lower part of his face.

"Gentlemen," said Klegg, "we're going about this like children in a schoolyard. Sit down, Mr. Macklin. No one wants you to do what you don't want to do."

The killer sat and crossed his legs. He put a hand inside his shirt pocket, remembered he'd quit smoking, and let it drop to his thigh. He was pleased to see Maggiore flinch at the gesture. The lawyer went on.

"You and I met just once, when I was going out and you were coming in. Until Mr. Boniface asked for you I had no idea what you were to his business. Being an attorney I prefer it that way. But as I understand it you've served him loyally for many years, which I take to mean that you respect him. I hope you'll look at this in that light and consider it a personal favor."

"We don't do favors, Mr. Klegg. It's one of the reasons we respect each other."

Klegg's expression petrified. He had changed personalities and was not at all the sly manipulator of Randall Burlingame's office. "Very well, if you want to put things on that level. What is your price?"

"It's not a question of price."

Maggiore leaned forward, resting his hands on his knees. "Why don't you admit it, Macklin? You're afraid of a bunch of pimple-faced punks with greaseguns and firecrackers."

"You don't know what being afraid is all about."

"Damn right!"

"Because if you did, you wouldn't be so proud of not being afraid." Macklin looked at the lawyer. "It isn't money and I'm not scared. It's not a thing I could do quietly the way I like. Too many people would see my face."

Klegg said, "Don't worry about it. This time the law's on your side. There will be some bad publicity and a lot of loud comment about the end not justifying the means, but they won't prosecute you at the risk of this deal being made public."

"My picture will be in the papers and on the eleven o'clock news. It'll be tough getting back to inconspicuous after that. We're talking about my retirement here."

"In other words," said the lawyer, "we're talking price."

Macklin sighed. "How many terrorists are there?"

"Eight. No, seven. They killed one of their own people."

"How good are they?"

"How good do you have to be with explosives and automatic weapons?"

"Better than you might think." He clamped his mouth shut against a yawn. His after-work lethargy wasn't retreating without a fight. "A hundred thousand."

"Ha!" Maggiore got up, put his hands in his pants pockets, and walked over to the window to look out through the gap in the curtains.

"Fifty up front. Cash as usual. I'll need operating expenses. If I need help I'll do the hiring."

"We don't pay by the job," Maggiore reminded him, without turning. "You're on salary like everyone else."

The killer ignored him, watching Klegg. "No outside interference. Whatever information I need comes through you."

"That's all arranged. Will you do it?"

"Yes."

The lawyer sat back, showing his dentures. "I'm sorry, Charles," he told Maggiore. "Michael asked me to make all the decisions on this one."

The man at the window said nothing.

"If there are no further questions we'll get to the briefing." Klegg picked up his case from the floor and undid the gold clasp.

Macklin left after an hour, big Gordy appearing as suddenly and silently as a genie to hold the library door open for him. Howard Klegg looked after him with a wrinkle in his high blue forehead.

"We covered a lot of details," he said. "He never took a note."

"I understand he doesn't." Maggiore got up from behind his desk, where he had sat unspeaking throughout the briefing. "I guess you'll be reporting back to Mike now."

"I'd like to tell him you're with him on this."

The Sicilian hesitated less than a second, then grasped the

hand that was extended him. "You don't have to tell him. He knows I'm a team player."

Klegg smiled and left. Gordy saw him out to his car. Maggiore adjusted the goose neck of a sun lamp mounted on the wall over the desk and switched it on. He opened his collar, sat down, and undid the catch that reclined the desk chair, relaxing with eyes closed in the lamp's warmth. A moment later he heard a soft footfall on the carpet in front of the desk and opened one eye to consider the young man standing over him.

"Did you get a good look at him?" Maggiore asked.

"Through the window. I'll know him again."

He opened the other eye. His visitor was in his mid-twenties, five-eight or -nine and a hundred and thirty pounds, with a narrow, babyish face that looked as if it had never felt a razor and a right eyelid that drooped mockingly. His hair was stringy and sand-colored and hung behind his ears to his collar from a prematurely thinning front. His suit was soft gray and fit him in such a way that the unmatched revolvers he wore in twin holsters under his arms didn't show. He had hairless pink hands and a thin voice that embarrassed him so that he didn't talk much.

"Freddo." Maggiore punched a button under the desk's glass top, switching off the sun lamp. "Is that your first name or your last?"

"Both."

"*Siciliano? Neapolitano?*"

Freddo made no reply.

"If you're not Italian, why do you use that name? Do you know what it means?"

"Cold."

The Sicilian waited for more, then gave up. He tilted his chair forward and rested his forearms on the desk. "Don't do anything just yet. Keep an eye on him. When it looks like he's getting ready to make his move, spliff him."

"Okay."

"I know how these deals work. When Macklin drops the ball and that boat goes up in flames, they'll find all kinds of ways not to make good on it. So Boniface stays where he is and I stay where I am. Who are you using?"

"I wasn't figuring on using anybody."

"No good. This isn't some fat laundryman you can slam with his arms up to his ass in dirty socks. Who you pick is your headache. Just make sure he's good."

Freddo nodded and withdrew on noiseless heels. Maggiore watched the door close and expelled some breath. Under Boniface, they waited to be dismissed before leaving. He breathed again, shook his head, and turned the sun lamp back on, twisting a little in the chair to put heat on his hump.

The Treasury agent on the morning shift tracked the shiny car through the small powerful lens mounted in the side of the van across the street and changed bands on his portable transmitter. While waiting for his call to be acknowledged he reached behind him and peeled his shirt away from his sticky back. Hundreds of millions in appropriations each year and Washington still hadn't gotten around to installing air conditioning in its field units.

The radio crackled. "Forty-six."

"Bealman, Treasury," he reported. "Just thought you Fibbies might like to know your boy's rolling west on Maumee in a silver Cougar, last year's model. Should be passing you about now."

"Roger, Treasury. We owe you."

"From your mouth to Randy Burlingame's ear. Out." Bealman changed bands again and felt his shirt clinging to his back. He had spent two weeks and filled a hundred and forty rolls of film with license plates and grainy faces in pursuit of evidence linking Charles Maggiore to a gun-smuggling ring in Chile, and that's where the air-conditioning money was going.

CHAPTER 7

FROM THE BRIDGE, ERIE WAS A great choppy pewter disc with gray fog like dirty cotton all around the edge. The boat's steam-whistle, normally hoarse and strident, had made a hollow plaintive hooting sound in the funnel of visibility, aborted when Don clapped the muzzle of his Luger to the base of Cap'n Eddie's skull where he stood at the handle.

"Don't."

"We have to blast every few minutes in this soup," protested the captain. "To avoid a collision."

"Just don't."

The tall old man released the handle and stepped away, following the motion of the gun.

Don had gone almost twenty hours without sleep and it showed in his face, drawn tight as upholstery with the crossed scar white on his cheek. He had tried to get some rest the afternoon before the operation began, but his brain had been racing and at length he had gotten up and laid out the whole thing one more time on the kitchen table in his apartment over the pawn shop, searching for flaws in the plan, using china plates to represent each of the boat's three decks and the bridge and making seasoning shakers do for the crew and the two security men. The plotting charts Siegfried had been using had by then been burned and the ashes broken up.

And yet now he didn't feel tired. If anything he was hyperperceptive, as alert and clear-thinking as if he had made use of the cocaine with which Mike—poor, dead Mike, the first to martyr himself to their cause—had supplied them all to help them through the tortuous hours. But he had no need for it yet. The sensation reminded him of combat.

The fog was a lucky break. It had been predicted and had been another factor on the side of moving when they did, but no one had much counted on its being thick enough to discourage surveillance from the air. The longer it held the greater their chances were of making it through the next—he inspected his heavy-duty wristwatch—fifty-nine hours and twenty-three minutes.

On the dance deck, Fay posed forward with her back to the railing and her ankles crossed, the M-16 resting on the angle of her thighs. The excursionists were crowded toward the center, standing against the little cubicle where snacks were sold and seated on the folding chairs with their heads down and their hands clasped between their knees, sneaking occasional glances up through their eyebrows at the small black Amazon holding them in check. The sobbing and cursing had played themselves out hours ago.

Most of the musicians on the bandstand had shed their scarlet blazers. Chester Crane, the leader, retained his. From time to time he put a hand up to his toupee to make sure it was still in place, but he hadn't said a word since Sol had pitched his bass player's punctured body overboard. Mike's blood was a swatch of rust on the railing.

Most of the bandsmen were hoojies, and not one of them was under 40. Fay bet herself that if she asked them for a little soul they'd throw fish at her.

Sol was aft in his shirtsleeves, the white cotton transparent against his skin where he had perspired through it while visiting the engine room below. He had waited until they were in the mouth of the lake, when no passengers without suicidal intent would risk swimming for shore. They had lost a few that way in the river—the deck was just too big for two people to hold—and Sol and Fay had wasted a few bursts in the water before Don had radioed orders down to ignore them. But anyone caught moving away from the center of the deck got a good look at the inside of the auto-rifles' muzzles.

It had been a close ninety at the base of the steep metal stairs leading down to the engine room, but when Sol had herded the sweating surprised personnel through the portal into the heart of the pistoning, oil-smelling works, the temperature had crept up past one hundred, and Sol had cut short his threatening speech for fear of warping the gun's cheaply constructed parts in the heat. The chief engineer, a tall knobby man in his thirties with a thick moustache and his naked shoulders and chest cooked to a glistening cherry color, had listened unblinking, his eyes on the gauges in front of him. Here was a place that was not a part of the world above the waterline; Sol had the feeling that nothing he did would change anything in this thrumming womb. On his way out he was surprised at how cool the original ninety degrees felt.

Now he smoothed back his damp platinum hair with his free hand and resettled the semiautomatic pistol he had taken off Mike in the waistband of his pants and considered his strategy for getting off the boat before the madman he was working for gave the order to turn it into driftwood.

On the second deck, crewcut Teddy shifted his weight from one sore ham to the other on the hard railing and changed hands on his .45 to mop off his right palm on his dress pants. He could feel the packet of cocaine in his left side pocket when he moved, and wanted to throw it over the side, but he didn't because he thought he might need it later in spite of his repugnance. In the service he had always avoided the company of his fellow officers when they smelled of marijuana or their eyes seemed too bright. Originally a defense mechanism to preserve his chances for promotion, the resolve had hardened over the years into the same kind of contempt he held for civilians.

But even it was nothing like the contempt he held for Ray, his partner on the other end of the deck. The rodentlike demolitions expert had something unclean about him that irritated the sensibilities of someone with bootblack and brass polish in his veins. Of everyone in Siegfried—God, the pedestrian melodrama of that name!—he despised this pimple-faced rat most. He personified everything about the group that Teddy found distasteful, and there was much of that. Fifteen years ago he might have been facing their like on the other side of a rifle at a place like Kent State. He sneered at their aims—his own had to do with simple revenge for being passed over in favor of inferiors—but he approved heartily of their methods. Fragging Mike in the presence of their hostages was a masterstroke, the burning of the Reichstag reduced to its purest terms.

Teddy knew no philosophy but parity. Don had known this when he recruited him, but he had lost no sleep over it because of Teddy's ability to gain access to necessary equipment and because his glittering hopes for early advancement had been dragged so low that he would follow Siegfried's course to its logical end.

Ray, riding aft of the second deck with a leg hooked over the rail and his pistol hanging heavily down his right side, a little motion-sick, thought in simpler terms, if he could be said to think at all. He had no talent or aptitude beyond his skill with explosives, and in fact he had as a boy been enrolled in a class for retarded children for five months until it was discovered that his problems were emotional rather than physical. He had entered college just under the wire and only his grades in those courses bearing upon his specialty had allowed him to graduate. He played timers, detonators, and nitric acids as if they were musical instruments, and if the officers who had investigated the fatal incident on the movie set in Malibu had been able to penetrate the dull shield that protected the animal workings of Ray's brain, they'd have seen that it was no accident. He had nearly as little regard for himself as he had for the rest of humanity. The cocaine he had taken lessened it further.

Right now he had only to raise his pistol and squeeze the trigger to activate the device that charged three and a half pounds of volatile gelatin molded under the entire length of the railing on the second deck.

On the top passenger deck, Larry was using his handkerchief often because he had exhausted his entire supply of cocaine in one toot and it was making his nose run and his eyes water. Thanks to Doris he had been on the stuff for months and had a higher-than-average tolerance. He liked the way it cleared his head, isolating each thought in a crystal cell that kept its edges clean and bright, and it made him smile in such a way that his hostages flinched collectively whenever he raised his .45 to scratch his cheek with the iron sight. It also shrank his doubts and fears into nothing more than an annoying, pulsating lump under the euphoria.

Mike's death formed the center of the lump like the grain of sand a pearl is molded around. He had not said ten words during the many meetings before the event, and Larry had come to think of him as a rather dull but important factor in their plan, when he thought of him at all. Mike's toadlike calm bordered on the soporific. Of all of them, he had seemed the least likely to rebel at the crucial moment and force Sol to kill him. Yet that was how Don had explained Fay's hasty report, transmitted shortly after the burp of gunfire sounded below, when he had relayed it to Larry's portable unit. Don had said that he had been worried about Mike all along and had asked Sol to keep an eye on him. Larry supposed that the ability to spot a traitor in his blandest guise was a requirement of leadership. But even the stimulant failed to make clear to him just what was Mike's transgression.

Doris meanwhile prowled aft, holding her M-16 like a furled umbrella and rubbing her upper arms for warmth. She had put on her sweater, but the thin expensive material was no match for the damp cold that was still in her bones from last night. The drug in her veins helped, but her extremities remained chilled. She had had circulation problems and an abnormally slow heartbeat since childhood. The condition had been the prime mover behind the exaggerated tenderness of her upbringing and the petulance that came as a result. She knew no standard of values beyond those given her by Larry, and that was why she was prowling the deck of an excursion boat full of hostages, looking to them like some hollow-eyed spectre from the deep with pale seaweed for hair and chewed nails against the plastic stock of death in a blue steel case.

All was quiet aboard ship. In the pilot house, Don sang his "Do, re, mi" song under his breath and contemplated the gray fog skidding past the windscreen.

CHAPTER 8

DANIEL OLIVER ACKLER.

Macklin figured he'd remember the initials even if he forgot the name. He wondered if it was an affectation, a cocky killer's idea of a grim joke, or if it was genuine and, if so, if it had had anything to do with his choice of occupations. Macklin liked it either way. If a joke, he would be the overconfident type, likely to swagger into Macklin's sights out of sheer hubris. If genuine, his decision to follow a vocation in keeping with his initials might make him superstitious, a believer in signs and portents, and therefore predictable in his actions. Macklin himself believed in no signs not sanctioned by the highway department.

If the information in the packet he had open on the work table in his study was reliable, Ackler was the man known to those passengers who had succeeded in jumping ship while it was still in the river as Sol, the same man who had pulled the trigger on a fellow terrorist as an object lesson for the hostages. He had come to the Detroit area four years earlier from places unknown and in spite of his youth had racked up an impressive number of independent hits, sometimes working for Macklin's own employers, but most times earning his fee from persons outside the organization with grudges and the cash to settle them. According to Howard Klegg, who had presented Macklin with the folder of typewritten data from his briefcase, Ackler was also the last man to see Jack DeGrew, bass violinist with Chester Crane and his Whoopers, alive.

So far as could be told from cold print, the young button man had just two weaknesses, vanity and an inordinate regard for automatic weapons. The first, which placed him in a professional hairdressers' chair twice a month to have his hair styled and dyed platinum, was something to keep in mind should Macklin meet him face to face. The second he could do something about right now.

He finished memorizing the information and tipped it, folder and all, into a square wastebasket under the broad oak library table he used for a desk. Immediately the basket growled and chewed the sheets into confetti and deposited the tiny pieces into a reservoir in the bottom. Then he rose, drew forth a key attached to a reel in the steel container on his belt and unlocked a green metal file cabinet in the corner next to the shaded window. There was a safe in the bottom drawer with a double combination lock whose numbers could be changed at will and soon he had it open and drew out the only item it contained, a new blue Smith & Wesson .38 revolver with a natural rubber grip, smeared with pink cosmoline and sealed in clear plastic. He had purchased it only that day from a private source for three times the list price to make up for the lack of legal paperwork. Coming up, he had known killers who sneered at his costly caution while patting the favorite weapons they had used on half a dozen jobs and given names like Eloise and Baby Blue, but all of them were pushing government time or feeding worms in unhallowed ground, nonstop from the little room where they drop the little cyanide pellet into the bucket of acid. One killing to a gun, and there was no percentage in being greedy.

Machine guns held no appeal for Macklin. Since the passing of the old Thompsons there was little aesthetically pleasing about the new sausage-shaped rattletraps stamped out of plastic and sheet metal in countries with no culture and muddy unidentifiable languages. And any idiot who could bend his finger and point could vomit a stream of lead over a broad area. It took something special to maneuver within revolver range of a dangerous target and let one well-placed bullet do the work of ninety hastily splattered ones.

And yet he was not a lover of firearms. He called them all guns regardless of fine definitions, and once he had this one out of its wrapper and had wiped it clean of preservative gelatin and tested the action and loaded it from the box of cartridges he kept in another file drawer, he locked it away again, along with an envelope containing fifty thousand dollars in hundred-dollar bills, hand-delivered by special messenger on Klegg's orders.

"Big shot executive type," said a voice behind Macklin. "What's in the safe, doubloons?"

He was deliberately slow in turning. He had observed Donna still asleep in the living room on his way upstairs and so had not bothered to lock the study door. Now she was standing in the doorway, still in the quilted bathrobe that needed cleaning, her gray-streaked blond hair sticking out at angles like burrs in a dog's coat. At 35 she had deep lines at the corners of her mouth and dark thumbprints under her eyes. She was glaring.

"How long have you been there?" His tone was dead calm.

"What's it matter? You think I don't know you keep guns in there? You think I don't know what you do?"

"I'm an efficiency expert."

That was what he wrote in the OCCUPATION blank on his income tax form, and it was how he was listed on the payroll at the camera-construction firm where he worked in Taylor. The company was one of the organization's legitimate enterprises.

"You're efficient, all right. You're always home, and when you're not and I call you at the office you're always in a meeting. Have you ever seen your office, Pete? Have you ever met your secretary?"

"You're drunk, Donna. You only call me Pete when you've been drinking."

"I drink because I'm married to you."

"You drink because you like it."

"I'm an alcoholic."

"You're a drunk. Alcoholics drink because they have to. You do it for the pure pleasure of getting numb. Don't romanticize yourself for just me. I'm a lousy audience."

"Okay, I'm a drunk. But I'm not a killer. Is that what they call you where you work? Killer?"

He said nothing, waiting her out. Her tirades never lasted long.

"I'll bet you like it as much as I like getting blasted. How is it pulling the trigger on someone, Pete? Do you get a boost out of the way their eyes bug out just before you do it, do you give them a chance to plead for their lives? Or do you prefer shooting them from behind? I guess that would be the safest way, the most efficient for an efficiency expert like you."

"It would be. If I were a killer."

"Stop playing! Don't lie about it like I'm a kid asking about sex. I want you to tell me what I know. Do you kill people for a living?"

"I'm an efficiency expert," he said.

She must have slid the heavy brass ashtray into one of the voluminous pockets of the robe before coming upstairs. He jerked his head right and the heavy projectile dusted his left ear. When she saw she'd missed, Donna screamed—a terrible animal shriek—and rushed him, clawing at his face with her long nails. But he turned his left shoulder into her and bowled her into the file cabinet, slamming shut one of the open drawers, and got her into a tight bearhug. Her blows bounded dully off his back, her screams tore his eardrums. He increased pressure and after a few seconds the noise died and she went slack in his arms.

She had fainted, with a little help from the alcohol in her brain. He picked up her feet, hoisted her into an unromantic fireman's carry, and bore her, his discs groaning, through the doorway and down the hall to the bedroom. He stopped once to lean against the wall and catch his breath, then finished the trip and dropped her, not gently, onto the bed. While the springs rocked to a halt he stood there wheezing and waiting for the black spots to fade. Sixteen and a half years ago he had swept her through the front door and up the stairs and still had enough energy to make love to her. She was heavier now, but she had been pregnant with Roger even then and no wraith. He determined to step up his weightlifting next session. Then he determined not to. What if it didn't help?

Donna was snoring with her mouth open and her hair in her eyes. He went through the pockets of her robe and excavated a crumpled pack of cigarettes and two books of matches from a wad of stained brittle Kleenex and gray lint and put them in his own shirt pocket. Then he backed out, closing the door behind him. He wondered where in hell Roger was.

His left ear burned where the ashtray had grazed it. He stopped in the bathroom to examine it in the mirror. The flesh was red. He wet a facecloth and held it against the ear until the pain lessened. Then he changed shirts, put on a fresh necktie, brushed back his thinning hair, and left the house carrying his jacket. It was a warm day in spite of the overcast.

He had left the gun in the safe and kept no weapons in his car. That was another way to end your career in a hurry, lugging unregistered firearms everywhere you went. He only carried one when he had use for it. Just now he was dry-stalking; the hunt itself would come later.

He spotted the federal men by the second corner. There were always two of them, and they always drove nondescript cars and followed no closer than a block behind. The gray Plymouth pulled over to the curb a hundred yards back while Macklin was waiting for the light to change, but no one got out. A high black four-wheel-drive pickup was stopped next to him in the right lane. Macklin let his car creep ahead a few feet, and when the green light came on he goosed the accelerator and cut across the pickup's path, angling right into the cross street. By the time the flustered truck driver blew his horn, the shiny Cougar was approaching the next street over and Macklin bumped the curb turning right again and cut across an empty lot, barking his suspension on the sidewalk. A minute later he hit one of the Mile Roads and blended into the late lunch-hour traffic on Telegraph. There was no sign of the Plymouth in his rearview mirror. He paid no attention to the brown Cordoba that pulled onto Telegraph half a minute behind him, nicking the red light, or to the young sandy-haired man behind the wheel, watching the road and the Cougar burbling along two cars ahead, his face tilted a little to see out from under an eyelid that drooped.

CHAPTER 9

HELLO GYP."

Wyler G. Ibsen, head tailor at Clovis Haberdashers on Greenfield, glanced up between the parted thighs of the fat man whose inseam he was measuring to see who had addressed him by his old nickname. When he recognized Peter Macklin, his perennial half-smile froze and the color slid from his face. The measuring tape slithered free of his thumb and forefinger and coiled on the carpet, but his hand stayed where it was. The tiny black moustache that made his round head look too big for his slight frame twitched and crawled like feelers.

"Oh—hello, Mac," he managed. "Guess I'm stuck here for a spell. Got appointments back-to-back till closing. Some friends are picking me up then," he added quickly, his half-smile flickering.

"That's okay. My business today is with your boss. He in?"

The question took a moment to ring up. When it did, Gyp

almost leaped to his feet. "Oh—Herb? He's in the office. In back."

"I know where it is." Macklin paused before turning. "It isn't that business," he said.

"Oh. Oh!" The smile became brilliant.

"Who was that?" asked the fat man, when they were alone again.

"Efficiency expert." Ibsen's hands were shaking so badly he had to use both of them to pick up the tape.

The fat man grunted. "Mine affects me the same way."

The "office" was really a working storeroom, jungled with cartons of Arrow and Van Heusen shirts and bolts of material lying at odd angles and accordions of tissue-paper patterns tacked elbow-deep to the lath-and-plaster walls. Macklin found the door open and Herb Pinelli, standing with one well-tailored leg bent and a patent-leather shoe propped on a crate stuffed with crushed newspapers and a clipboard on his knee, checking off a list of items on a typewritten sheet with a fat green fountain pen. He didn't look up as Macklin approached. "Pull up a box, Pietro. It's good to see you."

Macklin remained standing. "Gyp said I'd find you back here."

Pinelli grinned at the clipboard. "When he sees you I bet he shits."

"I can't think why. I've never had any business with him."

"He gets himself into some trouble six months ago, boffing the sister of a numbers man in Pontiac. The numbers man, he sends two niggers to wait for him in the alley with iron pipes. I come out first. They don't come back."

Macklin said, "Then he's got no reason to spook."

"You are not two dumb niggers with iron pipes."

Macklin warmed to the compliment in spite of himself. Pinelli was a big man in a snug vest and shirtsleeves with French cuffs and gold studs, and he brushed his silver hair straight back without a part, accentuating the Indianlike planes and hollows of his face. He was a well-preserved 60, retaining the strong Sicilian accent of his boyhood and an adolescence spent in New York's Little Italy. It was said that he had killed his first man at the age of

16. He scorned firearms of any kind, and legend had it that before his retirement from heavyweight work he could decapitate a man from behind with a single backhand slash of his seven-inch blade. He had large powerful hands and his old shoulders were stacked with muscle. For the past fourteen years he had been using them to build up the haberdashery business he had named for his late wife Clovis.

He lowered his foot to the floor, set aside the clipboard, capped the fountain pen, and clipped it to his shirt pocket, looking expectantly at his visitor. He never shook hands, a thing for which the much slighter Macklin was grateful.

"Daniel Oliver Ackler," Macklin said.

Pinelli touched the other's lips with two fingers and moved past him to close the door. He then tugged on the chain to an overhead fixture, banishing darkness from the windowless room. He was standing so close now that Macklin could smell the raw oysters on his breath. The old man believed they kept him vital.

"Wildcat." He spat out the word like filth in his mouth. "One of these beardless fish-eyes with no loyalty to no one and a purse for a soul. *Serpente.* You are not working with him?"

"Just the opposite. I'm after anything I can find out about him. Who he is, where he came from, who he hangs out with. The information I have is sketchy and comes from a questionable source."

"I am retired, Pietro. I do not keep up."

Macklin slid into the Sicilian dialect. "Come, Umberto. Retired athletes follow the sports pages. That great gray head of yours is a computer. It is one reason you are still alive. What have you heard?"

Pinelli laid a hand like a steam shovel on Macklin's shoulder. "You are my friend," he said in English. "*Mi amico*, which is more. If I had a son he would be you."

"You have a son."

"A young man in the state of Washington shares my name. He sends back the Christmas presents I send to his children. You are my son. Who taught you that you do not stab with the knife, you push? I have, how you say it, an investment in your well-being. So I say, forget about this Ackler. He is not worth spilling purple legion blood over. Leave him to the barbarians."

Macklin returned to English. "You forget I'm not Italian."

"Not in your name or your birth or your father's father. Here you are Italian." He doubled his other hand into a great fist and touched Macklin's heart. "So I say again, forget about this Ackler."

"Is he that good?"

"Good, who's to say who is more good? He is young, not thirty, and you are forty."

"Thirty-nine."

"I sheathed my knife at forty-six. I know now that I was a lucky man for six years. The hands, they slow. The eyes dim, the ears thicken."

"You heard me coming well enough just now."

"Ackler would have known your footfall the moment you entered the store. You see? Everything is relative." The big man sighed, a little theatrically. "You are now where I was when a young man with an Irish name came along—"

"Scots."

"—came along to remind me that the longer you remain alive the closer you are to death. Fine clothing has interested me since the day I bloodied my first silk shirt. So I withdrew my savings, of which there were not much considering the high cost of crash cars and good drivers, and invested in the little sideline that is now my life. Follow where I lead, Pietro. Do not end up naked in a tray with your insides showing."

"All I know about clothes is how to work a zipper. Also I'm strapped. Most of my savings has gone into keeping my wife in booze and my son out of jail."

"How is the boy? Roger."

"I haven't seen him in days." Macklin paused. "Ackler."

Pinelli blew some more oyster-fragrant air. "All I know of him has been told to me by others. I do not listen, understand. But I hear. One year ago he is not known here. Eight months ago, nine, his name is whispers on the air. You remember a man named Fishbein?"

"Vegas accountant. Pumped full of holes at Metro Airport

last January on his way to a congressional hearing in Washington."

Pinelli grinned his old wolf's grin. "You, too, hear."

"I listen."

"The federal marshals, they drive a bulletproof car right into the lobby of his hotel in Las Vegas to pick him up. From there they go straight to the loading ramp of a private jet. At no time is he in the open, except during the five-minute walk between planes in Detroit. A man steps out from behind a pillar and swings out a light machine pistol, one of these Swedish things with no more craftsmanship than goes into a good Boy Scout knife. A two-second burst, and then he is gone between luggage carts before the marshals can draw their weapons or even say holy shit. Fishbein is on his face in a puddle of blood and brains."

"That wasn't Ackler," Macklin said. "The Warren police ID'd a stiff they found in the trunk of a parked car a couple of days later as the killer."

"They find a dead man who matches the description the marshals give. The marshals, who you must understand are looking very foolish now, but perhaps a little less foolish if the killer is not still at large, go to the morgue and glance under the sheet and say, 'Yes, that's him.' But I ask you, when a man appears before you as on a puff of wind with death stammering away in his hands, how much time will you spend looking at his face? Do you remember what was learned from the corpse?"

"Nothing. His features were battered and his teeth had been knocked out and his fingers cut off. There was no way to identify him from records."

"Was there nothing else?"

Macklin started to shake his head, stopped. "Was he an addict?"

"Excellent!" The big old man was beaming like a college professor before a bright student. "His arms are full of old punctures and they find traces of heroin in his system, enough to kill a Hollywood film crew. Now, Fishbein's testimony would be disastrous to the Las Vegas interests. Who would risk someone so unreliable as a dope fiend to remove this threat? But the alleys are filled with young wrecks. Our man had but to find one whose height and weight and coloring resembled his own and then keep him supplied—tethered, if you will pardon the poetic indulgence, on a leash of white powder until the time came to end the investigation. An extra few grains in the needle, a short drive to Warren, a leisurely walk back, and Daniel Oliver Ackler is as one born again. I applaud the simple beauty of it even as I abhor its mercenary motive."

"Who hired him?"

"Those animals out West. They have no sense of family. Employing a wildcat, bah!"

"What else has he done?"

Pinelli shrugged, straining the seams of his vest. "His signature is his audacity. Select any five daring murders committed over past months in which the killer slipped away. Four will be his."

"Where was he before he came here?"

"New York. Philadelphia. I have heard him referred to by the nickname Baltimore, but perhaps the oriole is his favorite bird."

"What about friends?"

"How many friends have you, Pietro?"

Macklin smiled. "Just one."

"He has fewer."

"Has he ever been seen hanging out with hippie types?"

"I do not know what a hippie type is. Once it meant long hair and a beard, but now that is how one describes a politician."

"Radicals. Revolutionaries."

Pinelli still looked puzzled.

Macklin blew some air of his own. "The kind of person that would grab a boatload of civilian passengers and make big noises about blowing it up."

"Ah!"

"You heard?"

"It's on the news. Eight terrorists. One was killed."

"Ackler killed him. Just to show the rubes who's in charge. He's going by Sol on the boat."

"If it is Ackler, someone is paying him."

"I have to know who. I don't walk into a room with the light off."

Pinelli pointed a finger like a cucumber. "Walk away from this one, my friend. What do you know about boats?"

"For a hundred thousand I can learn."

"What is a hundred thousand? It will not even cramp you in your coffin."

"Are you going to help me, Umberto? If not I'll look for someone else. But yours is the only information I trust."

"I have told you all I know."

"Who's your source?"

The big man breathed noisily in the silence. The room was close and Macklin felt the illusion that all the air in it was going up Pinelli's tomahawk nose. Finally the retired killer took out his fountain pen and picked up his clipboard and leafed to a fresh page. He wrote something, unclipped the sheet, and handed it to Macklin. It contained an address in River Rouge.

"Talk to the man you find there. No names."

"What can he tell me?"

"Much more than I. He has seen Ackler."

Pinelli had an inspiration and reached behind his back, pulling something from inside the waistband of his pants under his vest. Macklin folded the sheet with the address on it and put it in his pocket to accept the item. He took hold of a smooth ivory handle and drew two inches of gleaming nickel out of black leather. Three more inches remained in the sheath.

"Be very careful with it, *mi amico*. It is sharper than a razor and never surrenders its edge. I have replaced the sheath three times. It came with my family to Messina and belonged to my father's grandfather, who threw Napoleon off the bridge at Arcole in 1796."

"*Grazia*, Umberto. I have knives." Macklin started to return it. Pinelli closed both his huge hands over Macklin's.

"Show it to the man you are going to see. That way he will know you come from me."

"I could have stolen it."

"In that case there would be blood on it." The old killer patted his hand. "*Buona fortuna, figlio mio*."

CHAPTER 10

RANDALL BURLINGAME answered the telephone in his office, listened for a moment, said, "Son of a bitch," and thumbed down the plunger, breaking the connection. Secret Service agent Bill Chilson, throwing a lot of light off his white shirtsleeves and bald head, started to ask something, but was cut off by the FBI director's upraised hand. Burlingame dialed a number.

"Treadaway? Me. Radio your men at Macklin's house to call in when he shows. Einstein and Schweitzer managed to lose him two blocks from Maggiore's place." His tone dripped acid.

When Burlingame hung up, Chilson said, "What is Macklin to Maggiore, anyway?"

"We ran his picture through the computer. Treasury man on stakeout at Maggiore's took it. The machine matched it with a file on Addison Camera in Taylor. It's a mob subsidiary. He's on staff there, some desk job. But if Boniface asked for him on this one you can bet he's a button."

"Seems to me that would show up on the machine."

"Only the ones who get caught." Burlingame played with his pipe. He hadn't recharged or relit it since Howard Klegg had left the office—he was cutting down—but the bowl was worn to a smooth deep rose color from much handling. "This other one, this spooky-looking one who showed up at Maggiore's a half hour ahead of Macklin and left a couple of minutes afterwards, he's not in the file. We Telexed his picture to Washington. Still waiting on that. I don't know where he fits in."

"Isn't all this surveillance just what we promised Klegg we wouldn't do?"

A smile tugged at the FBI man's lips. "I've been waiting for a chance like this as long as I've been here. When this is over, no matter how it winds up, we'll have a stronger line on the way these boys work than we've had since Joe Valachi."

"They'll find out."

"Oh, they know. You don't duck two experienced field agents by accident. I expect Klegg to come in here any time and pound the desk, but in the end they won't do anything about it. Boniface wants out."

"That part surprised me," Chilson said. "I never knew you to make a deal."

"We haven't just been scratching our balls since the gate closed on him. There will be a team of field men waiting for him when he steps outside to arrest him for tax fraud and eight other charges that will keep him under glass till they wheel him out toes first."

"Meanwhile what happens to those people on the boat?"

"You mean what happens to HEW Secretary Clarence Turnbull's daughter Carol. We're working on it."

"Working on it how?"

"We've got the dope on a recent theft from the National Guard Armory up in Grayling. Three M-16s, four Army Colts, six cases of ammunition, and about five pounds of gelatin explosives with caps. Guard has a warrant out for a Captain Philip MacKenzie, who's been AWOL since the stuff was discovered missing. His description fits one of the terrorists. It's our first solid lead."

"How does it help?"

"If we can find out who he was hanging around with before he dropped out of sight we might be able to put a name to each of the people who are holding that boat. It helps to know who you're fighting."

"What do you mean by fighting?"

Burlingame sat back in his chair, straining the buttons on his vest. "I think you're better off not knowing, Bill. Just so that when this breaks, however it breaks, you'll be able to say your people had nothing to do with it."

"If anything happens to that girl, I come back from Washington with my head under my arm."

"Your capacity isn't investigative. I'll take the heat."

"I hope you can, Red," Chilson said. "It gets harder to take the older you get."

Still leaning back in his seat, the FBI director blew several smoke rings before he realized he'd filled and lit his pipe. He looked at his hands accusingly.

The address Herb Pinelli had given Macklin belonged to a crumbling warehouse on a street with broken paving that opened off West Jefferson and dead-ended on the River Rouge. It was charred brick with high segmented windows gone blank with grime and exposure, and it would have started out by housing cases of liquor smuggled from Ontario during Prohibition, but in the intervening years it had not quite been converted into apartments. Cheap curtains moved in some of the windows as Macklin climbed out of his car and waded through calf-deep fog from the Rouge and then slid sideways through a two-foot space where the great steel fire door was propped open with a cement block.

His soles scraped a concrete floor the color of river mud, the noise echoing right through plywood partitions on either side of a narrow aisle. From where he stood he could hear six television sets and a radio playing seven different programs. The doors to the various apartments had been cut straight out of the plywood, hinged, and fitted with cheap white china knobs and locks with keyholes big enough to stick in a finger and turn the tumblers.

He didn't. He walked all the way to the end of the makeshift hall, smelling cooking smells and concrete mold and sawn wood and, he swore, bootleg whiskey sixty years gone, stopping at last before a door with a cheap metal plate screwed to it reading MANAGER. The lock was different from all the others, new-looking and brass, a dead bolt. He knocked lightly. The whole wall shivered under his knuckles.

"Who is it?"

A rerun of *All in the Family* was playing next door, and the voice was so low and whispery under the canned laughter that it had to repeat itself before Macklin was sure it wasn't just a gust of wind brushing a high windowpane. It seemed to originate from just behind the hairline crack between the door and the wall.

"My name's Macklin. Herb Pinelli gave me the number of this building and told me to talk to the man I found here. I didn't know it was an apartment house."

"Go away."

It seemed a strange thing for the manager of an apartment building with obvious vacancies to say to a stranger.

"You know Herb Pinelli?"

"Never heard of him." The whisperer went off into a fit of coughing. It had fluid in it and a measured cadence, as if he had had plenty of practice.

Macklin glanced down the hall. Three numbers down a door moved shut when he turned his head. He inserted his back between it and the manager's door and put his lips almost to the crack. He could barely hear himself under a margarine commercial jabbering away in the adjoining apartment.

"If you open the door I'll show you Herb sent me."

"Sure, I open the door, you cave my face in."

"I could sneeze it open. But I'm polite."

"Try it. I got a .357 Colt magnum in here for the *gesundheit*."

"Then you won't lose anything by opening the door. Unless you don't have any gun in there at all."

There was a long stretch during which Macklin kept his ear

close to the crack. Next door, Edith was explaining to Archie how she'd managed to dent a man's car with a can of cling peaches.

"Stand away."

Macklin straightened and took a step backward. There was a succession of metallic snaps, clicks, and jingles, then the knob rotated and the door moved inward three inches. A small steel chain hammocked in the space between. Darkness beyond, rheumy eye-whites bluish in a smear of dusky face, a splash of red flannel.

No words were spoken. After a pause, Macklin slid Herb's knife out of its sheath on his belt under his jacket, reversed the ends slowly, and extended it handle first through the space. A dirty brown hand accepted it. The door closed.

Seconds passed. The killer was about to knock again when something tinkled and the door swung wide. He was looking at a short black man in a faded shapeless bathrobe with a fringe of hair the color of chalk teased up over a bald crown. His eyebrows were thick and mealy, his nose flush to his face as if pushed by an insistent hand. Coils of whisker like trench wire clung to his jawline. He was holding the knife by its handle like the weapon it was. His other hand held a Louisville Slugger with its top four inches gone and silver duct tape wound halfway up its length.

A stench of urine and daily deposits of sweat going back several weeks unfurled and smacked Macklin in the face like a moldy towel.

The manager gestured him inside with an impatient jerk of his head and closed the door behind him, manipulating the locks and chains. "Where's the magnum?" Macklin asked.

"Ain't got one. Guns scare the shit out of me. I like baseball." The black man gestured with the bat.

"Nice place you have here."

Part of a window extended below the raftered and plywood-boarded ceiling, but it had been painted over from inside and no lamps were lit, making ominous hulking shadows of the piles of ragged clothing and stacks of newspapers and magazines in the corners and on the furniture, which included a bed with an iron frame, a painted dresser, a folding card table with a torn vinyl top, and a two-burner stove with dead flies preserved in a layer of grease on the surface.

"I know it's a dump. I could get better, you think I'd live here? What's Herb Pinelli's middle name?"

"I didn't know he had one."

The black man drew a split fingernail down through his coiled whiskers. Then he held out his palm with the knife balanced on it for Macklin to take. "I guess you're from him, all right. If he's got one, only him and someone that studied would know what it is."

Macklin returned the weapon to its sheath. "If we're through playing who won the pennant, I want to talk to you about Daniel Ackler."

Some of the blood went out of the manager's face, turning the brown a dead beige. "What'd Herb tell you about me and Ackler?"

"Nothing. He wouldn't even give me your name. Just this address."

"He gives it to you, you give it to Ackler?"

Macklin took the paper with the address written on it out of his pocket, showed it, and tore it into little pieces, letting them flutter to a thin carpet with all the color trod out of it. "I'm lousy with numbers," he said. "Can't even remember my own telephone. It's Ackler I want. He doesn't have to know who told me about him."

"I don't know nothing but what I said to Herb."

"Is he after you?"

"Christ, no. That's why I'm living in this here luxury penthouse apartment, because he ain't after me."

"Can I sit down?"

"Watch you don't scratch the finish on that there Chippendale."

The killer tested the broken overstuffed rocker with his hands braced on the scaly arms before trusting his weight on it. When he lowered himself onto the cushion he kept sinking until his knees were higher than his belt. He crossed his legs to a chorus of senile groans from the superstructure. His host leaned back against the stove with his arms folded across his chest. He had leaned the baseball bat against the loose oven door. His ankles were bare and painfully thin above rundown slippers.

"I don't care why he's after you," Macklin said. "I'm going to kill him. Or he's going to kill me. Either way he doesn't know my source. Unless I find him some other way."

Barney Miller was starting on the other side of the partition separating the apartments. The bass notes of the theme *spong*ed through the thin wood.

"What are you—cop?"

"I'm a killer."

"Oh," said the black man, twining and untwining whiskers around his index finger. "Oh."

"That make a difference?"

"Some. You drink?"

"Not when I'm working."

The manager grinned for the first time, and Macklin would just as soon he hadn't. There were things in his teeth. "Now I know you're not cop." He moved the baseball bat, opened the oven door, and hoisted out a green gallon jug with a screw top and a smeared china mug. The two-dollar wine made a gurgling noise going into the mug, like blood from a slashed jugular.

CHAPTER II

THE SPOOKY-LOOKING MAN WITH THE thinning blond hair and one lazy eyelid watched the middle-aged man in the untidy off-the-rack suit step outside the warehouse and glance up and down the street before striding to his car. That was what gave them up, that quick once-over they shared with their opposite numbers on the other side of the badge. The uninitiated, noticing the gesture, might take Macklin for a cop; he had that sad, well-worn look. Freddo himself was often mistaken for a professional athlete because of his fluid grace and good clothes. It was an impression he never tried very hard to correct.

He followed Macklin's car for six blocks until it nicked a light on the red and Freddo had to stop or be smashed by a U-Haul van barreling through the intersection. He drummed his fingers on the leather-covered steering wheel until the light changed, then squirted ahead, dusting the fender of a Volkswagen Rabbit attempting a left-hand turn in front of the pack. He drove several more blocks, craning his head around, tried a number of side streets, then gave it up and went back the way he had come. He was irritated but not upset. It was a hazard one ran when tailing someone alone. The smart shadow always kept an alternative.

He parked two streets north in case someone might remember seeing his car and walked back to the warehouse-apartment building with the fog boiling around his ankles like a special effect from a Universal horror film.

Port Huron, for chrissake.

That was where the old black man had said Daniel Ackler was living, in a cottage on the lake, when he had gone up there to deliver an envelope full of cash for the general contractor for whom the black man had mopped floors until he was promoted to messenger. He wasn't supposed to know it was money, but he had peeped. He couldn't say why his employer had sent it to Ackler, but Macklin was free to draw whatever conclusions he wanted from the fact that the firm's major competitor went bankrupt shortly after its president vanished. The janitor/courier/apartment house manager had made a poor thing of concealing his nosiness from Ackler, and he'd been in hiding ever since. The grandeur of his current title was somewhat dulled by the knowledge that he had made more money mopping floors.

The wildcat killer had been entertaining a house guest at the time of the visit, but the black man retained only a vague impression of a tall, youngish man with styled blond hair and a sleek moustache passing into another room just as the messenger entered on Ackler's invitation. He didn't remember seeing a scar, X-shaped or otherwise, but the rest of the description jibed with what the escaped hostages had said about the man in charge of the terrorists aboard the Boblo boat. It also fit any one of a hundred pedestrians one could see in downtown Detroit any hour of the day. In any case, Macklin had no wish to make a 120-mile round trip by road and lose two and a half hours to look at what was probably by now an empty rental cottage on Lake Huron.

And yet he knew he would do just that, if his next step failed to yield anything worth biting into.

The thought of biting set his stomach growling, and he remembered grudgingly that he hadn't eaten in twenty-one hours. Well, he could use the break. He doubled back to Outer Drive and took the Southfield Freeway into Dearborn.

The woman who answered the bell was thirty, with green eyes and black hair that was red in sunlight, parted in the middle and caught behind her neck to spill in a loose pony tail down her back. It wasn't a style Macklin particularly cared for, but it was the way she usually wore it, and it had been twenty years since he had looked for his last ideal. She was slender, almost painfully so, and nearly as tall as he in sandals with modest heels, but there was nothing masculine about her softly rounded features and full lower lip under a minimum of makeup. She had on an outfit that looked to him like a black sweatshirt and matching jeans, though it would go by a French name and cost more than his best suit. When she recognized him she snaked her arms around his neck and kissed him. Sharp teeth speared his lower lip like thorns.

"Hello, Christine. What's for lunch?"

"Is that all you can think of to say after not seeing or calling me all week?" She leaned her forehead against his, the corners of her mouth upturned mockingly.

"I've been working," he said. "What's for lunch?"

She bumped him with her pelvis. "I missed you."

"What's—"

She placed a scarlet-nailed finger against his lips, stopping the question. "I'll rustle up something. But it'll cost you."

"I'll pay my way."

She closed the door behind him and led him into the apartment by his hand. It was a long living room with a bedroom opening off to the left and a stainless-steel-lined dimple at the end that was the kitchenette, just big enough for two to stand in if they didn't move and kept their arms down. But the carpet was rich pile and the furniture was new. She left him to go into the kitchenette, and he wandered around the living room with his hands in his pockets, studying the pictures he had seen before on the walls and looking through the end window at the view he had looked at a hundred times. The morning *Free Press* lay open on the table in front of the window to the Help Wanted section. Several items were circled in black Magic Marker.

"Still looking?" he asked.

"No, I just like to mark the words I know."

"Stop that sarcastic crap. You're getting to sound just like Donna."

"Whoops, we're touchy today." A skillet on the stove snarled when a sandwich steak hit the grease. While it was cooking she came out and folded the newspaper and moved it to the telephone stand and started setting the table.

"They going to call you back at the plant?"

"They'll have to call back the workers on the line first," she said, "and they haven't done that yet. Clerical staff comes last."

He dug a roll of bills out of his coat pocket and peeled off some twenties. "Hundred see you through the week? I haven't been to the bank."

"I've still got some of what you gave me last time."

"I don't see how."

"Sandwich steaks," she said brightly. Then she jumped a little and hurried back into the kitchenette to turn his steak over.

He snapped the rubber band in place and dropped the roll back into his pocket. "I don't know why you won't let me open an account for you. Just till you're working again."

"I wouldn't like being kept."

"Now you sound like a novel."

Christine put the pattie on a roll and served it with a glass of milk. They sat down at the table. She watched him pick up the sandwich. "Aren't you eating?" he asked.

"I'm funny. I ate at lunchtime."

There was no more conversation. He finished eating and she cleared the table and then they went to bed. The curtains were drawn and when she slid naked between the sheets to join him the dull light sifting through the fabric lay violet on her polished skin. They moved together, placing learned hands in familiar places, and when he finally entered her she took in her breath and dug in her heels high on his back. Afterward they lay with their legs intertwined and Macklin's arm around her, his hand fondling a firm breast.

"I can't marry you," he said. "Donna would make a fight of the divorce and I can't afford open court."

"I don't want to be married. I've been there and I didn't like the scenery."

"Just living with someone isn't the same as being married."

"It is in everything important. Someone dies, someone else lives, and she has to shop for the casket and give away his clothes."

She had been living with a smalltime loan shark in Troy when they had met at a dinner party at Michael Boniface's house. It was there that Boniface, the traditionalist, had given the shark the kiss of death. Macklin had never seen the custom in practice before and had always thought it showy and a nuisance, as it put the intended victim on his guard, but when the old man did it, it seemed chivalric and exactly right. Macklin had refused the assignment on his principle never to kill someone he knew, but he agreed to lay the groundwork. Soon he was sleeping with Christine, against another of his principles. The cowboy they eventually sent so botched the job on the loan shark that the police picked up a clear lead and Macklin was called in to mop up. The cowboy was bones in the Detroit River now and Christine remained unaware of Macklin's role in her lover's death.

He kissed her forehead. She stirred and said, "That felt like good-bye."

"I'm still working. How much can you expect for a sandwich and a glass of milk?"

"What, no tip?"

He grunted. It was as much of a laugh as he ever allowed himself. *Save your emotions for private moments, Pietro*, Herb Pinelli had counseled him long ago. *They only make you human, and humanity is not a commodity in our market.* But the old killer hadn't told him how to break them out of storage when those private moments came. He squeezed Christine's breast gently and got out of bed, sucking in his stomach while he drew on his pants. Soon he would have a belly like a house painter.

Christine watched his muscles twitch as he reached for his shirt. "Call me?"

"I'll try. I'm going to be busy for a while."

It was as close as they ever came to discussing his work. Often he wondered how much she knew. She had never asked him what he did for a living, not since they had met. When his tie was done up he draped his coat over his arm and leaned down to kiss her. "I'll try to call," he repeated, while their lips were still touching.

When he had gone she lay awake for a while. Then she napped.

Because there was no back way out of the warehouse, a two-by-four having been spiked across the great doors opening onto the loading dock, Freddo left through the front door. The silk lining of his suit jacket felt cold as iron touching the patches where he had sweated through his custom shirt and he welcomed the cool moisture of the river mist on his face after the close humidity inside. The stuff was still thick enough to make shadows of the industrial buildings on Zug Island across the Rouge, but he could smell the acetone pouring out of the tall stacks. At night the island glowed from the foundry fires and reddened the bellies of low clouds like St. Elmo's Fire, but today it was as gray as old pewter. Freddo scowled at the black cinders as large as dried peas that had collected on the Cordoba's hood and roof but made no attempt to brush them off for fear of scratching the finish. He got in and drove away in search of a car wash. And a telephone.

Anna Dietrichson had seen River Rouge grow up around her from a semirural village of Ford workers to an anonymous appendage to the Motor City, and she didn't approve or disapprove of any of it so long as her joints didn't ache. She had not got on with her neighbors when the population was predominantly European, and so felt no resentment when the blacks moved in, or when Arabs and other peoples whose muddy-sounding languages she couldn't begin to identify came in to join them. She had, in fact, been seriously inconvenienced only twice in her sixty-year residency: once when Isadore, her husband of forty-two years, died, forcing her to go on welfare, and again eighteen months ago, when the apartment building she had lived in since her honeymoon was condemned and she was evicted.

This would make the third time. Cockroaches were something people all over the world learned to live with. Electrical failures were so infrequent now, compared with the early days of alternating current, that she barely noticed them. But when the gray pain was in her bones and there was no hot water in which to soak them, a confrontation was at hand. When she tired of banging on the pipes in her second-floor room in the converted warehouse with the crescent wrench she kept as protection against burglars, she buttoned her ragged sweater and snatched her hard-rubber cane out of the antique umbrella stand near the door and commenced the long journey down to ground level and the manager's quarters.

She rested twice on the stairs, and at the base she leaned against the flimsy stairwell wall and listened to her heart pounding irregularly in her ears. After five minutes she opened the door into the hallway just as a man in a soft gray suit like no tenant in that building ever wore passed by and continued to the exit. She saw only his long thin back and blond hair to his collar with pink scalp peeping through at the crown, and then the fire door closed behind him, cutting off her view. Someone from the city, she thought. If they were getting ready to condemn this place too . . .

She clunked the manager's door with the crook of her cane. To her surprise it opened a few inches under the slight impact. It had always been locked before. She waited, and when no one answered she nudged the door open a little farther with the soft rubber tip. She could always claim it moved by itself. It stopped after three more inches and would move no farther. By that time she could see inside far enough to know what was blocking it.

"Mother of God." She crossed herself for the first time in thirty-seven years.

CHAPTER 12

PORT HURON, WHAT'S HE WANT IN Port Huron?"

Charles Maggiore's voice, filtered through the telephone wires, sounded fat and contented. Freddo supposed he'd fallen asleep under the sun lamp and been awakened by the bell.

"Some soldier named Ackler," Freddo said. "He's got a place up there, a cottage on the lake. That's as much as I got out of the jig on Rouge before I lost him."

"Okay."

"Okay what?"

"Okay means okay."

"Oh."

"Who you got with you?" Maggiore asked.

"Nobody so far."

"Make it somebody. I don't want any missed chances. If you don't nail him the first time you won't get another try. I got a number in Pontiac you can call if you don't have someone in mind."

"I got someone."

"Okay, use him. I don't want to hear from you again till you tell me just one word and that word is yes, you got it?"

"Yeah."

"Okay." The line clicked and buzzed.

"Thinks he's Scarface Al." Freddo hung up on his end, then lifted the receiver again and dialed a number in Detroit. Leaning on his elbow on the shelf of the open-air booth, he watched a kid in white coveralls buffing the glistening Cordoba with a yellow chamois. When a voice came on the other end of the line he said, "Link?"

"Yeah. Freddo?"

"Get your shit. I'm picking you up in twenty."

"Heavy shit?"

"Heavy as you got." He pegged the receiver and tipped the kid with the chamois five dollars for remembering to buff under the windshield wipers.

None of the half-dozen diners in the Peacock's Roost was paying any attention to the organist. It was two hours to the dinner rush and the dark young man at the keyboard was using the down time to experiment with some chords the owner didn't allow when people were listening. Slim and swarthily good-looking from a little distance, he had tobacco color in the whites of his eyes on closer examination and his cheeks were a purple relief map of burst blood vessels. Although he was just thirty, there was a light sprinkling of dull gray in his curly dark hair, anchored by scimitar-shaped sideburns to his jaw. When he wasn't playing he was constantly flicking imaginary cobwebs from his face with his fingers, and sudden noises of whatever volume made him jump. At one time he had been organist for a rock band that hadn't missed a chart for the past six months, but drugs and alcohol had made him late for too many rehearsals and when the band went to Los Angeles to sign a recording contract he had been left behind. Now he played requests for couples celebrating their golden wedding anniversaries, and every other one was "Moonlight Serenade."

"John Scavarda?"

He looked up from a variation on "Lullaby of Birdland" he had borrowed from Elton John to see an exhausted-looking man with ordinary features of a slightly wolfish cast standing on the other side of the organ. His necktie of no particular color was at half-mast and he had his hands in the pockets of a dark suit that needed pressing.

"Johnny," corrected the organist. "You look like 'The Little White Cloud That Cried.' Or maybe 'Love Me Tender.'"

"I'm not making a request. I understand you were one of the last people to see Jack DeGrew before he turned up at the Wayne County Morgue."

Scavarda stopped playing and leaned back on the bench, swirling the ice in a glass of tea laced heavily with bourbon. "Cop, huh? I been wondering when you cats would get around to me."

"Everyone thinks I'm a cop. Howard Klegg gave me your name."

"I don't know any Howard Kleggs today. Try me tomorrow."

"He's a lawyer. He represents Michael Boniface. Whose main man while he's on a long holiday is Charles Maggiore. Who has a working relationship with a bookie named Ernest Starvo, also called Fort Street Ernie. Who just now is sitting on eighteen bills in markers signed by Johnny Scavarda. Care to talk?"

When the organist hesitated, the other man skinned two twenties off a roll he had produced from a coat pocket and poked them into the empty tip glass on top of the organ.

"Not here," said Scavarda, rising and transferring the bills to the inside pocket of his dinner jacket. "I got a break coming. Step into my office."

They left the dais where the organ stood and went out through a side door into an alley smelling of urine and rotting garbage and the dry musk of rats. None of the people eating inside had glanced up as they threaded their way between tables.

Scavarda lit a cigarette with quick nervous fingers and inhaled. "Who are you?"

"My name's Macklin. When word hit the street that DeGrew was the charbroiled stiff the police scraped out of that car torched off Eight Mile Road, you told Starvo you saw him getting into a car that fit the description, with a man whose description fits Daniel Oliver Ackler."

"I don't know any Ackler. And I didn't say the car fit the description of the one burned. I don't know a Chrysler from an Idaho potato."

"Klegg says different."

"Not knowing him I wouldn't call him a liar."

"You've got a snug lip for a man with my forty dollars in his pocket."

"Make me a request. I'll play any tune you want except 'MacArthur Park.' I hate that fucking song."

Macklin moved quickly. Scavarda was spun around, his cigarette flying and showering sparks, and a hand grabbed the collar of his dinner jacket and yanked it down from his shoulders to pin his arms behind him. One of the buttons plinked off brick and dropped on its edge and rolled to a stop amidst the litter from an overturned garbage can. Something pricked the flesh under his chin.

"Of course, I could learn to like it," he managed to gasp. " 'Someone left the cake out in the rain . . .' "

"Don't be funny, Johnny. As a stand-up you're a great musician." Macklin was talking through his teeth. Moisture trickled down Scavarda's neck into his shirt collar. "Where'd you see DeGrew get picked up?"

"In front of the Hyatt Regency in Dearborn. We were getting set up for a gig. I was subbing on piano for a guy that was getting married—"

"Save it for your memoirs. Did you recognize the man who picked him up?"

"Didn't know him from Beethoven. Look, I don't have a change of shirts here." Blood had veined his white collar.

"What'd he say?"

"He said he was with the union. Right away I didn't like

him, those guys are pricks. Said he got a complaint that Jack had sat in on bass for a private party in Grosse Pointe for less than scale. Jack climbed in next to him to argue about it and they drove off. I had to lug that elephant case of his inside. I was gonna burn him when he got back. Only he didn't."

"Say where they were going?"

"No. C'mon, man, my break's over. I need this job."

Macklin held his grip. "What else did you hear?"

"There wasn't nothing else. C'mon, man!"

"Guy in the car said DeGrew bent a rule, DeGrew said he didn't, they took off?"

"Yeah."

"People don't talk like that, Johnny. They take time getting to the point. What else?"

"There wasn't nothing else."

The knife dug a little deeper.

"Scavarda! Get your ass in here. We're losing customers."

The voice came from a second-story window overlooking the alley. Its owner's face was cut off from their view by a tattered awning over the side door that had been there since before the building across the way was erected. Macklin released the musician. Scavarda rubbed his neck, smearing the blood, and fished a white handkerchief out of an inside pocket to staunch the flow.

"That's all for now, Johnny. I may be back."

"Thanks for the warning."

"A little cold water will take that stain right out of your shirt," Macklin said. "But catch it before it dries."

"Yeah."

The killer poked another twenty-dollar bill into the other's breast pocket.

Scavarda prowled a black patent-leather toe among the spilled trash in the alley, found the button that had popped off his jacket, and retrieved it. He fiddled with it, looking down at his fingers. "I did hear something else."

"Figured you did."

"It isn't much. The union guy said something about Jack's being a hard fish to reel in. It sounded like fisherman's lingo."

"Could be. That it?"

Scavarda nodded, looked at his spotted handkerchief. The bleeding had stopped. The hole was only a pinprick. "Well," he said, and went inside, leaving the door open. Few people found it in them to close doors on Macklin, no matter how many flies gained entrance in the process.

Alone in the alley, Macklin used a clean cotton rag he found among the litter to wipe the blade of Herb Pinelli's great-grandfather's knife. More and more these days he found such repetitious acts helpful to his thinking, like an old man in a home rolling his wheelchair back and forth.

He'd heard the fishing was good around Port Huron.

CHAPTER 13

AS THE CAPTURED STEAMER GHOSTED OVER
the gunmetal water, trailing shreds of fog from its
mast and the flagstaffs flying the Canadian and
United States colors, "Cap'n Eddie" Fielding worried about only
one man in the pilot house, and it wasn't the one who called
himself Don.

The chief hijacker leaned against the chart table at the back
of the octagonal enclosure with his thumb hooked inside his belt
next to where his Luger rested, eyes bright, one ear cocked
toward the portable transceiver that crackled from time to time on
the table with his partners' random comments. He spoke little and
never moved except to shift his weight when one limb threatened
to fall asleep or to grip the automatic pistol's butt when one of the
other men moved too quickly. He was a dependable terrorist.

The man who worried the captain was Phil Holliday, his first
mate. They had been friends, or as close to friends as a
commander and his subordinate could ever be, for four years, and
yet the old sailor was certain with the conviction of ten thousand

days and nights spent on the water that Holliday lacked that last inch of what it took to command a ship under this particular stress. Rather, he fit the popular misconception of a ship's captain as a man of independence, resolve, and self-confidence bordering on massive arrogance. Only those who had been in the position knew that all of these things must be tempered by the ability to compromise. Cap'n Eddie had not risen from deckhand on an iron coffin of an ore carrier to his present authority without learning how to take orders. From his vantage point at the rear of the pilot house across its width from Don, the captain had ample opportunity to watch Holliday's back grow stiff and the nape of his neck redden as he stood at the windscreen watching for approaching craft. His helplessness clearly chafed, and Cap'n Eddie feared the inevitable blow-up.

"I always had the impression the captain ran this tub," Don said, breaking the reverie. "You've got a man on the wheel, a man to look out, and another man to look out for what the lookout missed. What do you do, just stand around waiting for someone to say 'Ahoy, the white whale'?"

His tone was bantering, with no animosity in it. The old sailor answered without rancor. "When there's a big blow or a pleasure craft coming the wrong way downriver, eight men up here wouldn't be too much."

"Yeah, someone has to blow the whistle."

"Captain Fielding is the best skipper on the river," Holliday snapped.

Don crinkled his eyes at Cap'n Eddie. "Kind of like having the best-looking legs on a girls' Olympic weightlifting team, huh, Popeye?"

"It's been claimed that if you can navigate the Detroit River, you can sail any body of water in the world," said the old man.

"It isn't like waving a pistol around and saying stick 'em up."

Lazily the armed man turned his attention to the first mate. "We don't need you, Wyatt. We've got a lookout and Barney Fyfe here to look out for the lookout." He inclined his head toward the young security guard seated glumly on the turning stool near the starboard hatch.

"I might not be as easy to hit as a fat bass player."

"Phil, for Christ's sake!" the captain exclaimed.

"You tell him, Popeye. Old Wyatt's quick on the draw for someone with dust in his holster."

The captain changed the subject. "Why do you call him Wyatt?"

" 'Cause his name's Holliday but he looks more like Earp."

"I guess he does at that, with that handlebar." Cap'n Eddie kept his tone light. "But maybe not as much as you look like Wild Bill Hickok."

He had struck the right chord. Don smiled slowly behind his own moustache. "You won't find my back to any doors on this bucket, old man."

"These bulkheads weren't built to stand up to Coast Guard bullets," put in Holliday.

Don said, "They'll have to find us first."

The fog had remained uniformly dense all day, as if the boat were towing its own cloud. Once they had heard the beating of helicopter blades overhead, but the noise hadn't returned and Don supposed that if it was a Coast Guard craft they were waiting for the curtain to lift before searching in earnest.

Holliday said, "This soup can't last forever. What are you going to do when the wind comes up and takes it away?"

"That's up to the Governor."

Cap'n Eddie adjusted the hearing aid attached to his glasses. Moist air was hard on the transistor. "Do you really believe the Governor will release those prisoners?"

"You better hope so, Popeye." Don lifted and resettled the Luger under his belt. "You better get down on your knees and pray to King Neptune he does just that."

The security guard stood up suddenly. The gun leaped into Don's hand. "What's wrong, Barney, you got a bite?"

"I have to go to the bathroom."

"Head," Holliday corrected automatically.

"Head, whatever. I have to go."

"So go."

The guard edged past Cap'n Eddie and descended the short flight of steps to the captain's quarters above the crown deck.

That had been the most complicated part of Siegfried's plans, seeing to the functional needs of the passengers and crew. There was a head for the captain and one for the crew and two on the dance deck for the passengers, and after they had been searched for weapons the hostages were allowed to visit them two or three at a time. The two-man teams on each of the three main decks took turns relieving themselves and watching their charges, and when Don felt the need he radioed Larry to come up and keep an eye on the bridge while he used the captain's toilet. The choreography worked. But eight hundred frightened people with bladders and sphincters ranging from healthy to minimal were a lot, and there had been a number of accidents that had done little to improve either the atmosphere or the dispositions of captive and keeper alike.

"Where are we going?" Holliday wanted to know.

"East."

It wasn't the first time the question had been asked or the answer given. This time the captain involved himself.

"For how long?" he asked. "We've only got fuel for twelve more hours. Erie's a big lake. We could drift for days before anyone rescues us."

"Nice try, Popeye. You could steam for four days and still have enough oil to burn Toronto."

Cap'n Eddie looked at him with the first faint blue glow of the dawn of admiration. "You did your homework."

Don said nothing.

A stuttering noise sounded below, as of an outboard motor revving up and then stalling abruptly. A scream, then silence.

Don snatched up his portable radio. "Who fired that burst?"

A pause, then Larry's voice crackled out of the speaker. "I think it came from the bottom deck."

"Fay?" Don released the speaker button, waited, pressed it again. "Fay, you there?"

"Yeah." She sounded breathless.

"What went down?"

"Nothing. Benny Goodman just tried something sweet."

"Who the hell is Benny Goodman?"

"Mr. Big Band. Crane. Nobody's bleeding, don't fret yourself."

"Easy on that ammo." He set the radio back down on the chart table just as the security guard came bounding up from the captain's quarters, tucking his uniform shirt into his pants. The guard's face was as white as the shirt. "Who got shot?"

"Sorry. You'll have to stay and see it again."

The guard gave Don a puzzled look.

Three tiers below, Fay was standing with her radio hanging from its strap on her shoulder and the smoldering muzzle of her M-16 almost touching Chester Crane's long thin nose. The bandleader sat spraddle-legged on the deck at her feet, his bald pate glistening through wisps of gray hair. His toupee had slid off finally and skidded ten feet along the highly polished boards. A ragged line of closely spaced holes stitched the back of the bandstand where Fay had fired when Crane had tried to jump her. Coming down hard from her last cocaine toot, she had been yawning bitterly and he had thought to catch her off guard.

"White boy," she said, "I don't know how you got this old."

He tried out his best Trocadero grin on her. It lost some of its glitter under the few lights allowed to burn on the dance deck. "Can't blame a guy for trying."

"Oh yes I can, Mr. Music. I got no sense of humor."

"Everything square, Fay?" Sol's voice rang out calmly from the stern.

She called back that everything was sweet. Her smile as she went on looking at Crane was brilliant against the old gold of her face. He watched her through squinted eyes. The smoke from the automatic rifle was making them water. Still grinning, she raised the barrel, holding the weapon horizontal, stepped back a pace, and sank to her heels, laying the rifle on the deck. Then she straightened and moved back another step.

"You call it, Baton Man," she said. "All you got to do is pick it up ahead of little Fay and fill her full of holes. You can move fast when you want to. For an old man with no hair."

Crane looked down at the weapon just beyond his feet for a

long moment before raising his eyes back to hers. "You're nuts," he told her. "Doped up."

"I'm stone cold. Pick it up, Señor Swing. 'Cause if you don't, Fay will."

He placed his palms on the deck and shook his head, gathering his feet beneath him. The woman shook her own head, mocking him, and moved to scoop up the rifle. He kicked out with one leg and felt the jar to his knee when his foot connected. She howled. It was a nasty thin tearing sound, like the shriek of an enraged cat. He launched himself up stumbling, spun around and ran, scattering passengers from his path. Ran with his shoulders hunched and his head sunk between them, his back burning where the bullets would go. Behind him the black woman was screaming curses. The rifle's loose parts rattled. He made for the railing. He was a strong swimmer, had kept in shape at an age where most of his contemporaries were retired or taking their mail in hospitals. If there was a boat nearby, if he could tread water while his arms rested. It was a better chance than he had at the moment. His hands gripped the clammy beaded steel of the railing and he tensed his muscles to swing himself over.

He almost made it.

CHAPTER 14

JUST ONCE I'D LIKE TO EAT IN A PLACE where the food was as good as the view," complained Bill Chilson, spreading butter on one half of a roll the approximate size and consistency of a cue ball.

Randall Burlingame sipped his wine and chuckled. "It comes into the building fresh, but a lot can happen in seven hundred and forty feet."

"It should take the elevator."

They were dining in the revolving restaurant atop Detroit's tallest hotel, decorated in leatherette and plush to resemble the inside of a candy box and just now overlooking through its tinted wraparound windows the shadowy skyline of Windsor across the river. Although it was not yet evening, a dusky gray screen blurred and flattened the details.

Chilson sneaked looks at the FBI bureau director over his meal of pressed sawdust masquerading as roast beef. He admired Burlingame, who, although he had been up since midnight, looked as fresh as if he had just had eight hours' sleep. Chilson himself had managed to catch a few winks at his room in the hotel, but he knew that the only break Red had taken was to shave and change shirts. He was an iron man, and if not for all that time wasted hassling with Hoover, would have been warming a chair in an office on the top floor of the Bureau's Washington headquarters years ago.

"What's the good news the Secret Service is bankrolling this gourmet dinner for?" Chilson asked.

"We've got a line on this Macklin." Burlingame put away a steaming forkful of mashed potatoes. He never blew on his food, never waited for it to cool. His companion decided his mouth and tongue were lined with asbestos. "He's a button like we thought, been with the Boniface family since old Papa Joe Morello got his tonsils taken out the hard way in Victor's Barbershop. Talk is Macklin worked the razor on that one."

"Christ, he must be fifty."

"Coming up on forty. He got an early start. Anyway, he's Boniface's chief samurai, and maybe the last of the loyal old guard. No wonder the old man saddled him with this one."

"Record?"

"One arrest eleven years ago, suspicion of ADW. It never got to court. Victim refused to identify him and then went away on a vacation he's still not back from. That just came in from Washington. We dug up an informant, someone close. Been feeding one of our field men for months, but it was all locked up in his own file and he's been out sick all week. Of course it's all hearsay. But good enough to work on."

"How does it help us?"

"It's the first chink we've found in Macklin's armor. If we hang on to it he may just lead us all out of this mess."

"Who's your informant?"

Burlingame stuck a covered wicker bowl under Chilson's nose. "Another roll?"

Smiling, the Secret Service agent shook his head and got off the subject. "So where do we go from here?"

"You I can't speak for. I'm going to lock up and go home. I'm not interested in finding out how long a man can live without sleep. Nightside will ring me if anything breaks. It won't for a while."

"What about Macklin?"

"We've got men watching his place. He has to sleep too, and those boys change their underwear now and again, not like the old days. He has to go home sometime, if only to see how the crabgrass is doing. They won't lose him again."

"What if they do?"

"They won't."

"But what if they do?"

"They won't, I said."

"How can you be so sure?"

"Because I'm tired and I need more sleep than I used to. If I thought they could lose him again I'd wind up counting the porpoises on the ceiling. They won't lose him again."

The view had shifted, and now they were looking west from downtown out toward the suburbs, where the skyline lay down and a crescent of orange sun splintered the fog into rainbows. Chilson said, "That's your secret, huh?"

"Bill, if I'd discovered it twenty years ago, I'd look five years younger. More wine?" He lifted the carafe.

Chilson started to shake his head again, then shrugged and raised his glass. Burlingame poured. Finally the Secret Service agent gave up and asked the question.

"You have porpoises on your ceiling?"

CHAPTER 15

PORT HURON WAS THAT UNIQUELY American phenomenon, the tourist city, feeding off transients in summer and then hunkering down to wait out the long winter under eight-foot snowdrifts while the icy winds skimming off the lake blew scraps of litter down its bleak deserted streets. Macklin had never been there in wintertime, and although he saw banks of permanent residences among the antique stores, fish markets, and souvenir shops, he always had the feeling that as soon as he passed them they were rolled up and placed in storage, to be unrolled again when the next visitor came. The fog dripping from the trees and cornices under congealing darkness added to the illusion of fairy-tale impermanence.

The address the black man in River Rouge had given him belonged to a small white one-story frame house with green trim, situated on an eighth of an acre near the mouth of the St. Clair River with similar cottages built so close on either side that a greyhound couldn't pass between them. There were lights on in the neighboring buildings. Macklin kept on rolling to the end of the pocked and rutted private road that dead-ended on the river, made a tight Y-turn between parked cars in an area as wide as a salt shaker, and drove past again and out of the neighborhood.

Half a block north of the cul-de-sac, two men sat in the front seat of a brown Cordoba parked in the entrance to a public landing site. The man on the passenger's side, in his early twenties with unnaturally bright red hair teased forward in a woodpecker's crest, a nose that turned up like Howdy Doody's, and freckles the size of pennies on his cheeks, peered through the gathering gloom at Freddo's motionless profile behind the wheel.

"You sure that was him?"

"It'was him," Freddo said.

"Ain't we going to follow him?"

"He'll be back."

"When?"

"When it gets dark. Relax, brother."

Lincoln Washington hated being called brother. It was bad enough he had been born with a name commonly associated with blacks. In moments of self-pity he blamed that for his errant life, and for the fact that he had fulfilled his first contract on a black Baptist minister. Two men who had called him brother hadn't lived to regret it. But when Freddo did it he said nothing. Washington liked to think it was because they were partners.

He shivered a little in the damp cool and moved to crank up his window. Freddo's wire-strung hand gripped his knee.

"Leave it down. We'll fog up the glass."

Washington left it down. In the cool dark they waited.

Macklin ate a fine black bass in a restaurant downtown with a lifeboat suspended from the ceiling and paintings of schooners under full sail on the walls. Uncharacteristically, for he hated attracting attention, he visited the salad bar twice. Soon he would be skipping a meal in preparation to move and he'd need the extra energy. He left a generous tip for the fat, cheerful waitress and drove back under a black sky to the private road outside town. The fog threw back his headlight beams like a wall.

Instead of turning into the road, he went on past and parked at a nearby landing site. There were two cars there already, looking dark and empty. Waiting for late boaters. He left the Cougar in the shadows at the other end where the license plate wouldn't be visible, glanced around, and started south on foot along the main road.

"Now," said Freddo.

The two men in the Cordoba had switched places, and now Link Washington was in the driver's seat. They came up from their slump below the level of the windows and Washington turned the key in the ignition, flicking on the headlights at the same time. The beams caught Macklin from behind. Freddo skinned his .44 Colt magnum out of the holster under his left arm and leveled the eight-inch barrel across the ledge of the open window on the passenger's side.

A black-and-white sheriff's patrol car swung into the line of fire, cutting off Freddo's view of his target. He dropped his gun below the window just as the spotlight sprang on and washed the parking area in white light.

"Move out slow," he told Washington.

"What if they try to stop us?"

"Let's all hope they don't."

The Cordoba coasted to the edge of the pavement, stopped, then swung out onto the highway, gravel crunching under its rear tires as it accelerated. The two uniformed officers climbing out of the scout car paid it only passing attention. The spotlight had come to rest on Macklin standing on the apron of the highway squinting into the glare.

"Car trouble, sir?" asked one of the officers. He was tall and tanned. Silver hairs glinted in his neat black moustache.

"I think it's the starter," Macklin replied. "I parked and took a walk to see if the salmon were running and when I got back it wouldn't start. I was looking for a phone."

"Let's take a look."

The man's partner was already standing next to the Cougar on the pasenger's side when Macklin opened the driver's door and the interior light came on. The partner's hand rested on the butt of his sidearm. Only the belt and the gun and the hand were visible through the window. Policemen were jumpiest around cars. They called it the kill zone. Macklin inserted the key and ground the starter. It turned over twice and caught with a low rumble.

"Seems okay now," observed the officer with the moustache.

"Must've been flooded."

"Can I see your license and registration?"

He got the driver's license out of his wallet and the registration slip from the glove compartment and handed them to Moustache. The partner came around the car and collected them and walked back to the black-and-white to use the radio.

"Have you got a fishing license?" Moustache asked Macklin.

"I didn't think I needed one just to look at fish."

After a few minutes the other officer returned with the papers. "No warrants."

Moustache returned them to their owner. "Sorry for the trouble. We've had some auto break-ins at these landing sites, radios and tape decks ripped off. Kids."

Macklin said nothing.

"You don't happen to know those guys that just drove off in the Cordoba, do you?" Moustache asked.

"No."

"Okay. You see someone coming out of one of these places without a boat or a trailer or a top carrier to put one on, you get curious. We'd of stopped them, except a man walking away down the road from one is curiouser."

When the officers were in their patrol car, Macklin backed around and left the site. It was nearly seven-thirty by his watch; at eight there would probably be a shift change and he could come back without fear of being questioned by the same men. He spent the time parked in a lighted shopping center lot on the edge of town, watching the evening browsers pass in and out through the electric doors and thinking about the brown Cordoba.

Those sudden lights coming from a car he'd thought was empty had sent ice up his spine and he had been about to leap into some trees at the side of the road when the sheriff's car came. Standing in the glare of the spotlight he hadn't been able to see who was inside the other vehicle or read its license plate as it pulled out. But he would remember the car.

Eight o'clock came and went. Inside the department store, a middle-aged man in shirtsleeves and a necktie saw out the last customers and locked the glass doors from inside. Cars parked on either side of Macklin's sprang to life. He pretended to doze until they had driven away. Employees came out of the big building and got into their cars and left. A few minutes later the lights mounted on poles over the parking lot went out and Macklin sat in darkness. A blue Chevrolet Impala stopped in front of the drugstore and honked its horn and a pretty blond pharmacist in a white slack suit and high heels click-clicked across the sidewalk and ducked in on the passenger's side and the car got rolling while she was still closing the door. Then silence crawled in like jungle vines reclaiming lost territory.

Macklin kept glancing at the luminous dial of his watch until it read half-past eight, reasonable time to expect Officer Moustache and his partner to go off duty and be replaced by others. Macklin started the engine, pulled on his lights, and returned to the highway. He checked his rearview mirror. Nobody was following.

The last car had left the landing site. He parked in its spot, nose out this time. Before getting out, he took off his necktie and turned up the lapels of his dark suitcoat and tied it around them to cover his white shirt.

Once during the trek back to the private road leading to Ackler's cottage he heard tires swishing on pavement around the next bend and slid into the foliage until the car passed without slowing, its lights brushing stark black shadows across the highway. Then as its taillights slid below the rise beyond the landing site he resumed his walk. His pantslegs felt clammy against his calves from the heavy dew on the grass and bushes.

A number of residences along the spiraling road down to the river were lit, and Macklin walked down the middle beyond reach of the yellow illumination spilling out the windows. A large dog tethered in front of a house trailer up on blocks barked as he went past and lunged to the end of its chain with a wham. Macklin shifted to double-time to get away before anyone investigated the noise. The dog quieted as soon as he cleared the lot.

Television sound effects racketed out of a cottage with no lights inside but the silver glow of the 21-inch screen. Two houses down from Ackler's a party was going on, with loud electronic music and tipsy laughter. That was a break. He wanted all the noise he could get. The lights had gone out in one of the next-door cottages, but they were still burning in the one on the other side. Macklin mounted Ackler's porch in shadow and rapped on the door. He waited five minutes, rapped again, waiting the same length of time, then squeezed around to the back on the side next to the dark neighboring house. In the faint light reflecting off the surface of Lake Huron's southernmost corner, he saw a back yard angling down to a dock from a weathered sundeck running along the rear of the house. Fog smoked up from the water.

Shielding the beam of his penlight with his hand, Macklin peered at the lock on the back door and grinned wolfishly. He hadn't seen one of those in fifteen years. It was the work of two minutes to slide the thick celluloid window from his wallet and insert it between the latch and the jamb as he leaned the doorknob toward the hinges. When the latch snapped back he glanced around quickly and let himself inside.

The air smelled stale, as of a house that had been shut up for days or weeks. Under it was an old cooking smell that told him he was in a kitchen. When he got so he could make out some of the room's more threatening shapes he moved along the walls and felt around the lighter oblongs of the windows, determining that the curtains had been drawn shut and weighted to the sills to discourage unwanted visitors from peering inside. Only then did he flip on his penlight and begin his search.

It was an ordinary kitchen, furnished with just the essentials under a fine film of dust. The living room, two bedrooms, and bath were hardly less ordinary, and just as securely curtained. The furniture was worn but clean, the framed pictures on the walls good prints of landscapes and maritime subjects by top-ranking American artists. They were bolted to the walls, and in fact everything that could in good taste be nailed down had been, after the fashion of rental home owners since the first lease was signed with a stylus. The mattresses on the beds had been rolled up, slipcovered, and lashed tight. There wasn't a personal item on the premises. All the drawers were empty and lined with newspapers weeks old. He lifted the receiver off the telephone on a stand in the living room. Dead.

A red-and-black FOR RENT sign lay on a low bureau near the front door. Macklin lifted the cardboard to read it in the beam of his flash, leaving a clean rectangle in the dust on the bureau top. He memorized the telephone number of the rental agency, replaced the sign exactly as he had found it, and left the house the way he'd entered, manipulating the spring latch so that it locked when he closed the door.

The walk back up the road seemed shorter. The party was still climbing steadily to a peak, jazzy theme music coming from the place with only the television set on told of a chase scene in progress, one or two of the homes that had had lights on before had gone silent and dark. Fishermen preparing for an early run in the morning. To avoid alerting the big dog across the road, Macklin cut around behind an unlighted house with no car in the driveway and a lawn that needed mowing. Then he started the steep climb up the bank to the highway. The place must have been hell to get into and out of in winter.

A car that could have been brown in better light swept along the shoulder from behind a cluster of cedars and ground to a halt across Macklin's path with a loud crunch, its rear wheels nearly lifting clear of the ground. A white face came to the open window on his side behind something black that gleamed. Macklin fell backward and rolled just as red and yellow fire lanced the night and a hard-edged roar drowned out the still-racing engine.

"Take your lead foot off the gas, shitface," shouted a voice Macklin didn't recognize, in the deafening aftermath of the shot. The engine slowed to a smooth idle.

He lay half-stunned on his back where he'd landed among damp weeds at the base of the bank and listened to the squeak of a car door opening. A foot chomped into gravel.

CHAPTER 16

FOR AN AGONIZING MOMENT HE couldn't get enough air and he was afraid his lungs had collapsed. Then they filled with a creak that seemed to him audible for yards. The wet, furry leaf of some noxious weed nuzzled his ear like a dog's tongue and when he jerked his head away, startled, the flesh where it had touched burned and tingled with the beginnings of rash. He yanked loose his necktie and flung it away and cool damp air spilled down his throat.

A smoky white shaft carved the darkness ten feet away, following the angle of the bank. When it swung his way he lay flat, holding his breath, and it grazed the tops of the weeds around him. Then it swung back and he heard footsteps in the gravel again growing louder. Mist curled in the beam of the powerful flash.

Macklin turned slowly on to his left hip and groped behind his back for the knife Herb Pinelli had given him. His fingers went inside the empty sheath. It had dropped out during his fall.

He felt the ground around him desperately. His hand bumped something solid and he closed his fingers around a two-foot length of fallen tree limb.

He couldn't hear the footsteps now. In their place, wet grass and leaves made slithering sounds against shoe leather and fabric. Macklin rolled back the other way on to his right knee and lifted his rude club. The illuminated lens of the flash grew elliptical, becoming round as it rotated back his way. He braced himself to spring.

"Who's out there?"

The shout came from behind Macklin and to his right, a man's voice, coarse with drink or sleep. At the same time a porch light belonging to a house on his side of the road blazed on. In its indecent glare, transfixed, stood a slight young man with long blond hair in a suit not built for traipsing through wet foliage. He held a foot-long police flashlight encased in black rubber in his left hand and a large revolver in his right. For a suspended instant his eyes met Macklin's. One lid drooped, and Macklin thought at first the man was winking at him. Then he backed out of the light. Quick footsteps in gravel, and then the engine that had been idling all this time swelled and a car door slammed and tires spat stones that pattered into the brush like fat raindrops. Gears changed automatically and the engine noise was smothered by distance.

Macklin became aware then of a noise that he had put down to a combination of his pounding heart and panting breaths. The chained dog down the road was barking and had been steadily since the shot was fired.

A fat juniper bush at his back made a bulky shadow in front of him, and he hugged the bush.

"Fuckers shining deer right out in the open," muttered the voice of a moment earlier. "Calling the sheriff."

The shadow moved and retreated back the way it had come. A door swung shut. When the porch light went off and darkness spilled back in, Macklin started up the road. Something gleamed dully in the grass at the side and he stooped and picked up Herb Pinelli's knife, mopping off both sides on his coatsleeve before sheathing it.

He kept to the edge on his way back up the highway, but no traffic greeted him. When he reached the landing site he sprinted the rest of the way to his car and opened the door. The interior light came on and found a gaping black hole in the dash with red and black wires hanging out like entrails.

Macklin grinned joylessly at his reflection in the windshield. While he had been busy breaking into an empty house and getting shot at, some of the local talent had made off with his radio.

Chester Crane awoke with a line of saxophones playing "Satin Doll" in his skull.

He hated the tune. It had been the band's signature in the waning days of Swing and he was expected to conduct it everywhere he appeared. Now he had reason to hate it more than ever. He groaned from the pain in his head and clamped his mouth shut against a rising tide of bile.

"Let it out," said a voice close to him. "Don't try to choke it back."

It sounded like good advice. He turned his head and splattered the deck.

Deck. How'd he know it wasn't a floor? Then he remembered, and cold fear filled the emptiness in his stomach. He opened his eyes and looked at the lights mounted on the ceiling, or whatever the nautical term was for the underside of the next deck. His eyes grated in their sockets when he shifted them to the concerned face in between. The face belonged to a young man with short dark hair and a square jaw, the kind they were making sex machines out of on television that season. Crane didn't recognize it.

"Can you sing?" he asked the face. His voice gargled. He swallowed.

The face rearranged itself into a puzzled smile. "Only in the shower. Why?"

"Doesn't matter. Once we get you up on that stand in one of those faggoty red jackets the girls won't care what you sound like."

"Thanks, but I've got a career. I'm going to be a doctor. You're my first patient."

As he spoke, the young man mopped Crane's vomit off the deck with one of the band's scarlet blazers. Crane was lying on the deck with what felt like another blazer rolled up and placed behind his head. He raised an arm weighted with iron and stroked his bald cranium, sucking in air through his teeth when his fingers touched a pulpy mass behind the crown.

"Where's my rug?"

"If you mean your toupee, it's safe. You'll have to wait until that lump goes down before it will fit."

"Am I shot?" The last thing he remembered was being chased along the rail by Fay and her M-16.

"No. The one they call Sol cracked you on the back of the head with the butt of his rifle. You've been unconscious for several hours."

"Tommy Dorsey got himself a boo-boo on his gourd," said Fay, and giggled.

Crane shifted his attention to the black woman standing over him with the automatic weapon cradled in her arms. It was dark out now and her teeth and the whites of her eyes looked brighter than they actually were as she went on giggling. She had made another visit to her pocket recently.

"You should've let me stay out," the bandleader said.

"I thought it best not to move you. You might have a concussion."

"What I have is a hangover. Without a night before to take my mind off it."

"Carol?"

A redhead who might have been pretty with make-up and some dental work on her prominent front teeth moved into Crane's line of sight and a fold of damp cloth was placed on his forehead. Sharp pain raked the bone along his sinuses and submerged itself in the broader ache behind his eyes. He smiled at the girl, and that hurt too. "Are you going to be a doctor too?"

"Nurse." Smiling shyly, she lifted the cloth and reversed it. She was wearing a pink sweater over a white summer dress.

"One of my wives was a nurse. The second one, I think. Hi. I'm Chet Crane."

"Carol Turn—"

"Turner," broke in the doctor-to-be. "I'm Ted Delano. We're engaged."

"Congratulations." Crane took his hand. It felt warm, and he realized then how cold his was. He shivered involuntarily.

"He needs a blanket," Delano said over his shoulder.

Fay stopped giggling. "So get one. I ain't no nurse's aide."

"Obviously not. The job takes character."

The muzzle of the M-16 came down. "Bite your tongue, Kildare. I got another clip in my pocket."

They stayed like that for a moment, Delano down on one knee looking up the bore of the automatic rifle in the woman's small hands. Then the transceiver she had slung from her shoulder squawked.

"Fay?"

She lifted the unit and depressed the speaker button. "Everything's tight, boss man."

"How's Crane?"

"Just snortin' bullets. Fine as pine wine."

"Sol?"

"The Spook is swell as hell and ringin' the bell. Holding the fort aft." She giggled.

"Don't stand so close to the powder, okay? It's got to last another fifty hours."

"You gots it, Massa Don."

She lowered the radio, and with it her toothy smile. Her face now didn't look as if it could support one. Stepping back, she nestled the rifle in the crook of her arm. "Go get your blanket, Dr. Jekyll. I won't kill no one till you get back."

The motel was one of a dozen in a neon-lit strip along the main highway that had succeeded in making a tiny, glitzy Las Vegas out of what had been a quiet Michigan port village. There were box-print curtains over the sliding windows in Macklin's bungalow, false maple paneling on the walls, and Plexiglas on top of everything a man could set a drink down on. Macklin broke the bathroom glass out of plastic, colored some water with bourbon from the flat pint he had sent the desk clerk after, and stretched out atop the bedcovers to sip and think. It was the first time in years he had drunk alcohol on the job. He was bending a lot of rules lately.

He had parked his Cougar behind the bungalow out of sight of the highway, but he was sure the man who had tried to kill him wouldn't make a third attempt the same night. Professionals knew when to back off and wait for a better chance. And he was a professional, or Macklin would have been aware of his presence long before he made his move, or at least he hoped so. Not a local either: Macklin knew every heavyweight in the area.

He drained his glass, looked at the bottle, thought better of it, and capped it. Then he lifted the receiver off the telephone on the bedside table and dialed the number of the rental agent whose sign he had seen in what had been Daniel Ackler's cottage, holding down the base with the hand gripping the receiver to keep it from jiggling off the table. He could never understand why the telephones in most motel rooms were so much lighter than instruments in other places.

"Hello?" A fat man's voice, thick and soft.

"Wisner Realty?"

"This is Maurice Weisner."

"I thought it was Wisner."

"That's how we're listed. I got tired of people calling me Wiener."

"I'd like to talk to you about some rental property you own on the lake."

"Call the office Monday."

Macklin said, "I thought this was the office."

"I have a line running into my home. Ordinarily I wouldn't answer it on Saturday, but my wife's visiting relatives and I can't stand to let a phone ring. We close at eight Fridays. Saturdays I don't work. I keep kosher."

"This wouldn't be work. I just want to ask you about a man who rented from you recently."

"I'm sorry. I can't discuss my business. I'll be happy to talk to you Monday."

"What's wrong with Sunday?"

"Sunday I'll talk to you. But I won't be so happy. *Shalom.*" The connection was broken.

Macklin looked at the electric alarm clock the management had thoughtfully provided him with at the rate of two dollars extra per night. Ten o'clock. He set the alarm for midnight, stripped to his underwear, folded his suitcoat and pants under the mattress for pressing, climbed under the covers, and went to sleep. It was a talent he had; he could will himself unconscious at any time among any surroundings for as long as he wanted.

He awoke fully a minute before twelve and turned off the alarm before it could begin buzzing. After splashing some water on his face in the bathroom he came back out and sat on the bed and dialed Maurice Weisner's number again. The rental agent answered on the sixth ring.

"Good morning, Mr. Weisner. I'm the man who called you last night. It's now Sunday. I thought you might be willing to discuss your business now."

"That was just two hours ago!" The voice wasn't as soft as it had been. "I've been in bed an hour. I have to be up early for church."

"I thought Saturday was your sabbath."

"It is. But most of my income comes from gentiles and I close most of my deals after services."

"Mr. Weisner, you sound like an ethnic joke."

"Just partly. I have a weak-willed mother and my son is a forest ranger in the Upper Peninsula. What is it that can't wait until a decent hour, Mr.—?"

"I'd rather not give my name just now. I want to ask you some questions about a man who was living in your lake cottage a few weeks ago."

"My firm owns sixteen lake cottages. You'll have to narrow it down."

Macklin gave him the address. After a pause Weisner said, "How'd you know we own that one? We won't be listing it until some improvements have been made."

"We all have our business tricks. About the renter."

"Just a moment. Why should I be standing here in my pajamas in the draft from the hallway answering questions from a midnight caller who refuses to identify himself?"

"Because you own sixteen lake cottages, and your insurance company won't pay if they all burn down and arson is found to be the cause."

This time the pause on the other end was much longer.

"Mr. Weisner?"

"I'm here."

"The man I'm interested in is under thirty and bleaches his hair. His name is Ackler but he might have rented the cottage under a false identity."

"That would be Mr. Charon."

"Charon with a C?"

"That's how he signed the papers."

Macklin shook his head at the paneled wall. His man was up on his Greek mythology and as original as ever. "How long did he stay and when did he leave?"

"He moved in at the end of June and left two weeks ago. Everything was paid up in cash and the house was in good repair. I should have more renters like Mr. Charon."

"Any visitors?"

"Some. I have other property on that road and sometimes when I drove past I would see cars parked out front. Oh, and he had a house guest for a few days in July. I met him briefly when I stopped in to ask if everything was all right. Blakeman. I remember the name, because I asked him if he was Jewish. You know, because of the 'man.' He said no."

"What did he look like?"

"Youngish, but older than Mr. Charon. In his thirties. Tall and blond. Real blond, not platinum like Mr. Charon. He had a scar on his cheek. The right one, I think."

"What else did he say?"

"Hello when I came in and good-bye when I went out. I wasn't there long. Mr. Charon said Mr. Blakeman would be doing some fishing while he was there. He was quite the fisherman himself, Charon was. He must have had a thousand dollars tied up in equipment."

Macklin asked a few more questions, garnering little more information. Finally he said, "Well, thank you, Mr. Weisner. I don't think I'll be bothering you again."

"I think I'll call the police now."

"Tell them someone stole the radio out of your car. They'll come quicker."

After hanging up, Macklin set the alarm for 6:30 A.M. and switched off the bedside lamp and lay thinking for a while before he dropped off. His last thought was that Blakeman didn't sound like an alias.

CHAPTER 17

GORDY CHARLES MAGGIORE'S leviathan bodyguard and man-servant, rapped softly on his employer's bedroom door and when there was no answer opened it and stood over the bed, blocking out the light from the unshaded window. Maggiore, a light sleeper since the New York gang wars of the seventies, stirred and sat up, rucking back the black velour sleep mask he wore over his eyes and screwing up his face in the morning bright. He had on a chinstrap to keep his neck from sagging and gray silk pajamas. "What time is it?"

"Seven o'clock, Mr. Maggiore."

"*Seven!* Damn you, Gordy, I said ten."

"Sorry, Mr. Maggiore. You told me to interrupt whatever you was doing when that Freddo called." He pronounced the name as if it belonged to a corn chip. Gordy had been raised in South Dakota and didn't speak a word of Italian.

"He still on the line?"

"Yes sir. Calling collect from Port Huron." The big man

drew a black satin dressing gown from one of the room's two walk-in closets and held it, lining out, while Maggiore stuck his feet into his slippers and then rose to let Gordy help him into the gown.

"I didn't even know there still *was* a seven o'clock in the morning." Leaning automatically toward the hump on his right shoulder, the Sicilian passed through a small dressing room into a parlor containing a lot of green chintz and a French telephone and took the receiver off the hook. The mansion had eight bedrooms and not an extension in any of them. He considered the instrument an invasion of privacy.

"Say it," he told the mouthpiece.

"No." Freddo's voice sounded far away.

"That isn't what I wanted to hear."

"I made two tries. The first time cops got in the way and the second time there were witnesses hanging from the trees. He knows I'm on his case now."

Maggiore cursed. "So why call me?"

"Just checking in. I didn't want you finding out he was still kicking and then sending in a back-up for me to trip over."

"I wouldn't do that."

"Bet you told Macklin the same thing."

Maggiore wished the killer would watch his mouth on the wire. Every week he had men in to inspect the telephone for taps and every other week they found one. "Where is he now?"

"Getting gassed up across the street from his motel. I'm calling from the motel cafeteria. I can see his car through the front window."

"Who you riding with?"

"Link Washington."

"Christ, I wouldn't hire him to empty bedpans."

"He takes orders. Guys like that are getting hard to find."

Tell me about it. "Okay, stay on him. He won't give you four shots."

"You said before he wouldn't give me two."

"So he's slipped. He made his bones when you were still shitting yellow. Remember that."

"All that means," said Freddo, "is that he's old."

"You should live to be so old." Maggiore hung up.

Gordy had started the shower in the huge bathroom off the master bedroom and slipped away discreetly. Maggiore stood under the scalding spray for five minutes, turned it off, stepped out of the stall, and admired his trim figure in the fogged mirror that covered one wall as he toweled and powdered himself, calculatedly ignoring the hammocks of aging flesh that dangled under his arms, his shriveled penis, and the lump of malformed bone on his shoulder that had won him the nickname Quasimodo in high school until the boy who had first called him by it was found with his skull crushed by a rock behind the gym. At 50 he was satisfied that he could pass for much younger.

He padded naked into the dressing room, where Gordy had laid out his clothes on the upholstered bench, and put on a yellow sportcoat over a black polo shirt and matching cords and slid suede moccasins onto his bare feet. On his way out through the bedroom, he tugged a drawer out of the bureau and untaped an alligator holster containing a short blue semiautomatic 7 mm. pistol of Italian make. He broke out the clip for inspection, made sure there was a round in the chamber, holstered it and snapped the holster on to a special strap woven into the lining of his jacket so that it fit into the inside pocket. He buttoned the jacket and looked at his reflection in the full-length mirror on the door to see how it hung. It hung well, concealing the weapon even when he raised his arms. All his clothes were tailored to accommodate either a gun or a thick wallet. He was the only man he knew in his position who owned a gun; most of his colleagues preferred to hire others to carry them. But Maggiore had lived through some bad times and knew that in such times the only things a man could truly count on were a good eye and a steady hand.

He hadn't worn the gun in months. No one knew he had one, not even Gordy. He always felt a little ridiculous carrying it, like some snake-eyed thug in a George Raft movie. But he knew Macklin never felt that way, and if Freddo went on missing opportunities there would be nothing else to stand between Maggiore and Michael Boniface's loyal hammer.

*   *   *

Freddo pegged the receiver on the pay telephone next to the cash register, clattered a nickel onto the counter for a foil-wrapped mint from a bowl of them next to the toothpicks, winked at the fat woman cashier, and left the motel cafeteria, swaggering a little. Despite a couple of false starts, he was already thinking beyond Macklin to the bonus he would surely get for the job and what he would buy with it. Maybe a sportier car. The Cordoba was all right for comfort and style and power, but it looked dull. If Macklin could get away with driving a silver Merc there was no reason for Freddo to maintain the traditional low profile.

That car was still parked at the pumps across the street. The uniformed attendant had finished filling the tank and had the hood up to check the oil. Macklin had gone around the side to use the men's room. That was one of the first things to go, the bladder.

The middle-aged killer was easy. He had proved that by letting Freddo get so close on two separate occasions. Freddo wondered if this was age or the fact that the competition was softer in Macklin's time. Maybe a little of both. He had suspected it long before this job; if Macklin were as good as everyone claimed he'd be drying the moss on his back on the Riviera by now, fat and retired with a wife half his age. It was a young man's game, this business of killing. Freddo had no intention of staying in past 35—by which time, of course, he would no longer have to.

He had left the brown car at a meter around the corner from the service station with Link Washington asleep on the passenger's side. After cruising through motel parking lots looking for Macklin's car they had taken turns sleeping and watching it throughout the night in case Macklin broke, and while Freddo felt refreshed after a total of three hours' rest and a shave and sink-bath in the same public restroom where Macklin was now wringing his mop, Washington had squirmed all night and not slept a wink. He was making up for it now, for he didn't stir as his partner opened the driver's door and slid in behind the wheel. He slumped with his knees above the dash and his chin on his chest, his freckles dead brown against his pasty face.

"Rise and shine," said Freddo, starting the engine. "Plenty of lonely spots on the expressway between here and Detroit.

They get a lot of accidents there; one more won't even wrinkle the weekend stats. C'mon, Link. You're driving." He pushed a hand against Washington's shoulder.

The other man's head slipped sideways and came to rest against the window. A dot of scarlet appeared at the corner of his mouth and melted down his chin. Freddo saw the rest of the blood then, soaking the front of Washington's rough Mackinaw and curtaining his neck from a clean line across his throat that opened neat as a pocketbook as his body settled.

"The trick is to bunch up the collar of his coat before the first spurt," explained the man in the back seat. "Otherwise it gets messy."

Freddo had quicksilver reflexes. Instead of turning immediately, he slung his right hand under his left arm and pulled at the butt of the .44 magnum. Before he got it clear of his coat, a fist seized his hair and yanked his head back hard enough to pop roots. Something hard and sharp prodded his jugular. A pair of tired eyes filled the rearview mirror.

"You're a lot closer to bleeding to death like your friend there than you are to pointing that cannon and squeezing the trigger," said a calm voice in his ear. "Take it out the rest of the way and toss it back here."

When Freddo hesitated he got another yank. He howled and pulled desperately at the gun, snagging and tearing the lining of his coat with the hammer, and flipped it over the back of the front seat. The heavy weapon bounced off the rear cushions and thudded to the floor.

"Now the other one."

"There isn't any—" His hair was pulled again and he gasped. The pointed thing nicked his flesh. He thrust his other hand under his right arm for the .22 long pistol he carried for close work. At the same time he jammed his heel down on the accelerator and threw the automatic shift into drive with his right hand.

The car shot forward across the intersection, shearing paint and metal off its left side on the thick bumper of a stake truck making a right turn. The enraged whomp of its horn shivered the Cordoba's window. Freddo spun the wheel and the car swung left, tires shrilling. Macklin lost his balance and sprawled across the back seat. He looked at the fistful of torn hair he was still holding and shook it off his palm. Freddo had the .22 out now and was steering wildly with one hand, the car slewing from side to side down the street, as he brought the gun around. Macklin lunged up on his knees on the hump of the driveshaft, seized Freddo's wrist, and twisted it. The revolver went off with a nasty flat loud crack. The bullet grazed the windshield and whanged around inside the car, skinning fabric off a padded window post and gouging glass out of the rear and left rear side windows before burying itself in the back of a seat. Macklin twisted again and the gun dropped to the floor.

Just then the world came to an abrupt stop with a horrendous wham and the heavy framework of the seat caved in Macklin's ribs and his fingers sprang loose from Freddo's wrist and the back of the rear seat came forward and pounded Macklin's back with the hearty violence of a long-lost friend and he fell in a tangle of too many limbs to be all his. Something hissed, like air escaping a torn lung. A piece of shattered glass dropped with a loud clink.

After a long time Macklin shook himself free of the dream he was having and sat up. He moved each arm and leg separately. No loose bones rattled or sloshed. Pain lanced his left side when he took in air, but that was no problem, he'd cracked ribs before. The back seat seemed a lot closer to the front than it had been. A man with no head was sitting on the passenger's side in front. Through a round hole in the windshield with the glass chain-mailed all around, Macklin saw what looked like a clump of carroty hair perched on the hood. The glass had finished what Herb Pinelli's knife had started. The hood was folded back almost against the windshield and an expanse of warped green metal blocked out the rest of the view behind a cloud of steam from the Cordoba's smashed radiator. The car had rammed the back of a parked delivery van.

The driver's seat was empty. Macklin hoisted himself forward, sucking in air against the stabbing in his side, and peered at the floor under the wheel. Freddo wasn't there either. The door on that side yawned open on twisted hinges.

Freddo. That was all Macklin had been able to learn about

the young man who had tried twice to kill him, the name he traveled under. The redhead he had surprised asleep in the car after letting himself out the window of the service station restroom and doubling back around the block had told him that much, then tried for a .45 Army semiautomatic pistol on his hip—a .45 auto, for chrissake—and Macklin, reacting too quickly, had slashed his throat with a single sideways jerk. A man could be too fast, he thought sourly, even in this business.

A crowd was starting to gather around the car. Blocks away a siren wound up and grew louder with each whoop. Ignoring the faces craning in through the shattered windows, Macklin kicked Freddo's big .44 under the back seat and groped between the cushions until he found the knife he'd dropped. He sheathed it under his coat and got out, tilting the driver's seat forward and wrenching the door open farther against the spavined frame.

"Mister, you all right?"

A bearded man wearing a billed cap and gray coveralls with *Bob* stitched in red across a breast pocket full of pencils was standing in front of him. Macklin placed him as the driver of the van. The beard looked artificial against the pallor of his face. He'd seen the decapitated head on the hood.

Macklin nodded and walked around him. A hand closed on his right arm.

"Wait, mister. You have to wait for the cops."

Macklin stopped and looked down at the hand on his arm, then at the face of the delivery man. After a beat the hand dropped. Macklin resumed walking. The crowd parted before him.

He quickened his pace, cutting through a drugstore parking lot and circling back to the service station where he'd left his car. Every breath he took needled his left side.

The attendant at the cash register rang up his purchase and told him he was a quart low on oil. He divided his attention between his customer and the police car speeding past outside the front window, its siren yelping. "Must of been some accident," he said. "Heard the bang clear over here."

"You've got rotten drivers in this town," Macklin told him.

"Weekends, you can have 'em. I get Monday and Tuesday off, when all the nuts are off the road."

Macklin eased himself behind the wheel of the Cougar with his teeth clenched. There was no scraping, and he was satisfied that none of the ribs was actually broken. As he pulled out of the station the handle of Herb Pinelli's knife pressed his right kidney. If anyone knew who Freddo was, he considered, it would be Herb.

CHAPTER 18

BILL CHILSON FOUND RED BURLINGAME in his shirtsleeves in the conference room with a nautical chart of the Greak Lakes spread out on the long walnut table and a group of agents in snug suits and silk ties, not one of whom looked older than seventeen. The granite Art Deco buildings of downtown Detroit huddled gray and brown outside a row of double-paned windows along the back wall. The fog appeared to be lifting, lying like meringue on a layer of golden sunlight.

The bureau chief didn't look up as the Secret Service agent entered, but motioned him around to his end of the table. He was holding a metal rule down on Lake Huron with one hand and bisecting a previously drawn line with a thick carpenter's pencil in the other.

"We got a possible fix on the boat," he said, apparently to the chart.

"Visual?" asked Chilson.

"Radio. They've got portable units aboard and they've been jabbering away like women for the past couple of hours."

"I thought they were observing radio silence."

"They are, ship to shore. But those walkie-talkies are little and cute and it's easy to forget how far a signal will travel on the water with fog to boot. Coast Guard puts them right here as of five o'clock this morning." He squashed a broad thumb down on the point where the lines crossed. "Steaming on their current course at an average cruising speed of six knots, that puts them two points to the southeast by now."

"How's the visibility out there?"

"Improving slowly. Fog's drifting back the way it came, and those Canuck bastards can have it."

One of the younger agents spoke up. "Excuse me, sir, but I was born in Winnipeg."

"Next time you write home, tell them to keep their fucking weather to themselves." To Chilson: "Coast Guard expects to have copters up by noon and will let us know direct as soon as visual contact is established."

"What then?"

Burlingame looked up at his friend for the first time and smiled his canary smile. "Sorry, Bill. Clearance."

"What about Macklin?"

"That's all, gentlemen," said the chief, straightening.

The other agents shuffled out. Burlingame watched them until the door closed behind them, then sniffed the air and scowled.

"They're supposed to be field men. When I find out which one of them is wearing that cheap cologne I'll put the punk on suspension." He turned to Chilson. "The Bureau's arrangement with Michael Boniface is classified information, Bill. Only you and I and the Mob and the brass in Washington know about it."

"Sorry, Red. I haven't been under cover in twenty years. My cloak's got mildew and my dagger's rusty."

"Yeah. Some nights when I have trouble getting to sleep I start thinking about it all, the compound code names and the security rituals, and I wonder what a grown man and a grandfather is doing running around playing Captain Midnight."

He rolled down and buttoned his cuffs and hooked his suitcoat off the back of a chair. Slipping into it: "Macklin hasn't shown since he shook our tail yesterday. That we're sure of."

"What's that mean?"

"Yesterday afternoon the police in River Rouge investigated a complaint off West Jefferson, in one of those old warehouses they've turned into apartments. They found the manager beaten to death in his office. Whoever did it used the baseball bat the poor bastard kept there for his own protection. Witnesses saw a man entering and leaving the building earlier whose description fits Macklin. One even saw him talking to the manager."

"From what you've told me about him, it could fit any one of a thousand men in this area."

"That's what I thought when it hit my desk. But just for the hell of it I sent a man around with a telephoto shot those Treasury men took of Macklin leaving Maggiore's place. Two of the three witnesses identified him from it."

"Do you think it has anything to do with this?" Chilson indicated the marked chart.

"I don't know. On the manager who was killed we turned a couple of stray ties to organized crime in the area, but it was strictly broom-pushing, and you can't hardly push a broom around here that it's not some Mob trash you're pushing. I can't spare the men to dig any deeper into a case that will as likely as not turn out to be nothing more than an unpaid loan."

"Bludgeoning doesn't sound like Macklin's style."

"Our information says he's pretty versatile." Burlingame produced his pipe from a breast pocket, charged it, and patted his trunk for a match.

Chilson flipped a match folder on to the table. "Anything on that spooky one?"

Lighting the pipe, the FBI man shook his head. "If he's an eraser he's not local. Washington's slow getting back to us on his picture. Back-up for Macklin, most likely. Either that or Maggiore's playing his own game. That snake has more than one head."

"Nice people we're dealing with these days."

"A numbers runner pumped full of holes and stuffed into an

automobile trunk at Metro Airport, a V.C. spy shoved out of a helicopter a thousand feet over a jungle in Vietnam; each one's just as dead as the other. Macklin and Maggiore are in the same business we're in. Why doesn't make any difference to the Sixth Commandment.'' When Burlingame had the tobacco going he returned the matches to the Secret Service agent. ''I didn't know you smoked.''

''I don't. We all carry them to light the President.''

''I didn't know *he* smoked.''

''One of our jobs is to see that nobody does.''

''Ah, hell.'' Burlingame blew a gray cloud. ''How'd a couple of swell guys like you and me wind up doing what we do instead of selling vacuum cleaners?''

''We took a civil service exam,'' said Chilson.

Macklin blacked out on the Edsel Ford Freeway near the New Baltimore exit.

He came around a second later with the vague euphoria of a man awakening an hour ahead of the alarm to see the gray concrete of an overpass abutment filling the windshield. His reflexes kicked in and he tore the wheel left, skidding sideways across the lane in front of a station wagon. The other car's brakes shrieked and the Cougar climbed the grassy inside bank and scrambled back down onto the pavement just before slamming into the thick beam that supported the center of the overpass. Macklin straightened the wheels and drifted back into the slow lane.

The station wagon roared past blaring its horn. The steering wheel shivered in Macklin's shaky grasp and his heart was bounding painfully off his ribs as if trying to force its way through the fissures. He drove another mile doing the minimum and pulled into a rest area to test his legs and splash cold water on his face. His reflection in the mirror over the sink was greenish.

After walking around the paved parking area for a few minutes, sucking in lungfuls of fresh air and holding his side against the sharp ache, he got back in and drove the rest of the way to Detroit with the window down and the radio going to help his concentration. There was nothing new on the Boblo boat hijacking, and the item had slipped to third place in the news report after a summary of the President's latest address to the nation and speculation on the Mayor's proposed layoff of a thousand Detroit police officers.

Instead of backing into his driveway in Southfield as he usually did so that the car would be facing out, he pulled straight in for fear the strain of twisting around to look out through the back window would put a rib through his lung. He unlocked the front door of the house and climbed the stairs. There was no sign of Donna in the living room and when he passed the open door of the bedroom he saw her bathrobe flung over the end of the bed. She had dressed and gone out. He didn't care where. He was grateful to be able to avoid another confrontation like the last. He didn't want to spend too much time there. If the police investigating that collision in Port Huron traced witnesses' descriptions of the man seen leaving the scene to that service station and the attendant remembered his license plate number, they wouldn't be long coming to Macklin's address. The dead man could have been killed in the accident but the .44 magnum under the back seat would be hard to explain. And yet Macklin hadn't been about to risk carrying away an unregistered weapon in broad daylight with all eyes on him.

He stopped two feet short of the door to his study. It was open a crack. He remembered locking it. And even if he didn't remember, he'd know it was locked because he always locked it when he left, even if it was for only a few minutes. While he was standing there thinking about it a vague shadow fluttered in the fan of sunlight spreading out from the crack across the hall runner.

He unsheathed the knife—he wondered if Herb Pinelli had ever had cause to use it as many times in twenty-four hours—and pressed a palm against the door, opening it silently on its well-oiled hinges. A man in a black T-shirt and faded jeans was hunched in front of his file cabinet with his back to the door. The muscles in his back twitched with the movement of his arms, their elbows close to his sides. Macklin heard the uneven clicking of metal against metal.

The killer leaned all his weight into his forward leg to pounce and a floorboard under the carpet moved under his foot. The infinitesimal noise made his man turn just as he leaped. His blade scraped sparks off a long glittering something in the man's hand and they collided, white pain throwing off sparks of its own in Macklin's side. He felt a black void opening in his skull and clawed at the man's face for support, bringing the knife in a short underhand arc toward a flat abdomen under a dark T-shirt.

"Dad?"

At the last instant he pulled back. The point snagged a hole in the black material. He dropped the hand with which he had been about to gouge out the eyes of his son.

At 16, Roger Macklin was as tall as his father and built slighter, but with hard knots of muscle in his upper arms. He wore his black hair long and parted in the middle, and because he had his mother's features it gave him a girlish look. His mouth hung a little open, but that was normal. A foot-long Johnny Bull screwdriver dangled in his right hand, and that wasn't.

Macklin smacked his son's chest with his open free hand, shoving him back against the file cabinet. A smaller screwdriver and a shoemaker's awl rolled off the top and clinked to the floor. "How the hell did you get in here?"

"I picked the lock. You going to cut my throat for it?"

Already his native insolence had supplanted fear. Macklin put away the knife and slapped the curl off the boy's lip. It was back almost immediately. "What do you want from my file drawers, drugs?"

"Money. I was going to ask to borrow some, only nobody was home."

"So you decided to help yourself. Where are you sleeping these days?"

"In the Goodwill box behind K-Mart."

Macklin slapped him again. Roger's head banged the tall cabinet.

"A friend's house," he said then, reaching up to flick blood off his split lip. The underside of his wrist was dotted blue.

"What's the matter, he can't supply you?"

"Not for free."

"What's it up to now, a hundred a day?"

"Seventy-five."

"Horse's ass," Macklin snarled.

The boy smiled. Macklin hit him again. Roger spat blood and lunged, then stopped short. His father stepped back and peeled off his coat.

"Let's do this right," he said, unsnapping the sheath holding the knife and tossing it atop his coat on the work table.

Roger said nothing. With one hand he slid open one of the jimmied file drawers, lifted out a box of cartridges, and flipped it to the floor at his father's feet. Some of the brass-bodied .38s tumbled out and lay gleaming on the carpet.

The boy said, "I didn't know you owned a gun. You never even went hunting."

"I'll be years dead before you know everything there is to know about me." Macklin unbuttoned his cuffs and turned them back.

"Yeah. Like what it is you do."

"I'm an efficiency expert."

"Bullshit."

Suddenly Macklin had had enough. He came forward and the boy raised his fists to defend himself. But his father shoved him aside roughly and unlocked the bottom drawer containing the safe and worked the combination and lifted the lid and drew out the Smith & Wesson. The barrel swung Roger's way and he whimpered and ducked, but it kept swinging to the side and down and when it was pointing toward a wooden crate full of potting soil on the floor Macklin pressed the trigger. The report slammed deafeningly inside the room. The dense black soil swallowed the bullet.

"Now you know why this room is soundproofed." Macklin shouted over the ringing echo. "You have to be in the bedroom next door to hear anything, and then it sounds like a door slamming down the block. I usually wear earplugs. Each time I get a gun I test it. One shot, one gun, and I never use the same one twice. There are eight spent slugs in that box of dirt. That's just since I replaced the last box."

While Roger watched, his father unloaded the revolver,

shaking the five cartridges and the empty casing out onto the table, then got his cleaning kit in a flat metal case out of the drawer that had held the cartridge box and cleaned the barrel.

"Does Mom know?" asked the boy.

"She suspects."

"That's why she hates you."

"She doesn't hate me." When the boy opened his mouth, he added, "Don't say 'Bullshit' again. You got away with it in here once."

"How come it's okay to kill people, but not to swear?"

Macklin held the barrel up to the window and peered through it with the cylinder swung out. "Did you study any biology before you dropped out of school?"

"Sure, but what's that—"

"Learn anything about alligators?"

"Alligators?"

"They live in swamps in Florida and South America and eat small animals."

"So?"

"So if we didn't have alligators we'd all be up to our asses in small animals."

"That's a copout," Roger said after a moment.

Macklin wiped off the gun and laid the cleaning rod and rag back inside the case. "No, it isn't."

"How long you been an efficiency expert?"

"Save that stuff for television. I'm a killer. I was a killer when you were born and I was a killer when I met your mother. Anything that happened before that isn't your business."

Roger grinned then. Seeing his own wolfish look reflected in his son's face startled Macklin.

"I never got to do show-and-tell in kindergarten," said the boy. "All the other kids had fathers who were firemen and plumbers and they got up and talked about it. I never did because I didn't know what an efficiency expert was. I could've been a hit."

"Now you know why I never told you."

"How come you're telling me now?"

"It doesn't matter any more. After this job everyone will know anyway."

"What's the job?"

Macklin didn't reply. He replaced the cartridges and flipped the spent shell into the potting soil and filled the empty chamber with a cartridge from the floor. Then he put the rest back into the box and slid the box into his pants pocket, where it made an unsightly bulge. He carried the cleaning kit back to the file cabinet and put it away and holstered the Smith & Wesson and snapped the holster to his belt next to the knife.

Roger said, "Take me with you."

"No."

"Why not?"

"I don't work with addicts."

A corner of the boy's lip turned up, starting the split bleeding again. "I thought maybe you were going to say you didn't want me to get hurt."

"You're too high most of the time to hurt."

"Look." Roger held out a hand as steady as a bough.

"Do that again in a couple of hours when the stuff's worn off."

"You're kind of old. You need someone like me to back you up."

Macklin took the thick envelope out of the safe, returned to his work table, and scribbled a name and address on the top sheet of his telephone pad. He ripped out the sheet and counted ten bills out of the envelope swiftly. Then he thrust them and the scrap of paper at his son.

"That's a thousand dollars," he said. "That's what the man whose name is on that piece of paper charges to dry you out. Use it for that or use it to put yourself in heaven for two weeks. But if you use it for that, don't come back here."

Roger stood there for a moment, holding the cash on his open palm. Then he fisted it and left. Macklin heard the front door slam a minute later.

CHAPTER 19

THE BURNING IN MACKLIN'S SIDE WAS AT high flame. Just the touch of his fingers sent a white bolt shooting clear to his back teeth. In the bathroom he turned the shower on high and stripped gingerly, unbuttoning his shirt with one hand and letting his pants drop and stepping out of them without bending. He used each foot to pry the shoe and sock off its mate, kicked them away, and stepped naked into the clouds of steam. There he let the hot spray pummel his side. He didn't remember hurting this much the last time this had happened.

Later he broke an Ace bandage out of the medicine cabinet and wound it around his abdomen, securing it with a safety pin. The ribs still throbbed but now he could think of other things.

Roger was beyond help. Macklin wasn't one of those fathers who neglected their children for years and then woke up and suddenly decided to turn them around. He had seen this coming from a long way off, back when things were hotter and he was working all the time and sometimes had to stay away from home for months rather than attract trouble to his family. Donna's drinking was a problem even then and her attitude hadn't welcomed the dual role of mother and father. Macklin's own father had worked in a junkyard; his calluses had made iron paddles of his hands and when the boy stepped out of line he wore their mark on his face for days. But a man to whom killing came easily feared to touch his son in anger, and Donna had little enough discipline of her own to spare any for the boy. When Roger wanted help, real help, he would have to seek it out himself or it would do no good. Macklin believed he wanted help the same way he believed that thousand dollars would end up in the hands of the drug therapist Macklin had recommended.

He dressed skin out in fresh underwear and a dark blue sport shirt and jeans and black sneakers—real sneakers with a suction-cup tread that gripped and held, not those slippery track shoes that were crowding them off the shelves in most stores—and put on a reversible windbreaker with the dark side in. Finally he transferred the revolver in its holster from his leather suit belt to the canvas web he was wearing with the jeans, tugged the elastic of the jacket down over the butt, and put Herb Pinelli's knife and sheath inside one of the slash pockets. It had come in handy for more than getting in a door. He tipped a handful of .38 cartridges out of the box into the other pocket and left after tidying up.

Where was Donna?

"You won't get a bushel of miles to the gallon, but the ones you get will be pure gold."

Smiling chipmunk fashion as if amused by his own words, the fat little used car dealer squeaked his swivel chair contentedly and gazed out the picture window at the square blue Oldsmobile parked next to the door. The car was four years old, a discontinued model, and starting to scab up around the rear wheel wells, but Freddo liked its 550-cubic-inch Cadillac engine and speedometer that topped off at 140, and he knew that it would probably do better. He said, "Stop selling it. You got the money."

Indeed he had, thought the dealer, eight hundred dollars in

hundreds and fifties straight out of the young man's wallet. It was a shame to have to let a good car go for so little, but that oversize fuel tank scared off a lot of customers and anyway, cash was cash. He watched the new owner signing the title transfer. Nice suit, a little wrinkled as if he hadn't had it off recently, thin blond hair, slight swelling and discoloration on the forehead. The dealer had been about to ask about that when the wallet came out. So much cash in hands so young with Detroit so close tended to discourage questions.

When the papers were pushed away the dealer craned his short neck to read the signature and stood, offering his hand. "Come back and see us any time, Mr. Metzger. We're a full-service dealership."

Freddo folded the bill of sale and title slip into his inside breast pocket and went out without shaking the hand. The Oldsmobile rumbled into life and squirted forward the instant he put it in drive. That meant the idle was high. He pulled out of the lot, detoured around the area where a wrecker summoned by the police was hitching up to what remained of the Cordoba, found a commercial garage on a side street and parked in front of the doors.

A pimple-faced teenager in blue coveralls with a smudge of grease on the end of his nose greeted Freddo in a cluttered office paved with concrete. Freddo spiked a hundred-dollar bill on a spindle layered high with canceled statements.

"I got an Olds out front needs idling down," he said.

The garage attendant's eyes were fixed on the skewered bill. "That's just a sixteen-dollar order, mister. I can't change no hundreds. You'll have to wait till my boss gets back."

"It's a twelve-dollar order. The hundred's yours if while you're adjusting the idle you accidentally knock loose all the anti-pollution equipment."

"That ain't legal."

"Excuse me. I didn't know I was doing business with Dick Tracy." Freddo reached for his money. The attendant's hand was quicker, covering it. Freddo straightened. "Ledger stays closed on this one, right?"

"What ledger?" The boy displayed brown teeth and got up to open the doors. The hundred was gone.

Out of boredom, Freddo stood by watching as the boy worked under the hood and then drove the car onto the hydraulic lift to free the catalytic converter. Judging by the look on the used car dealer's face as Freddo had counted out the eight hundred under his nose, he'd have been glad to yank the environmental baggage that curtailed speed and performance free of charge, but Freddo had used the Lyle Metzger identity to make the purchase and since the request was suspicious he didn't want to waste an alias he might need later. He had had driver's licenses and Social Security cards under three names besides his own, acquired on birth certificates issued to children who had died in infancy, but he had been forced to tear up one set of identification after abandoning the wrecked Cordoba. Police would trace the registration to an Italian youth killed in an apartment fire in Philadelphia in 1960.

He was angry, too, about the .44 magnum he had been forced to leave in the car. It was a good gun and still unblooded. But he didn't worry about having left fingerprints on it and all over the car. His prints weren't on file anywhere. And he had held on to the .22, now nestled in its holster under his right arm. It was accurate and effective within thirty feet, his usual working distance.

It saddened him a little to have lost Link Washington. Loyal fetches were rare. The redhead must have been dead to the world to let Macklin get behind him like that. Well, he was sure enough dead to the world now.

Freddo thought about calling Maggiore again, then rejected the idea. The cocoa-butter bastard would just sneer at him like before. So the old man had a little more tread on his tires than Freddo had given him credit for. So he had outsmarted Link. An orangutan with arrested development could outsmart Link. The whole episode so far was an ugly wrinkle in Freddo's smooth record of nine quiet kills.

He wanted Macklin badly.

* * *

The silver Cougar's right signal flashed.

"He's turning right," said the man riding on the passenger's side of the gray Plymouth a block behind.

"Oh, is that what that blinking light means," said the man at the wheel dryly.

"Well, close it up. This is where we lost him yesterday."

The driver used the center turning lane to pass a foreign hatchback poking along in front of them and turned right a fraction of a second behind Macklin. "He's going to know we're tailing him," he said.

"He knows now, shithead."

The two cars crossed the street where they had been separated the day before, the Plymouth just barely squeezing through on the yellow. They might have been chained together. They undulated over a series of hills and hollows. The Cougar slowed down and sped up and slowed down again. The driver of the Plymouth tapped his brakes to avoid ramming the car ahead.

"Don't give him any slack," barked his passenger. "If we blow it again our ass is grass."

The driver touched the accelerator. The cars were as one angling down the first of a brace of steep hills. A small city of brick splitlevels showed behind a skin of trees on either side of the paved road. At the bottom of the hill the Cougar's brake lights flashed on.

The driver of the Plymouth stood on his brakes. They locked with a hideous wail of rubber on concrete. A car following a short distance behind braked and slewed sideways, nearly clipping the rear of the Plymouth. Then the Cougar's lights went off and a puff of black smoke escaped its exhaust pipe and it tore up the next incline. The roar drowned out the idling of the Plymouth's engine.

"He's rabbiting! Step on it!"

The Plymouth hesitated, then snarled and shot forward and up. The speedometer needle climbed to sixty.

"Oh, shit!" the passenger exclaimed. "Back up! Back *up!*"

The Cougar was rolling backward down the hill, its sleek rear filling the Plymouth's windshield. The driver of the Plymouth stamped on the brake pedal and slammed the automatic transmission into reverse while it was still moving forward. Something shrieked and the car shuddered and shot backward and struck the car behind broadside as it was maneuvering back into the right lane. A tire blew with the force of a grenade and the Plymouth sat groaning on its left haunch.

Meanwhile the Cougar swung on two wheels into a backward U-turn, paused, and took off the way it had come. The horn tooted twice as it passed the scene of the collision.

The driver of the Plymouth sat with both hands still on the wheel, watching the driver of the car he had hit wrestling an angry six-foot-three out onto the pavement. He looked at his passenger.

"You tell Burlingame, okay?"

CHAPTER 20

CLOTHES MADE A DIFFER-
ence. The plain-
clothes security
guard at the Detroit Public Library who hardly glanced at
Macklin when he wore a suit looked at him hard when he entered
in his windbreaker and jeans. Macklin walked with a hand in his
rear pocket to cover any bulges the gun might make and took the
stairs to References, where the telephone directories were kept.
Once he strapped on a weapon, he kept it on until the job was
finished. It was like a new pair of shoes you had to walk around
in for a while before you got used to each other. Everything about
a man changed when he was wearing a gun: his stride, his
posture, the way he sat and got up again, even the timbre of his
voice. The process of assimilation was just as long no matter how
many times he had carried one in the past.

There were four Blakemans listed in the metropolitan
directory. One was named Frances, another David, and the other
two had only initials for their first names. They were probably

women. He copied all the names and numbers into his pocket notebook anyway and pulled down the reverse directory, with the numbers listed in numerical order followed by the names. There were two listings for the David Blakeman number. Bold print identified the second entry as the Born Again Redemption Center on Gratiot.

It sounded religious. Macklin put the reverse book back on its shelf, drew down the *Yellow Pages*, and looked it up under Churches. It wasn't listed. He frowned at the racks of books for a moment. On impulse he turned to Pawn Shops and found a small display advertisement for the Born Again Redemption Center. "D. Blakeman, Prop."

He used a pay telephone on the ground floor to call the pawn shop, canting his back against the wall next to the box to conceal the revolver and meet the guard's gaze imperiously until the guard looked away. When no one answered after six rings he hung up and left.

He missed the place on his first pass down the right block on Gratiot. He'd been looking at the signs and addresses at street level, where he expected to find signs and addresses. The second time through he spotted it, three circles and BORN AGAIN lettered in flaking silver on a second-floor window. He parked in a city lot one street over and walked back.

Steep stairs as old as Prohibition led up from a street door between dark walls smelling of old paint and cigars and rubber from the stairway runner. Senile boards winced under his weight. At the top he followed a hallway floored with hardwood made dull by too many coats of varnish to a door at the end with BORN AGAIN REDEMPTIONS painted in black on the frosted glass under the inevitable three circles. No light showed through the glass. Macklin tried the knob. Locked. He stood there for another moment, then turned. As he did so a door down the hall closed with a click.

He approached the door. Solid and paneled, it had been abused with varnish like the floor. Several coats had been applied since the last time the tarnished brass numerals 203 had been removed, so that the thick dark liquid had dried to form an uneven collar around them. Macklin thumped the door three times with a knuckle.

It was opened almost immediately, flung wide by a short broad woman with hennaed hair and large feet in a man's brown loafers spread wide so that her skirt of no particular color stretched between her knees without a wrinkle. Over a green-and-orange floral print blouse she wore a thick blue sweater mangled at the wrists and missing all but its top button, which she had fastened. Her jowls were loose, she had circles the size of bar rings under her eyes and a gray moustache that went like hell with her orange hair. She looked like a bulldog that had been kicked in the face once and had never forgotten it.

"If you're asking me where he went I don't know," she told Macklin. "If you're asking me when he'll be back I don't know that neither. A den of thieves, that place. I bet you're a thief too."

"What makes you think so?" He stood back a little from the doorway. He was almost two feet taller than she and didn't want to frighten her into putting the door in his face.

She squinted up at him again, and Macklin guessed she was nearsighted. Her forehead was corrugated from years of squinting up at people. She was probably afraid glasses would spoil her looks.

"No, you ain't no thief," she said then. "You're too old."

"There are old thieves."

"Not around here. Not the ones come to Blakeman's selling other folks' stereos and toasters and TV sets. Most of them are *black*." She leaned forward on the last part and mouthed the word *black* soundlessly.

"No kidding."

He had tried to keep the mockery out of his tone, but the old lady had good ears. Her mouth came shut with a snap and she drew her face in so that the fat of her neck folded up around it like a turtle's. "You're a policeman, ain'cha?"

Macklin held his answer, turning over the question for thorns.

"Don't tell me you ain't," she said, "because I can spot a policeman quick as I can spot a thief. Not that there's a difference. I seen my share of them going into Blakeman's. They find a place busted into and then go in and help themselves before they report it. Then they come up here with the stuff in bags and come out empty-handed and whistling."

"They come up here in uniform?"

Her features caved in as if she'd just smelled something bad. "I said they was crooked. I didn't say they was stupid. I told you, I can spot them. I spotted you."

"You sure did. How come you know so much about them?"

"Because that's how they used to do it in my old neighborhood when I was a girl."

"Maybe things have changed since then."

"Mister, it would take a lot more years than I got to change that, and then it wouldn't change. How old you figure I am?"

He guessed late sixties. "About fifty."

She hoisted her jowls in what she imagined was a sweet smile. "Sixty-two, sonny. A lot older than you'll get, you keep messing around with puke-pots like Blakeman."

"I hope to do a lot of messing around with him soon." He lowered his voice a full octave. "Internal Affairs wants to shake all the rotten apples out of the barrel. We were counting on Blakeman as an informant, but since he's not here we'd be grateful for input from an observant citizen such as yourself."

She drew in her face again and brought the door forward eight inches. "I ain't getting mixed up in no investigations. That ain't how I got to be sixty-six."

"I thought it was sixty-two."

Her jowls blew out. The door swung. Macklin blocked it with the flat of his hand. "You didn't give me a chance to explain the department's new compensation policy."

The pressure against his palm slackened a notch. "Talk English, mister. You saying you'll pay?"

Macklin lowered his hand. The door didn't budge. He separated a twenty from his roll and held it up. A pudgy red hand snatched it away and the door sprang open wide. Conquering the urge to count his fingers, he stepped across the threshold.

"Sit down, mister. I ain't had a man in here except the guy to fix the TV since my husband passed away in 'sixty-seven. Right during the riots it was, though it didn't have nothing to do with them, it was cancer got him."

"Thank you, Mrs.—?"

"Fardle. But you can call me Audrey."

He got away from Audrey Fardle after an hour, bloated with cheap doughnuts and expensive information, and drove to the haberdashery on Greenfield, where once again he had to settle Gyp Ibsen's fears about his presence there before the natty little tailor told him Herb Pinelli was having lunch down the street. Macklin walked the block and a half and found the old killer curling fetuccini around a fork at the back of the restaurant. He rose and greeted Macklin warmly, but again without shaking hands, and waved him into a chair. A swarthy young waiter suddenly appeared next to the table.

"Do not order anything Italian," Pinelli counseled, reseating himself. "The chef is Finnish."

"You're eating Italian."

"I have to. Once you are in business you will find that if you are fortunate enough to have established an image you must live with it. The clam chowder is exquisite."

"Thanks. I'm not eating."

"Ah, you are working. Wine, then. What you Americans used to call the Dago red before you became so sensitive."

"Coffee's fine."

"*Dio mio*, I forgot that rule." Pinelli looked up at the waiter and began to order in Italian. When the waiter said he only understood English, he rolled his expressive eyes and asked for coffee with cinnamon. "The cinnamon takes away the bitter taste," he told Macklin.

"I like the bitter taste. If I didn't I wouldn't drink coffee."

"You are an exasperating man, Pietro. Very well, a cup of battery acid."

When the waiter had withdrawn, Macklin looked around as if surveying the decor, then got the sheathed knife out of his pocket and passed it across the table. Pinelli secreted it under the tails of his blue camel's-hair suitcoat. Leaning back: "It was of use?"

"*Molto*. I thank you, my friend. I couldn't have gotten in another way."

"There is one who found another. But here is your coffee."

Macklin searched his friend's hawkish features as the waiter placed a steaming cup and saucer and a silver cream pitcher on the table in front of him. When they were alone again, Pinelli pushed away his plate and stretched an arm to refill his glass from the half-liter of red wine on the table. His well-tailored coatsleeve masked the play of his old muscles.

"An assassin made his way into the manager's apartment in River Rouge yesterday and hit him with a ball bat many times. The radio said he was pronounced dead at Detroit Receiving Hospital. That means he probably was dead when the police found him."

"It wasn't me," Macklin said after a moment.

"I did not think it was. Why would you use a bludgeon when you had an excellent knife? Also dead men are unreliable messengers."

"I'm sorry about your friend, Umberto."

"He was not a friend. Someone who owed him a favor asked me to hire him to clean up around the store. He knew what I did before I sold clothing and this frightened him at first. I calmed him. We talked. We were friendly. We were not friends."

"Do the police suspect anyone?"

"The radio did not say."

"That means they do." Macklin sipped his coffee. It tasted bitter and for a moment he wished he'd let Pinelli order the cinnamon. Then he decided it wouldn't have helped. "I know who it was."

"Not Ackler. Even he could not be on a boat in Lake Erie and in River Rouge at the same time."

"Not Ackler. If I'm right, the same man tried to kill me twice last night. He's the reason I'm here. Have you ever heard of a pro calls himself Freddo?"

"Only four or five," said the other, showing the grin that Macklin never saw anywhere else except in the mirror. In the early days he had imitated everything there was to copy about the old killer, and some of the mannerisms had stayed with him, most noticeably the grin. Not humorous, it was a lightning glimpse behind the civilized mask they presented to the world. "One of the first things I taught you, *figlio mio*, is that the successful killer is less than a shadow, blending with the landscape like the stain of breath passing from glass. He avoids ostentation in all its forms. We will not discuss the car you drive, which we both know distresses me. These sly names, these reverse euphemisms so beloved of the men who make movies and of the children who see them, they will tangle about your limbs and make you stumble. Freddo, fah! All the art has gone out of our profession."

"This one is about twenty-five and blond, built like a survivor of a Nazi concentration camp. He has a lazy eye. His voice is as high as a girl's. Wears sharp suits. Drives—drove a new Cordoba, brown. Carries a .44 magnum and a .22 target gun in shoulder rigs. He had a partner he called Link. He doesn't any more," Macklin added.

"You killed the partner?"

"Yes."

"He had red hair and freckles, looked like that puppet on the old children's television program? Happy something?"

"Howdy Doody. Yes. You know him?"

"He was what the police like to call a layoff. The man who stands at the door holding a gun on the squares while his partner goes in and snuffs the mark. You do not trust such a man alone on any but the least important contracts. That he lived so long is evidence of the decay in our work."

Macklin smiled at his friend's elephantine attempt at TV crime parlance. "What about Freddo?"

"I think I would remember such a man as you describe. He is new or an outsider. The organization is getting to be like a college football team with all this recruiting out of state. The partner was called Lincoln Washington. A black man's name, although he was not black. A native who farmed out."

"Connected?"

"In the loosest possible way. He was with the Boniface family for a time, but the old ties are not as tight as once they were. I am surprised you had not met earlier. Carlo Maggiore sponsored him back when Maggiore was just a lieutenant."

Macklin scowled at his reflection in the coffee in his cup.

Pinelli reached across the table and patted his friend's hand. "Do not waste time wondering why you are being stalked, Pietro. Perhaps some pinball *capo* caught you looking at his favorite whore. Just watch your back and your front as always and be prepared like the snake with two heads to strike in both directions at once."

"Thank you, Umberto. You are a good friend."

He withdrew his hand. "I am old and too free with advice. You have learned what you set out to know?"

"I've made a start. I know the name of the man who hired Ackler and I have descriptions of the other terrorists, if I can separate them from the descriptions of the petty thieves and unemployed Ford and GM workers who did business with the man."

"That is not enough."

"I know. That's the other reason I'm here. I'm a killer, not a detective. I don't know what to do next."

Pinelli drained his glass and mopped his lips with a linen napkin, shaking his great silver head slowly. "My words must ever be the same, *mi amico*. Give it up and come to work with me. With my knowledge of fabrics and your talent for persuasion we will sweep up, as they say."

"I can't do it."

The big old man moved a shoulder.

"You won't help me?"

"I cannot. I am no more detective than you, and when you get to be my age you will learn not only that you do not know everything, but that you have forgotten most of what you did know. It is most distressing."

Macklin glanced at his watch. "I have thirty-six hours." Before rising, he leaned across the table and kissed the big gold ring on the old man's left hand. The old-world gesture pleased Pinelli. "*Arrivederci, padre mio*. Don't let your enemies see your back."

"I would welcome nothing less. It is the way lions die. *Addio*, Pietro."

Macklin walked back to the clothing store and climbed into the Cougar. The engine turned over a dozen times without starting. Cursing, he got out and flung open the hood. While he was examining the ignition wires a man in a blue uniform appeared at his side and placed an item the size of a quarter and shaped like a black asterisk on the cowling over the fan. "This might help."

It was the rotor from the Cougar's distributor. A thrill of electricity shot up Macklin's spine. He shouldered the uniformed man in the chest and spun to the right away from him. Another officer in uniform was standing on that side with the fender between them and his service revolver drawn.

Macklin's own gun was jerked from its holster then and a hand slammed him forward so that the radiator punched him in the stomach and he sprawled face down across the engine. White fire licked up his side. His legs were kicked apart and he was frisked and cuffed and something was said to him that he couldn't hear for the pain pounding in his ears. But it didn't matter. He knew his rights.

CHAPTER 21

THIS ISN'T A POLICE STATION," MACK-
lin said.

The scout car had stopped in a
playing card-size parking lot behind a yellow brick building with
a scuffed-iron fire door in back stenciled NO ADMITTANCE. He
was hustled out of the back seat, still cuffed, and, while the
partner held the door open, he was shoved inside by the officer
who had drawn on him earlier. The dark interior smelled of stale
cooking grease. That put them near a kitchen.

"Oh, we're moving up," responded the officer who had
held the door. "Next month we're getting an unlisted number."
He stabbed a wall button worn concave and it glowed sullenly
behind a cross-hatching of greasy thumbprints. Behind the wall
an elevator car clanked and wheezed to a halt. While they were
waiting for the doors to open, one of the officers released
Macklin's wrists from the handcuffs. Then the doors gave way
with a grating noise and he collided with the back wall. The doors
closed.

Another button was punched and the car shuddered and began to rise. The light inside was strained through a cake of grime on the overhead fixture and it was a few seconds before Macklin realized that the officers hadn't entered with him. He peered at the man with whom he was sharing the car. Tall and strongly built, he wore a three-piece suit tailored to draw attention away from his paunch. He had a broad hard face and a high forehead topped by close-cropped hair with a pale reddish tint. His hands were in his pockets and he wasn't smoking, but the car smelled of pipe tobacco. The man gave Macklin the perfunctory glance of a fellow passenger, then took a hand out of one of his pockets and pushed another button. The car stopped with a sinking sensation of inertia. The doors remained closed, and when Macklin looked up at the old-fashioned indicator he saw that they were stuck between the sixth and seventh floors.

"You look like a detective," Macklin said then. "But you don't dress like one."

"Thanks, I'll consider that a compliment. My tailor picks out the colors and fabric. I just go there at the time we set and put on what he tells me to. I could give you his name." His eyes traveled down and up the killer's casual attire.

"Would he tell me who you are?"

"Sorry. My name's Burlingame. My friends call me Red. You can call me Mr. Burlingame."

"I've heard of you. I've never seen your picture."

"I have other men stand in front of cameras for me. Hoover and I used to fight about that a lot. He liked publicity. But you never know when you might have to go back into the field." He put a hand to the peeling yellow fiberboard that paneled the car. "Believe it or not, this is one of the better downtown hotels. The fanciest places always seem to have the worst service elevators."

"I know the building," Macklin said.

"I thought you might. We own this one. We use it for interrogation when we don't want to run the press gauntlet at headquarters."

"You always use the elevator?"

"Only when I don't want to be interrupted."

"I never heard of an FBI chief conducting interrogations."

"Normally I don't. But you're a hard man to pin down. You managed to shake two of my best agents twice. I don't mind telling you what a blow it is to the Bureau's pride to have to ask the local police to put out an APB on your car."

"I'm surprised they agreed."

"Oh, we're on much better terms since Hoover died. The old fart would never cooperate with the locals and got zilch back. He didn't care. He wanted a national police force with himself as chief. Why'd you kill the old man in River Rouge?"

Macklin said nothing. His face suddenly felt as if it were wearing an ice mask.

Burlingame unbuttoned his coat and spread it. "I'm not wired. Neither is the elevator. Anything you say in here stays in here. So long as I like what I hear," he added, and smiled sheepishly. "That rhymed, didn't it? Sorry."

"Is that why I'm under arrest?" He'd thought they'd traced him from the accident in Port Huron.

"Oh, you're not really under arrest. That was just for anyone who happened to be watching. The Detroit Police couldn't care what happens in River Rouge if it doesn't tie in with something of theirs. We're still a provincial people after all."

"I haven't killed anyone in River Rouge lately."

"We have witnesses. You were seen entering and leaving the building and talking to the victim less than an hour before the body was found. That's about as close to the well-known smoking gun as I've seen in thirty years of investigations."

"The witnesses are wrong."

"It wouldn't surprise me." Burlingame produced a blackened briar and a disreputable-looking pouch from a bulging vest pocket and filled the bowl. "I'd offer you a cigarette but I gave them up when the current surgeon general took office."

"I don't smoke."

"You're lucky." He struck a match on the fiberboard. "I don't think the witnesses were mistaken. I think they saw you. I just don't think you did it." He puffed the tobacco into life.

"Must be my stalwart profile."

"Leave the snappy patter to the experts, Macklin. Our information is you're basically humorless. No, the Rouge murder

143

wasn't your style, too spontaneous. The killer used a weapon that was already on the scene. You don't shit without casing the toilet for three weeks first.''

Macklin made as if to stretch his legs, moving a little closer to the elevator's control panel. If there was space enough between the seventh floor and the top of the car, if he could get the doors open and hoist himself up. Just thinking about it made his side ache. He had a dozen years on Burlingame, though. If there weren't any agents or officers posted on the next floor. "You sound like my biographer," Macklin said.

"You're in a business that draws attention. Who killed him if not you?"

"Why should you care? It's not federal jurisdiction."

"Not officially. But ever since Howard Klegg visited my office yesterday morning, everything that involves you interests us. Stay clear of those buttons; I'm armed."

The killer moved away and leaned back against the tacky railing. "You're the one with all the experience in investigation. You tell me who killed him."

"I think it was the man who's been following you since you left Charles Maggiore's sweet little cottage in Grosse Pointe yesterday. The one who looks like he should be crawling out of a grave on the cover of an old E.C. comic book. Am I right?"

"What do you know about him?" Macklin asked quickly.

"Only that he arrived at Maggiore's before you did and left right behind you. We thought at first you were working together, but that was before we found out you're a loner. You're standing on a rug and your boss is holding on to one end of it. And I know why."

"My boss is Michael Boniface."

"*That's* why." Burlingame stabbed a blunt finger at him. "Maggiore doesn't take to the idea of going back to being a lieutenant. Who would? But if you pull off this Boblo thing and Boniface walks that's exactly what will happen. There's still a lot of loyalty to the old man among the family, so Maggiore can't just refuse to go along with the deal. What he can do is pull in a mechanic from outside the organization to skag you. The deal falls through, Boniface stays behind bars, and Maggiore's feet stay on Boniface's desk."

"Complicated."

"It's simpler than it sounds. How do you think he got where he is? In New York he had a history of having to go take a leak just about the time a lifetaker was coming into the restaurant to ventilate the men he was having dinner with. He's a corporate survivor just like any rising young executive you read about in the *Wall Street Journal.*"

"So why kill someone in Rouge?"

"That wouldn't be part of the plan. Since you were there earlier, I would consider it a judgment call. The spook was following your tracks and got carried away."

Burlingame paused to bat smoke away from his face. The ventilator wasn't working properly and the car was filling with haze. Macklin's eyes were starting to fill. The FBI man put his pipe back in his mouth and blew up some more clouds.

"Why don't you help me with this next part, Macklin? We're supposed to be working together. What did the man tell you before he was killed?"

"We're working parallel. It's not the same thing as together." He made as if to scratch his nose, rubbing his right eye with a knuckle.

"Don't be a damn fool. Two men digging separate holes take just as long getting to China as one. We're fucking around with eight hundred lives here. But I guess that doesn't mean much to a murderer."

"You've never killed anyone?"

"Actually, no. My last field job was the Brink's robbery."

"No one ever killed anyone on a job you assigned?"

"What's the matter, you never split a hair?" Burlingame smiled a small fat man's smile, the equivalent of Macklin's lupine grin. "Okay, we're both killers. The Justice Department and the Sicilian Boy Scouts have enjoyed a long and profitable partnership. We don't call you rats any more and you don't call us G-men. So what are we fighting about? Let's pool what we have."

"You first."

"Uh-uh. It's my elevator."

Macklin sniffled discreetly. His eyes were running into his nose and mucking up his thoughts. After a moment he said, "Put out that grease fire, will you? You're giving the walls cancer."

Burlingame knocked out the pipe against the railing, showering sparks to the grimy floor. He crushed out the live ones with the sole of a black wingtip. Macklin said, "I bet you get a lot of answers that way. Gas them out."

The FBI man shrugged.

Macklin told him what he'd learned since talking to the apartment house manager in River Rouge, including his conversation with Daniel Oliver Ackler's former landlord in Port Huron and what Audrey Fardle had told him outside David Blakeman's pawn shop on Gratiot. He left out Freddo's two attempts on his life and the collision and his interview with the organist at the Peacock's Roost. The story was easier to tell without the options.

"Okay, that's the *Reader's Digest* verson," said Burlingame, when it was finished. "Let's hear the uncondensed one."

The killer folded his arms and crossed his ankles, half-sitting on the elevator's railing. Burlingame fingered his cooling pipe and nodded.

"My turn. I could have saved you a lot of time and maybe a couple of cracked ribs if you'd come to me at the beginning like I asked Klegg. Yeah, it's the way you move, like you're carrying raw eggs in your pockets. I cracked three of my own playing football in college and I moved the same way for two weeks."

"What color shorts have I got on?"

"White jocks. They're the only kind you ever wear." The FBI man went on without pausing. "Blakeman is thirty-six and a Vietnam vet with two purple hearts and a DSC rec that never came through because the army doesn't award important medals to psychos. A piece of fragmentation grenade put half of that X on his cheek; army surgeons made the other half taking it out.

"What the khaki shrinks call his psychological profile places him a shade to the conservative side of Charles Manson. Delusions of grandeur with pathological tendencies. That's what a hundred and forty pages in his medical file boils down to. Local cops questioned him twice on suspicion of receiving stolen property in his pawn shop, but no charges were ever filed for lack of evidence. We'd have had all this sooner but we're computerized now.'' He made a face and put away his pipe.

"He's the one they call Don.''

Burlingame nodded. "We matched witnesses' descriptions with Blakeman's known associates and came up with some possibles. The kid of the group has got to be John Carlisle. He's a teenager with rich parents in Grosse Pointe, no criminal record, and runs with an older girl named Melissa Stein. She's got a history of arrests for shoplifting and one drug bust, no convictions. Her folks have money too. She'd be the blond twist on the boat.

"The black woman is Tonda Kalu, right name Purifying Buchannan, Fay on the boat. As much as she hates anything white I'm surprised she bothers to brush her teeth. Federal agents put holes in her Panther boyfriend on Mt. Elliott four years ago. She did eight months in the Detroit House of Corrections for harboring and campus cops threw her off the Wayne State grounds a couple of times for circulating hate literature. One bust for soliciting, even black revolutionaries have to eat. We got a positive ID on the one calls himself Teddy. His name's Philip MacKenzie and he's a captain in the National Guard wanted for desertion from Grayling, where a number of weapons and explosives were removed from the armory on a forged requisition the day he went AWOL. Their demolitions man is James Delbert. They want him in California for parole violation because he left the state. San Quentin hosted him for over a year on a manslaughter rap. Seems he blew up another employee while they were laying charges for one of those car-crash-and-boom pictures Hollywood likes so much. He's either Ray or Mike; the witnesses weren't sure.''

"What about the one they killed?''

"Franklin Green, musician. His job was finished after smuggling the weapons aboard in his instrument case, so they dusted him. He was a heroin junkie and therefore a liability. Musical bastards, this bunch: Doris, Ray, Mike, Fay. Sol.'' The pause before the last name was significant. "He's the only one we can't put a name to, the one killed Green. Howard Klegg said you know who he is.''

"Klegg mentioned me?"

Burlingame snicked his teeth with his tongue, the first sign of impatience he had shown. "I mean the collective you, meaning you guys. Klegg said he was an independent contract killer and that he knocked down the band's original bass player so Green could take his place. Just a few minutes ago you said you'd traced one of the terrorists to a beach house in Port Huron. That doesn't fit with any of the information we have on the others. What's his name, Macklin?"

"Who's your informant?"

The FBI man frowned his puzzlement. This time it was Macklin who made the impatient noise.

"The one who filled your file on me," he said. "Somebody had to. I haven't seen any agents going through my underwear drawer lately."

"You know I can't tell you that. Who would come forward if we started running to the very people we get the information on and pointing fingers?"

"You've done it. When the people you had information on had information you wanted worse."

Burlingame smiled. "The collective you. *I* haven't."

The killer straightened, crossed his ankles the other way, and leaned back again with his arms crossed.

"You forget you're standing on shit, Macklin." There was now no evidence that a smile had ever lived on Burlingame's square face. "Those officers are still downstairs. I can remand you to them and they'll kick you over to River Rouge for the murder of the apartment house manager."

"It won't stick."

"You'd be surprised what you can make stick when you've got the glue. Oh, hell." He unbuttoned his vest. The atmosphere in the elevator was cloying. "You've got the background you wanted on Siegfried. You'll be dealing with one pro, two semis if you count Blakeman and MacKenzie and their combat training, and two dangerous amateurs, Tonda Kalu and Delbert, the Beast That Blew up Hollywood. Frankie and Annette aren't worth losing sleep over. It's no good to you if you don't know where to find them. I do. Let's trade."

"I can't believe one man's name is worth this much dope," Macklin said. "What have you got in mind, Burlingame?"

"Oh, hell," he said again, and pushed another button on the control panel. The elevator lurched and began descending. "The Bureau is just coming back from all that bad press in the seventies. We haven't had our pick of recruits in years. The good men are nearing retirement, getting careful, and the new men aren't good enough. I haven't a man I'd trust on a boat full of innocents with a blooded killer aboard."

The car settled. Burlingame held his thumb on the Close Door button and said, "I'm going to have to go ahead with you, Macklin. You're the only professional I've got."

CHAPTER 22

LARRY WISHED THE BOAT WOULD
start moving again.

It had been at anchor sever-
al hours now under Don's orders, groaning as it drifted against
the taut pressure of the chain. The engine was shut down, and the
gentle undulation of the wooden hull on the flat waves shifted the
sodden potato chips lying lumped in the 18-year-old hijacker's
stomach. There was nothing to eat aboard but packaged snacks
from the concession stand on the bottom deck, delivered to the
upper levels by big-eyed passengers with loved ones below, and
Don had forbidden smuggling more nourishing food up the
gangplank for fear of arousing suspicion before their first move.
Larry's glittering high had given way to a black void as the
cocaine wore off. His head hurt and he yearned for some
movement of air over the bow to stop his lungs from creaking. He
wished he hadn't accounted for his share of the powder in his first
blow. He wondered if he was an addict, like Mike was or like the
crater-faced wrecks he had seen snuffling around that boarded-up

151

store on Erskine the first time Doris had taken him to meet her connection.

Doris.

His sweat was a greasy sheen on his face and plastered his body like a clammy shroud under his clothes. The bends of his elbows made wet tearing sounds when he straightened his arms, and the checked butt of the heavy .45 was slippery in his palm. It did no good to change hands and wipe the palm on his pants; his glands were stuck open. Even his toes squelched in his shoes.

He wondered if Doris had anything left. She could leave her hostages for a few seconds. Most of them were lying or sitting on the deck, not even bothering to look at their captors any more, and any who had it in his head to take a flying dive off that topmost passenger deck into the middle of Lake Erie wasn't going to be a problem. He called her. It came out a croak. He hadn't spoken in hours. He cleared his throat, wet his mouth as well as he could, and called again. That time it rang out clearly, if a little too loud. Some of the passengers started and looked up at him.

Doris' blond head appeared around the base of the crown deck that separated them. "Yes, John?"

"Larry," he corrected automatically, angrily. Well, it didn't much matter now. Don had said their names would all be known to the authorities after thirty-six hours. "You got any stuff?"

"A little."

"Bring it here."

She hesitated. Her head disappeared for a moment, and then he saw her walking his way along the railing, holding the M-16 across her body in both hands like a balancing rod. She looked like someone's kid sister playing soldier and Larry would have smiled if he thought he wouldn't look like a death's-head. He felt the hairs in his nostrils standing out as if reaching for what was coming.

"Doris, get back to your station."

Larry saw the girl stop and look up. He followed her gaze. Don was leaning one hip against the railing of the starboard bridge wing with a heel hooked on the bottom rail and the Luger in his right hand resting on his raised thigh. The extended cartridge clip protruded four inches below the pistol's square butt. Larry had watched him convert the gun to full automatic in five minutes one afternoon.

"John"—Doris corrected herself—"Larry wanted—"

"I know what he wanted. Go back."

"But he needs it."

"No one needs coke. It isn't like heroin."

But after a second, Don slipped two fingers of his left hand into his pants pocket and came up with a flat cellophane package, which he flipped over the wing. Larry watched the package turning end over end in a long arc, felt the weight of his heart on his tongue when a breath of wind pushed it toward the outside railing, then lunged forward as it dropped straight down and landed on the edge of the deck with a flat smack.

Don divided his attention between his own prisoners in the pilot house and those on the top passenger level while Larry knelt with his gun in his pocket and spilled a little of the powder on to the deck and separated it into lines with the razor he carried and then snuffed up two lines through a tightly rolled dollar bill. He scooped the remainder back into the package and stood, his eyes glittering in the sunlight that was just beginning to break through the overcast. "Keep it," Don told him, when he resealed the cellophane and made as if to flip it back. "Just try to make it last another day and a half, okay?"

Larry said he would and Don was turning back away from the railing when the boat lurched to starboard, throwing him hard against the painted metal. He grabbed the top rail to keep from pitching over, almost losing his gun, spun around, and loosed three shots in a half-second burst into the pilot house. One bullet starred the windscreen. Another splintered the oak paneling on the port side. The man at the wheel, who had spun it in an attempt to hurl Don overboard, cried out and grasped his right arm above the elbow. The other men in the pilot house stood back against the walls with their hands raised.

The wheel man swooned, blood streaming down his arm and pattering to the deck. The weight of his body turned the wheel and the boat swung into a slow starboard drift. Covering the others, Don strode in past his portable radio and unpegged the microphone to the public address system. His voice, clear and loud and quivering with emotion, rang through the boat.

"We got a comedian up here. If there's a doctor aboard this tub he might think about coming up and bringing his bag with him. Otherwise we'll all hear a splash."

He replaced the microphone, watching the old captain and the glaring mate and the pale and shaking lookout and the security guard staring at the deck. The wounded man was semi-conscious, slumped on one knee at the base of the wheel with a hand clasping his injured arm. There was a lot of blood.

It had been a mistake to take Larry along, Don thought. He wondered if it would be a mistake to keep him along.

CHAPTER 23

FREDDO WONDERED WHERE the G-men had gone.

Parked across the street and down the block from Peter Macklin's house in Southfield, he abandoned the pretense of reading his road map and folded it and socked it into the glove compartment of the blue Oldsmobile. It was obvious no one was watching. With his jacket and tie off and his hair tucked up under a cloth cap he had bought in a five-and-dime on the way down from Port Huron, he had walked casually up one side of the street and down the other, letting his gaze slide inside the few cars parked along the curbs, and convinced himself that no federal men were watching the place. There was a bare chance they were forted up in one of the other houses on the block with binoculars and cameras with telephoto lenses, but he doubted it. That was for big operators of Maggiore's stamp, not for street soldiers like Macklin. And it still required a radio car for the tail. Freddo felt like the guest who had read his invitation wrong and come one night late for the party.

He had stopped off at the room he rented in the city to put on a fresh shirt and exchange his suit for a tailored blazer and checked pants and break his spare .44 magnum out of the false ceiling he had rigged in his closet. He had hardly hoped to find Macklin at home afterward, but if the FBI were still in residence he would have had hopes the master of the castle would show up. The feds were dumb as telephone poles but all that sitting around on their piles generally paid off. He didn't like their not being there. He never thought he'd want to see a cop.

There was more than money in it now, or even simple ambition. No old man in a floppy suit let himself into Freddo's car and spilled his partner and walked away to write his memoirs. This was a new sensation for Freddo. Poor old Link had had to work himself up a good hate every time he hit someone or helped someone else make a hit. He used to stand in front of a mirror and pretend his reflection was the mark and make his eyes bulge and his face red thinking up all this crap the mark would be handing him, then barge out the door like a big-ass Mexican bull. You couldn't even talk to him until afterward when he was like a wet rag with a mouth that wouldn't stop. He wasn't what Freddo called a natural. But Freddo could eat half a sandwich, get up, go out, drop the nickel on the stiff whoever he was, then come back and finish the sandwich and wait for the news on television. He wondered if Macklin was like that. Well, he'd give him another half hour and then go try something else.

Twenty minutes later a woman came walking around the corner on the side of the street where the house was, carrying the kind of striped paper bag liquor stores sold their merchandise in. She had a dumpy figure under a blue blouse that needed ironing and a roll of flab jiggled over the top of the wide plastic belt that went with her dark skirt, and at first Freddo paid her no more attention than a bored dog would spend watching a caterpillar climb a blade of grass. But she slowed her pace as she neared Macklin's house and when she turned into the front walk, juggling the bag under one arm while rummaging in a big black purse, he sat up, blinking.

While he was at Maggiore's house waiting for his first glimpse of Macklin, Freddo had gone over a folder full of material on the killer, and among the driver's license pictures and telephoto shots taken of him getting into and out of his car and walking down the street, there had been a family photograph, shot against a professional blue backdrop and gleaned from some commercial photographer's file of negatives. It had shown a younger Macklin, less tired-looking, with more hair and a wary smile on his face, standing behind a chair containing an attractive tawny-haired woman with a dark-haired boy of eleven or twelve at his side. This woman was heavier and broad streaks of gray showed in her home bleach job, and anyone could see by the way she walked that she was a lush. He thought at first she was the housekeeper. But it was the kind of neighborhood where servants attracted attention, which wasn't Macklin's way.

If this was what had become of his wife Donna, Freddo could see why Macklin didn't spend much time at home.

Hardly had the door closed behind the woman when another actor entered the scene. He appeared from between houses on the opposite side of the street and strode across with a nervous, jerky gait, yanking his head from side to side in a way that said he wasn't looking for traffic so much as seeking to avoid detection. His sudden appearance on the woman's heels suggested that he had been waiting just for her arrival, and Freddo cursed himself for not having seen him earlier. He watched the youth look around one last time on the front stoop, then pull the door open and duck inside quickly.

He had grown at least a foot and lost his baby fat, but Roger Macklin looked a lot like his mother in the old picture.

Freddo sat watching the house and drumming his fingers on the Oldsmobile's steering wheel. Assimilating. In the old days, he had been told, there had been some unwritten rule that no matter how hot things got, a man's home and family remained off limits. Those were the days when fat greaseballs in loud silk suits with garlic on their breath kissed each other in restaurants and sent flowers to each other's funeral "from the boys."

He was glad the old days were gone. He touched his underarm holsters and reached for the door handle.

* * *

The secretary in Randall Burlingame's outer office said "Yes, sir" into the intercom and removed a finger with a plum-colored nail from the speaker button. She measured out a frosty smile for the lean bald man. "You can go in now, Mr. Chilson."

"Thanks, Miss MacNamara."

He was rewarded when the smile chipped loose from her face. "Gabel."

He shrugged and walked around the end of her desk. It actually blocked any direct entrance to the private office, making Miss Gabel a kind of Cerberus at the gate to Hades. Except that she was too good-looking in her polished porcelain way to be compared to a dog with three heads.

On his way in, Chilson passed a man coming out in a light-colored windbreaker and jeans. He looked like a repairman for the telephone company and the Secret Service agent's eyes flicked downward automatically to see if he was carrying a toolbox. But his hands were empty.

"I see you've had the British workman in your house, Watson," Chilson said, closing the door and shaking Burlingame's hand. "He's a token of evil."

"When are you going to stop reading that Conan Doyle crap?" grumbled the FBI chief.

"As soon as the secret agent business gets as good. Who was that, one of your deep cover men?"

"That was Peter Macklin."

"You're kidding." Chilson glanced back stupidly at the door.

"I'd have introduced you, but he's in a hurry."

"He looked like a telephone repairman."

"That's the idea. In the murder game it's called dressing for success. Is this important, Bill? I've got a lot of work kicking me in the behind."

"Why was Macklin here?"

"We adjourned here from the hotel. The charts were here." As he spoke, Burlingame walked back to his desk and folded the great chart of the lakes he had shown the Secret Service man that morning.

"You let him see it? You told him where the boat is?"

"He'll need it. Look, Bill, I'm really swamped." He pulled at the top drawer of the desk to put away the chart. The drawer came all the way out and spilled papers onto the carpet. He threw the drawer down in disgust.

"Did you kiss him before he left?" Chilson asked in the silence that followed. "Or do they still do that?"

"It was the victims that got kissed. This is my case, Bill. It has been from the start. Your involvement is strictly courtesy. If one hostage aboard that boat loses a toenail it'll be my head in the basket, not yours."

He had been shouting, and it was a moment before either of them realized the intercom was buzzing. Burlingame jammed down the switch. "What is it, Louise?" He spoke quietly, recoiling from his own outburst.

"Is everything all right in there?"

"Swell. Why?"

"Someone in the next office asked if you were rehearsing *The Ring of the Nibelung*."

"Louise, you're fired."

"I'm a civil servant, Mr. Burlingame. It would take an act of Congress to fire me."

He turned off the intercom and scowled at Chilson. "I'm beginning to understand why people hire someone like Macklin."

"I didn't mean to come on like Jack Armstrong," Chilson said gently. "I forgot how far your neck was out on this one. But there has to be a better way. What about that plan you wouldn't tell me about?"

"There never was a plan. Not really. That's what I didn't want to tell you." The FBI man cocked a hip on to the corner of his desk. "The Bureau has standard procedures for dealing with hostage situations in tall buildings and airliners parked on runways. Give us a crazed Philippine national barricaded in an underground bank vault with a Russian pineapple and a pregnant teller and we'll have them both out quicker than you can make a legal withdrawal. We even have commandoes trained specifically to scale the Washington Monument just in case someone threatens to blow it up like that nut did last spring. But for seven kamikazes holding eight hundred citizens aboard a floating firecracker on one of the Great Lakes, we're strapped. They'd hear a helicopter or a power boat coming for miles and turn the whole works into burning flotsam in less time than it takes me to light my pipe."

"That's hardly an indication of speed," the other commented.

Burlingame ignored the crack. "One man might get aboard, but it's what he does when he gets there that will make all the difference. He sure wouldn't do it for love or patriotism. But he would for money. That's Macklin."

"There are more desirable alternatives."

"Name one."

"I just got off the phone with my boss. He had an idea all ready."

"I won't release those prisoners from Jackson."

"It's not your decision to make. Only the Governor has the power to issue pardons and commute sentences. I'm driving up to Lansing to see him this afternoon."

"The Governor does what the federal revenue sharing people tell him to do. The Director in Washington is with me on this. He has files. Not like Hoover had files, but he has files nonetheless. There's a hooker in Chevy Chase whose name whispered in the right ears is as good as a presidential veto. Those cons don't walk until I say they walk."

Chilson said, "I didn't realize so much of the old fart had rubbed off on you."

Burlingame's face turned a dark cherry color. But instead of shouting he looked down at his desk and realigned the edges of some typewritten sheets in a stack on the blotter. When he raised his eyes the flush was gone.

"Back when I wore a crewcut and you could nick your finger on the lamination on my ID, I thought rules were the berries," he said. "They were what separated us from the gorillas in uniform in places like Mississippi. My first assignment was as auditor to a bureau chief named Yerkovich in Yuma, Arizona. He was a foul-mouthed, cigar-chomping tin Napoleon who had been with the bunch that shot Dillinger and anyone could see he was going to die in Yuma, because he didn't look like any of the agents who got their pictures in the papers when the big busts went down. One day he sat me in a chair and stuck that cigar a quarter-inch from my right eyeball and said there weren't any rules. That was just something the Bureau wanted your criminal element—he said it just that way, your criminal element—to believe in. They thought they could lie and cheat and commit mayhem and we couldn't, and so they swaggered into Interrogation clicking their gum and grinning. They came out six hours later with two black eyes and the gum stuck on the end of their noses, and that's why Dillinger was dead and not still robbing banks in Indiana.

"It was two years before I believed a word of it. Those two years cost me a partner and a reprimand for 'recreant display' during a loan office robbery in Baton Rouge. Read that 'coward.' I refused to shoot an unarmed bandit standing at a window. Five seconds later the unarmed bandit swung a sawed-off shotgun out from under his overcoat and blew my partner into Sunday without even bothering to open the window. It's still in my file, otherwise I'd be cooling my Guccis on a desk three times this size in Washington."

"Red, I never thought you were that kind of agent."

"There aren't any other kinds outside training."

"Bullshit. We never did things that way in the Service."

Burlingame sighed theatrically. "You Service boys put on striped ties and comb your hair and have tea with blue-haired old ladies who write letters to the President telling him to go fuck himself. When it looks like you might get a spot on your cuffs you come to us."

Chilson had been leaning forward over the chair in front of the desk with his fingers sunk into the upholstered back. Now he straightened.

"I'm talking to the Governor. He can put the wheels in motion, buy some time."

"Go ahead. When the seventy-two hours is up Siegfried will just tack on a new demand, and when that isn't met they'll make a waterspout out of the Boblo boat."

"How can you be so sure?"

"Because I've been wading ass-deep in David Blakemans since the first Marine set foot in Vietnam."

"What about Peter Macklins?"

"The Macklins of this world just go on and on. If Cain had had a choice he'd have paid someone to take out Abel for him."

Chilson took his eyes from his old friend's to read his watch. "I'd better get going if I'm to have dinner with the Governor." He moved to the door. "Orders, Red. If Carol Turnbull gets killed there'll be two heads in that basket. One bald."

The FBI man nodded. He was still perched on the edge of the desk. "I guess you know this conversation didn't happen."

"It hasn't been that long since I had tea with my last blue-haired old lady."

Burlingame sat there a long moment after the Secret Service agent had left without saying good-bye. Then he got up, turned around, and slammed the flat of his hand down on the desk hard enough to sting himself and jar the telephone receiver out of its cradle. A second later the intercom buzzed.

CHAPTER 24

CHRISTINE FINISHED unwinding the ban-
dage from around Macklin's midsection and gasped. "What did
they use, a baseball bat?"

"It was an accident." He was sitting stripped to the waist on
the edge of the bed in her apartment. Under the reddish burns the
bandage had made, a pattern of purple bruises had spread
amorphously across his abdomen. There were other, older scars
on his back and upper arms and chest that she had never asked
about. Her probing fingers found a spot that made him take in his
breath. He grabbed at her hand and she slapped his wrist.

"I know what I'm doing. Not all of Carmine's clients paid
up with a smile. I got enough practice on him to qualify for my
nurse's license." Carmine was the loan shark she had been living
with until his violent death.

She untinned a roll of adhesive from the bathroom medicine
cabinet. "I wish I had some linament."

"That stuff just raises blisters and burns like hell so you think it's doing something. Just tape me up."

"Well, raise your arms."

He did so, and she wound the white adhesive around his ribcage until it felt like tight armor. When she was done she put down the empty spool and stepped back. "You look good in a girdle."

"You look good out of one."

She squinted at him. His shoulders sagged and the failing light sliding through the window at his back found strands of silver in his mud-colored hair. "Don't go starting things you can't finish," she warned him.

"I was counting on you helping."

"I'm afraid I'll break something."

He raised his head a millimeter, and though his face was in shadow she knew he was grinning. "You damn well better try."

Afterward he was sorry, and he lay on his back with his chest heaving and little bursts of pain going off in his side like timed charges. Christine sighed sleepily, laid her head in the hollow of his shoulder, and drew a bare thigh across his groin that took his mind off his agony. He slept.

The telephone's keening ring found a place in his dream, and he didn't stir until the bedsprings moved and he heard Christine padding into the next room. The ringing stopped.

Grunting, he hoisted off the covers and sat on the edge of the mattress for a moment and stood and stepped gingerly into his shorts and jeans. The sun was not yet down, shedding rose light tinged with gray into the room. Christine, on the telephone, was standing with her back to the bedroom door and he paused in the doorway to admire her long back and curving buttocks with the marks from the bedsheets tattooing her smooth white skin. He had first been attracted by her skin. He hated tans.

She must have heard his bare feet brush the carpet, because she turned with the receiver in her hand and held it out. "It's for you. A man named Burlingame."

He cursed, took two steps, and seized the receiver. "Who gave you this number?"

"Never mind that," said the familiar voice. "Can you talk?"

"Second." He looked at Christine. She nodded and walked past him into the bedroom, trailing a scent of sandalwood and feminine musk. The door closed. "Okay."

"You should have told me his name was Freddo, Macklin. It might have given us a place to start."

"Who's Freddo?"

"We left that shit back in the elevator," Burlingame rasped. "He's the growth on your ass, or I've wasted myself in the wrong business all these years. He just called."

"Called where?"

"Called where. Called here. My office. He says he's got something that belongs to you."

"As for instance."

"He wouldn't say. But he said he was calling from your house."

Macklin felt the ice mask.

"Macklin?"

"What else did he say?"

"Just to go back home. He'll call you. That was the whole message, just that he's got something of yours and to wait for his call. It's your family, isn't it? Macklin?"

He cradled the receiver. After a moment the telephone rang again. He picked up the receiver again and lowered it, severing the connection, then took it off the hook and laid it on the telephone stand.

Christine had on slippers and a lacy blue robe when he went back into the bedroom. She watched him draw on his shirt and when he looked at his socks on the floor she knelt and helped him into them and his shoes and tied the laces. He said, "Where'd he get your number?"

"I was going to ask you that. What are you doing, writing it on men's room walls?" She rose, the smile dying on her face when she saw his expression. "Peter, what is it? Bad news?"

"I'm on the books at the federal building. I didn't know I was on the books there before today. No one knows I come here. I didn't tell anyone."

She tried the smile. "What are you saying?"

"You tell me."

"Peter, I didn't tell anyone."

"Burlingame knows I wear white Jockey shorts."

"I didn't know that was actionable."

The back of his hand made a loud crack against her face. She staggered back and put a palm to her reddening cheek.

"I told you before to cut the sarcastic crap. What did they do, threaten you with accessory? Or was it a straight cash deal?"

"Murdering bastard," she muttered.

"What?"

She said it again, louder. The rest of her face had flushed to match the imprint of his hand on her cheek. "You killed Carmine and then you moved in while my thighs were still warm from him."

"I didn't kill him."

"You knew someone was going to and you didn't say anything. It's the same. I hear things. People talk. To everyone but the police."

"That's why you turned informant?"

"I didn't. If I'd thought of it I would have."

"How come you still opened your door to me if you didn't?"

"Because I love you and it stinks."

"Oh, Christ."

"It happens," she said. "Maybe it never happened to you. There's nothing good about it. It's like being addicted. If I could get out from under I would in a minute."

"Lying bitch." He cocked his hand. She backpedaled swiftly, stepped on the hem of her robe, and fell, the material parting and uncovering her nakedness. Tears slicked her cheeks.

"I guess you'll kill me," she said.

"I only kill when I'm paid."

"Whore."

"You pay a prostitute," he corrected. "You don't pay a whore. You take her and leave."

He snatched up his windbreaker and reached for the Smith & Wesson he had left on the same chair. The holster lay empty. He swung around and looked at Christine, standing now with the gun in one hand. He froze.

She smiled. Her eyes were wild. "So much power." She raised the gun and opened her mouth to put the barrel inside.

He sprang, tromping her toes in her thin slipper. She screamed and he got her wrist between his thumb and forefinger at the break and twisted and the gun thumped the floor. In the same movement he swung his right shoulder into her body and she exhaled and stumbled backward. This time the wall kept her from falling. He picked up the revolver and shoved it into its holster.

"I'll just find something else," she said. Her robe remained open. Her breasts rose and fell rapidly.

"As long as it's not my gun." He hesitated, about to say something more. Then he left. He heard her on his way out of the apartment.

He took his time driving north on the Southfield Freeway while the sky purpled and the lights of one shopping center after another strung the landscape. Behind a gauzy haze the sun eased down like an old man lowering himself into scalding bath water. By morning the fog would have lifted completely.

It was dark when he reached his neighborhood. He parked in an empty service station two blocks south and got out and took off his windbreaker, reversing it to its dark side before putting it back on. He loosened the revolver in its holster and started walking. No one had summoned him home to wait for any telephone call.

The air held the slight chill of autumn testing the ground for winter. At the corner before his house he turned, then cut through a neighbor's back yard and swung first one leg over a white picket fence and then the other and crossed a patio paved with flagstones and entered his own back yard with cold dew seeping through the canvas of his tennis shoes. Something crackled. He stopped.

"Raise them hands or they're gonna be combing your brains out of the grass into next week."

The voice was high, girlish, half whisper. He couldn't place its source. He moved his hands away from his body.

"I said raise them."

He raised them to his shoulders.

"You shouldn't of killed Link," said the voice.

There were no fences or hedges or trees in Macklin's yard. Over Donna's protests he had cut down the one cedar that had stood there when he bought the house, explaining that it obscured the view. Actually he had borrowed the idea from feudal lords who had sought to discourage intruders from gaining access to their castles from cover. There were no lights on inside the house, but the slight glow from a neighbor's upstairs window found a triangle of shadow where Macklin's back door stood ajar. There was no place else for Freddo to be hiding.

"You said you had something that belongs to me," Macklin said.

"They're tied up inside. That's some boy you got, Gramps. After you give him that thousand he comes back to squeeze some more out of the old lady. I figure after I'm done with you I'll save him for last."

"I thought it was me you wanted."

"This way the cops'll be looking for some nut that jerks off to old Donna Reed reruns. Mass murder is getting to be Michigan's chief export."

Macklin moved his right foot a little as if shifting his weight. If he could move fast enough, get the open door between them for half a second. He spoke to cover the slight movement. "I guess you want me pretty bad."

"Nothing personal. Just business. Stay put or I'll start with your kneecaps."

He had pushed it too much. He set his feet. In the darkness inside the doorway was a darker patch of shadow, manshaped. "It's personal," he said. "Otherwise I'd be dead now."

The door opened farther. The light from the far window found a high forehead, the bridge of a nose, white shirt, gleaming metal farther down. "Back up. Keep backing up till I say stop."

Macklin obeyed. His feet felt icy in his soaked shoes. He had retreated five feet when Freddo called for him to halt.

For a long time neither man moved. The television in the house next door was tuned to a religious program and the twenty-third psalm came straining through the window. Finally Freddo stepped forward and closed the door behind him. He was jacketless, the dark leather straps of his twin underarm holsters harnessing his upper body. He looked emaciated and his narrow face with stringy wisps of fair hair trailing down on either side and shadows in the hollows made a death mask in the poor light. Ten feet from Macklin he stopped.

"We'll do this right." He twirled the big .44 western style and snugged it into his left holster, raised and resettled it. Set his feet.

Macklin lowered his arms. "You're kidding."

"Anytime you feel lucky."

"I'm unarmed."

"Like hell."

"Someone's holding a gun for me. I was going to get it when Burlingame called. You can frisk me."

A thin vertical line cracked the smooth marble of Freddo's forehead. Finally he nodded and moved to slide the .22 target pistol out of his right holster. Macklin scooped out the Smith & Wesson and shot him three times in the chest.

The long-barreled revolver bobbled out of Freddo's hand and they hit the ground together. He lay twitching on his stomach, one eye staring up at Macklin. A dot of blood darkened the visible corner of his open mouth. The mouth was working.

Someone had turned off the twenty-third psalm. There was an outline at the window of the house next door.

"Who hired you?" Macklin demanded. He was standing over the wounded man with the .38 smoking in his hand.

"I needa doc'or," said Freddo.

"I'll get you a doctor. Who drew up the contract?"

"I can't breeve." He coughed. A string of bloody saliva stretched between his mouth and the wet grass.

"Was it Maggiore?"

"Mashy."

"Maggiore?"

"Mashorry. Yeah. Getta doc'or."

Macklin leaned down, grinning. "Die, you rat-faced bastard," he said.

KILL ZONE

* * *

He found Donna and Roger sitting back-to-back in hard chairs in the kitchen. They had been gagged tightly with dish towels and their wrists and ankles were bound to the chairs and each other with copper wire from the garage. Wild eyes stared at him when he switched on the light.

"I don't have time to untie you," he said, reloading the Smith & Wesson from among the cartridges in his pocket and dumping the spent shells into his other pocket from old habit. "I'll let the police do that. If our neighbor is as civic-minded as he is religious he's called them already."

Donna hummed something frantic through her gag. He holstered the revolver and stepped forward and loosened the dish towel.

"Son of a bitch," she snarled. "I suppose you killed him just like all the others."

"No, each one is different."

He reached into his shirt pocket and withdrew the thousand dollars he'd taken off Freddo. His thousand. Some of the bills were stained dark on one corner. He approached Roger, who shrank back in his bonds, and poked the bills into his son's jeans pocket. "Don't come running to me if the police take it off you."

He went upstairs and got the rest of the fifty thousand out of the safe in his study. Then he went back down to the kitchen and folded ten thousand in hundreds into the flour canister on the linoleum counter. He could hear a siren now, a long way off. He looked at Donna. "I never wanted this here."

She spat at him.

CHAPTER 25

HE DROVE THE COUGAR TO A CHAIN RESTAU-
rant on Lahser and waited in the parking lot. During
the next fifteen minutes, three people came out and
got into their cars and left and two more parties drove in. None of
the cars was more than five years old. A few minutes later a
fourteen-year-old GMC pickup with a six-foot-high cab and holes
rusted through its rear panels trundled into a space thirty yards
down and a five-foot-high man with a handlebar moustache got
out tugging down the hem of his zip jacket and went inside.
Macklin gave it another five minutes, then left the Cougar with
his key still in the ignition and hoisted himself into the driver's
seat of the pickup and tried the wheel. It turned both ways. The
vehicle had been built before the development of the self-locking
steering column. He stripped two wires under the dash and had
the engine started in thirty seconds. He had dropped out of school
at 16 to go to work for an automobile repossessions firm, and
except for some cosmetic computerization and a couple of
clumsy security devices, cars hadn't changed all that much

inside. By now there would be a BOL bulletin out on a silver Cougar with Macklin's plate.

Just to tangle the chain of investigation, after twenty blocks he switched to a cream-colored Dodge Dart of similar vintage parked at a curb in a residential district and left the pickup in its place. In a shopping center lot on Twelve Mile Road he traded plates with a blue AMC Spirit and drove away feeling cleansed. Stopping at a bank of public telephones outside a service station on the corner of Telegraph, he dropped a quarter into a slot without getting out of the car, dialed a number from memory, and spoke for a few minutes with a man whose voice sounded as if he had a fishbone caught in his throat. Then he took Telegraph south to I-75.

He changed cars once again in Toledo and followed the shore of Lake Erie east. Around eleven o'clock his back began to ache from all the driving and he stopped to stretch his legs and drink a cup of black coffee at an all-night diner. The waitress traded ribald jokes with a party of rowdy truckers in a corner booth and paid him scant attention. He left a modest tip. His stomach growled on his way out but he wasn't eating.

Stars were peering through breaks in the overcast when he entered the Sandusky city limits. He left the car in a small factory employee parking lot during a shift change and walked to a motel, where he rented a room from a sleepy clerk for two hours' sleep and changed a ten-dollar bill into dimes and quarters. After awakening he washed his face and shaved with bar soap and a disposable razor he'd stopped to buy on the way. He threw away the razor and used the pay telephone in the hall around the corner from the registration desk to call Randall Burlingame's Detroit office long distance.

"Macklin, where the hell are you?" The FBI man's voice was wound tight, and Macklin guessed he hadn't been home. "All hell's busting loose here. The Detroit police want you for murder."

"It was self-defense. I'm calling to see if you've got a fix on the Boblo boat as of this morning."

"Listen, we can smooth over the thing in Southfield. The stiff was wearing a Colt Python in a shoulder rig and there was a

.22 revolver found nearby. Just come down here and we'll have you out in an hour."

"Can't make it. Where's the boat?"

"I'm dangling from a bush over the rapids on this, Macklin. If it gets out we engaged the services of a hunted murderer, Washington will saw it off at the roots."

"Burlingame, I don't care."

"You will if the Bureau disavows responsibility for your actions. You'll be a guest of the state into the next century."

"I'm looking at that now. For the stiff in River Rouge."

"You're off the hook on that one. An old lady in the building found the manager's body. She saw a man leaving his apartment just before. She didn't see his face, but the description she gave matches the stiff at your place. That doesn't mean you won't go down for that one."

The operator cut in, demanding money for the next three minutes. Macklin fed quarters into the slot.

"Macklin, where are you?"

"Where's the boat?"

"Fuck you."

Macklin checked his watch. "Eighteen hours, Burlingame."

The FBI man swore again and left the line. A moment later he came back on with a new set of chart points. "Got those written?" he asked.

"I got them." Macklin didn't bother to say he never wrote anything down.

"One favor?" asked Burlingame. "Seeing as I'm about to blow my pension and violate policy by interfering in a civil murder investigation, will you at least call me before you move? I'd sort of like to look like I know what's going on when the reporters get here."

"I can't promise that."

"Who the fuck said anything about promises? Say you'll try."

"I'll try."

"Okay. And Macklin?"

"I'm running out of change, Burlingame."

"Macklin, I don't care. I just wanted to say that if the Bureau had ten men like you, the J. Edgar Hoover Building would still be a swamp."

Not having a topper, Macklin hung up.

He left the motel and walked northeast. The wind freshened his cheeks and buckled his windbreaker and grew stronger with the scent of moisture and fish as he walked. Sunlight flashed metallically between buildings, reflecting off water, and then he followed steep cracking pavement downhill to a row of sagging docks glittering with millions of fish scales with the choppy cold blue surface of Lake Erie yawning endlessly beyond. Men in T-shirts and filthy jeans and khakis were at work, had been for hours despite the sleepy red disc of the sun still struggling with inertia over the water, climbing up and down ladders and across gangplanks carrying cans of fuel and boxes of tackle and ice chests. In spite of his workman's clothes and rumpled look, Macklin felt as out of place as any landlubber.

Finally he found the dock number he wanted and walked to the end, where a thirty-foot launch slightly lower than the dock rode the water, with *Wolf Larsen* stenciled across the fantail. A fat man with lumpy white-stubbled features under a crushed yachting cap sat in the back of the open cabin pouring beer down his throat from a gold can. He was naked to the waist and wisps of white hair stirred against rolls of shocking pink lard on his chest. His feet, planted firmly on the deck, were large and bare and the square toenails were as thick as horns.

"Captain Stephenson?" Macklin asked.

The fat man looked up at him, screwing up his face and shielding his eyes under a hand cross-hatched with old dirt and tar. He looked like a bloated Popeye. "*Mister* Stephenson," he corrected, in a voice furry with phlegm. "You get busted down from chief petty to ABS three times in eighteen years in the Coast Guard and you get so you don't ever want to hear no officer's titles. Who are you?"

"My name's Macklin. Manny Felder gave me your name. I talked to him on the phone in Detroit last night."

"Manny, how is the thieving kike bastard?"

"Doing okay. He's semiretired now, turned over the tug and the salvage business to his son Aaron. He said to 'tell that lard-butt Scandihoovian he still owes me five hundred from that poker game two years ago Christmas.'"

"He's got it backwards. He owes me. Only Yid I ever knew could tell a sextant from his abbreviated dick. How do you know him?"

"He helped me dump a load of cement into Lake St. Clair a couple of times. With someone inside."

Stephenson paused with the beer can halfway to his lips, squinting up at Macklin. Then he slugged down the rest of the contents, crumpled the can, and flipped it over the side, where it bobbed on the surface a long time before shipping enough water through its opening to sink. "I don't deep-six cold meat," he said, and burped. "They fine the shit out of you for just dumping garbage into the lake. I was to get caught I might lose my skipper's license."

"You had it yanked once for thirty days already. For smuggling Havana cigars and Russian caviar into the United States from Canada."

"I still got friends in the Coast Guard or I wouldn't've got it back at all. I get into accessory to murder one, that shit, they don't know me from Davy Jones."

"I'm not doing any dumping today. I want to hire your launch."

"There's a marina a hundred yards down the beach. They rent everything from rowboats to minesweepers."

"Marinas keep logs."

"So do I."

"Not always, according to Manny."

"Manny talks a lot for a Hebe. When you figuring on going out?"

"Tonight after dark."

Stephenson lifted the lid off a battered cooler full of ice and gold cans and popped the top off one, spraying the inside of the boat. "Can't help you."

"Why not?"

"Tonight I'm taking a doctor from Dayton out after coho. Fancies himself a dark fisherman." He tipped up the can. It gurgled twice before he lowered it.

"Cancel him."

The sailor patted his huge pink stomach and burped again. "Let me give you some free advice, just in case you ever decide to get into this business. Don't ever cancel a doctor. None of 'em knows the first fucking thing about anything once they get out of that white coat, and they pay and pay and pay anyone who looks like they do know."

"This one paying a thousand?" Macklin took out his roll, to which he had added from the envelope in another pocket, and skinned off ten one hundred-dollar bills. Stephenson watched him, marble-blue eyes glittering in folds of pink fat.

"I don't stand in front of no bullets," he said. "I'd bleed Budweiser."

"You won't get near any shooting."

"How long's the trip?"

Macklin gave him the chart points he had gotten from Randall Burlingame.

"That ain't no thousand bucks' worth," Stephenson said.

"I want you to throw in a crash course in skin diving. Manny says you used to be an instructor."

"You ever been?"

"Never."

Stephenson chuckled, his stomach a bellows. The chuckle turned into a bubbling cough and he hawked something up from his square toes and spat over the side. "Forget it. I might could turn you into a diver that won't suck in a double lungful of Lake Erie and go to stay with the bottom-feeders his first time out alone. In about six weeks. There's an undertow out there will suck you under like Granny Gums' best blow job."

Macklin unwrapped another five hundred. "I've got fifteen hundred says you're a better instructor than that."

Stephenson drained the can, tossed it after its predecessor without bothering to crush it, and hoisted himself to his feet, rocking the boat violently before he got his hands on the rope ladder and climbed up to the dock. Macklin was surprised to see that he was barely five feet tall, and nearly as broad. "Where are you going?"

"I got a place on the beach," Stephenson said, closing a sandpapery paw on the money in the killer's hand. He stank of fish and sweat, none of it fresh. "You wasn't planning on doing no skin diving without equipment, was you?"

CHAPTER 26

LIFE IS A MESS.'"

"What?" asked Macklin. He was poised on the rope ladder, handing down fins and a mask and a wet suit and a safety vest and a knife in a waterproof scabbard to Stephenson, who stood in the boat to receive and stow the items. They had selected the equipment, some of it mildewed and evil-smelling, from various niches and corners in the sailor's cluttered fiberboard-and-aluminum shack on a patch of littered beach a quarter-mile from the docks.

Stephenson said it again. "'It is like yeast, a ferment, a thing that moves and may move for a minute, an hour, a year, or a hundred years, but that in the end will cease to move. The big eat the little that they may continue to move, the strong eat the weak that they may retain their strength. The lucky eat the most and move the longest, that is all.' Know who wrote that?"

"Cole Porter?"

"No sir, Jack London. He had Wolf Larsen say it in *The Sea Wolf*. Know that book by heart. It's the Great American Novel and the best story there is about life on the water. Cast off that line.''

"I always heard it was *Moby Dick*." Macklin slipped a loop of hemp made green and stiff with dead plankton off a dock piling and tossed it to Stephenson. Then he climbed down into the boat. The hull slid on the water and his stomach shifted a little the way it did when a fast elevator came to a stop with him inside. He would have to get used to that before nightfall.

"*Moby Dick*, shit. Melville would of had a cute little story there if he flushed all that bilge about the wonderful history of whaling and spent some time developing Ahab. Christ, you don't even see the fucking white whale till the last third of the book. No, it's *The Sea Wolf*." Coiling the line aft, he raised his voice to a singsong tenor. " 'What can I tell you? . . . Of the meagerness of a child's life? Of fish diet and coarse living? Of going out with the boats from the time I could crawl? Of my brothers, who went away one by one to the deep-sea farming and never came back? Of myself, unable to read or write, cabin-boy at the mature age of ten on the coastwise, old-country ships? Of the rough fare and rougher usage, where kicks and blows were bed and breakfast and took the place of speech, and fear and hatred and pain were my only soul-experiences?' I nearly shit my pants when my old man read that to me when I was six.'' He slipped into a bright orange life jacket that came to within eight inches of tying in front, tossed another to Macklin, and clambered into a seat upholstered in tough Naugahyde behind the helm, rocking the boat alarmingly. The big inboard started with a pleasant belching rumble when he turned the key. Macklin sat on the bench at the rear of the cabin. They pulled away from the dock and swung in a long arc toward open water. Wind teased Macklin's hair.

He raised his voice over the whining engine. "You ran away from home to take up the sailing life, right?"

"Hell, no. Home was a sixty-foot sealer built in Frisco in 'ninety-eight with a steam clanker and quarter-inch boiler plate bolted to the inside of the hull. My old man floated good hooch across the lake from Ontario during the dry time. I bet I personally loaded a million gallons of Old Log Cabin by the time

I was eight." Steering with one elbow, the fat man opened a fresh can from the cooler. He had laid in two more six-packs from the tiny refrigerator in his hut. "He was a terrible old man. Used to get drunk every Tuesday night and screw my sister. Someone smothered him with a pillow when he was dying of cancer in 'forty-six."

The engine pounded Macklin's eardrums for a half hour before Stephenson cut the throttle and killed the noise. There was water all around them with no sign of land and only one other craft in sight, a sailboat whose bright-colored sheet stuck up like a sharkfin out of the far horizon. Seagulls swooped at the water and made rusty creaking noises through their sharp beaks.

"Strip to your trunks," Stephenson ordered. "You won't need the wet suit before tonight."

"The water won't get that cold even at night." Macklin took off his windbreaker and unbuckled his belt.

"You don't know shit about hypothermia. You can freeze to death in water warm enough to bathe in."

Macklin flexed his bare shoulders contentedly in the heat of the sun and made no comment. His companion was no expert on bathing. The killer had put on his clothes over a pair of black swimming trunks in his size that Stephenson had found for him in a hamper smelling of sweat and mold. He had unwound the tape from around his ribcage and left it on the floor of the hut. Now, nearly naked, he felt as fragile as old crystal. He used melted ice from the beer cooler to wet his feet and put on his fins.

Under Stephenson's close supervision, he donned mask and snorkel and practiced the awkward feet-first dive and the side and flutter kicks throughout the morning and into the early afternoon, resting between workouts while the fat man guzzled beer and held forth on atmospheric pressure versus water pressure and quoted Jack London. Finally Macklin hauled himself into the boat with every muscle in his body aflame and, he swore, steam rolling off the heat in his injured side. The wall of his mouth tasted like rubber from the mouthpiece of the snorkel and his head ached from blowing his nose constantly to equalize the pressure in his ears. He was a fair swimmer, but it had been two years since his last time in the water. He was starting to wonder if the hundred thousand was worth it.

"Okay," Stephenson said, launching another crushed can out past the fantail, "let's see them hand signals again."

"Shove the hand signals. I won't have anyone to signal tonight."

"Okay. You're the one wanted the complete course in one day. How's the ribs?"

"They dissolved three dives back."

"I got just the thing." The sailor, who was sitting on the bench next to Macklin, leaned back, shoving out his massive belly, and rummaged a hand under the captain's seat, coming up at last with a square fifth of Jack Daniel's with four inches of liquid gone from the top. He thrust it at Macklin, who shook his head.

"C'mon. You want me to throw more *Sea Wolf* at you?"

"Christ, no." Macklin accepted the bottle, uncapped it, and took a swig. The liquor burned a furrow down his throat, dozed in his stomach for a moment, then started the slow warm crawl up his spine. He took another short drink and handed it back. Stephenson rubbed the mouth with the heel of a filthy hand and accounted for two inches in a single slant. He lowered the bottle, drew his forearm across his lips, and jerked a thumb back over his left shoulder. "She's out there someplace."

"Who?" Without thinking, Macklin took back the bottle and drank. The inside of his skull was starting to echo. He hadn't eaten in almost twenty-four hours and the stuff was going straight to his brain.

"The Boblo boat. Don't you listen to the news?"

The killer said nothing, searching the old man's broad flushed face and faded eyes.

"I was in charge, I'd fly a helicopter in low and drop a bomb on her, blow them fucking Commies past hell to Philadelphia."

"Could be that's why you're not in charge."

The fat man stabbed a black-nailed finger at him. "That's the thinking got them people on the boat in the fix they're in. You ever wonder why you never hear about no terrorists taking no Russian citizens hostage?"

"Because the Russians would fly a helicopter in low and drop a bomb on them."

"Damn right. None of this negotiations shit." He tilted the bottle. The stubble on his chin glistened. Passing it back: "Oh, it's tough on the hostages the first two or three times. After that the fuckers get the message and lay off. I said the same thing when Hitler went into Czechoslovakia, but who listened to me? I damn near enlisted in 'forty-two. But I was tied up shipping black market beef in from Amherstberg."

Macklin spilled whiskey on his bare chest and grinned. "Stephenson, you're a floating piece of shit, you know that?"

"Colorful, though."

They slumped with their backs against the hull while the sun dried Macklin's body and struck sparks off the blue waves. The fog had lifted entirely. More sails showed on the horizon. A speedboat ripped past below the curve. Five minutes later its wake slid under the *Wolf Larsen*, rocking it gently.

"You like putting the touch on folks?" Stephenson asked finally.

"You like taking doctors out after coho?"

"Yeah, I get you." He drank and offered the bottle to Macklin. The killer declined. Stephenson tried to put the top back on twice, screwing at empty air, then flipped it over his shoulder and finished the rest of the contents in two swigs. The bottle slapped the water an instant later. " 'Their generation,' " he said.

"What's that?"

"Conrad. *The Nigger of the Narcissus*. 'Their generation lived inarticulate and indispensable, without knowing the sweetness of affections or the refuge of a home—and died free from the dark menace of a narrow grave. They were the everlasting children of the mysterious sea.' Conrad, he knew. Just like London. They were sailors before they were writers."

"I wish a killer had written something I could quote."

Stephenson unzipped his baggy mouth to show black spaces among his orange teeth. " 'The Jews are the ones that will not be blamed for nothing.' Jack the Ripper wrote that one on a brick wall."

"He was an amateur. Good professionals die forgotten. Like good presidents."

The sailor lowered an anchor fashioned from a motorcycle engine block and they napped in the shade of the cabin with the lake moving under them.

Macklin awoke in the first chill of evening with the red eye of the sun watching him warily over the water to the west. A stiff breeze licked up his spine and played among the curls of white hair on Stephenson's great paunch across from him. The sailor was snoring with his mouth open. Immediately Macklin checked the plastic bag inside his trunks, into which he had placed the Smith & Wesson and all his cash, including what remained of the fifty thousand Howard Klegg had paid him. Everything was there. He reached for the wet suit lying like a rubbery octopus on the deck. A brass snap clinked, bringing Stephenson awake with a start. He was an even lighter sleeper than Macklin.

"How's your head?" asked the killer. He was climbing into the suit.

"In my hat. How's yours?"

"I haven't had a hangover since high school. How about a couple of quick lessons while we've got light?"

"They're your ribs."

Afterward he toweled off, traded the wet suit and trunks for his clothes, and they put in to shore, where the two carried an eight-foot skiff with oars out of a lean-to in back of Stephenson's hut and stowed it aboard the launch. The sailor stopped to put on deck shoes and a greasy linen wrapper and build himself a sandwich with cold cuts and sliced french bread from his refrigerator, but again Macklin declined to help himself. He had slept off the alcohol, and with the hollowness in his stomach his head felt as clear as alpine air. He could feel his adrenaline level climbing.

The moon was high and heel-shaped in a sky pierced with stars when they set out. Tiny drops from the bow wash pelted Macklin's face like ice crystals, smarting and forcing him to lean forward into the shelter of the cabin. His face stiffened in the cold nighttime lake air.

It was a very long trip to the chart points he had given

Stephenson, or it seemed that way. But after what felt like two hours, Macklin glanced down at the luminous dial of his watch and saw that they were less than forty-five minutes from the dock. He knew nothing of how far out those points were or how long it would take to reach them. Twice he spotted lights on the horizon and thought they belonged to the captive boat. But when he pointed them out to Stephenson he was told they belonged to ore carriers on their way down from the iron mines in Michigan's Upper Peninsula to the foundries in Sandusky and Cleveland.

When he did see the lights of the Boblo boat he thought they were just waves flashing under the moon. They were gone that fast behind the earth's curvature as the *Wolf Larsen* dipped between ground swells. Then he spied them again, ghostly on the edge of the disc of water, and grasped Stephenson's shoulder. The sailor nodded energetically.

"Seen it. Pleasure craft, probably."

"How close are we to those points?"

"Hell, we're right on top of them."

"Stop."

Stephenson throttled down. The engine slowed to a burble, coughed, and stopped. Wind hissed across the water. Waves slapped the hull. Starboard of the bow, the distant lights blinked on and off behind the rolling of the lake. Macklin stripped and climbed into the wet suit, stowing the plastic bag containing the gun and his money under the waistband. He clamped his jaw to keep his teeth from chattering when the cold damp rubber touched his skin.

"It's a long row," Stephenson warned him. "Hit a wave wrong, you'll capsize sure."

"Take the bow, will you?" Macklin grasped the skiff by the stern and lifted.

The sailor helped him hoist the small boat over the side and lower it into the water. "You ain't rowing back."

"I don't plan to. As soon as I'm out of sight you can go home." He gathered the rest of his gear under his left arm and held out his free hand. "You're going to need a new rowboat."

Stephenson took the hand in a horned grip. "You said I

wasn't going to be dumping no bodies into the lake. I'll hold you to that."

"Bosh," said Macklin, and when the fat man stared at him: "I read *The Sea Wolf* when I was ten."

"Then you know that was Larsen's last word."

Macklin climbed carefully into the skiff—had it been only hours since the feel of water beneath his feet had made him uneasy?—stowed his gear under the middle seat, undid the line from the ring and tossed it to Stephenson, who caught it one-handed. In the pale green glow from the boat's instrument panel the sailor's bulk carved a starless hole out of the sky. Macklin pushed free of the larger craft, unshipped the oars, and rowed away into the darkness. Behind him the *Wolf Larsen* undulated on the waves until its profile slid below the curve. Then its engine made a liquid rippling sound in the distance going away.

CHAPTER 27

ALONE ON WATER AS BLACK AS the sky, Macklin knew the fear he had sought to make Charles Maggiore understand two days earlier.

There was no light anywhere except the chains of reflected moon on the hungry waves and the feeble interior glow from the Boblo boat—no running lights burned on its hull—and every time a movement of the skiff put the rolling lake between them, Macklin was sure he'd lost even that dim beacon. And whenever it did come back into view it was always the same distance away. He wondered with a cold stab at his heart if it was indeed anchored as he had thought or still under power. If the latter, it would soon be out of sight, leaving him stranded on one of the most unpredictable bodies of water on the planet. Death was nothing. In a world that was ninety percent water, man's most primitive terrors had to do with being cast adrift on an endless sea under eternal night.

He brushed his chin against the smooth bright vinyl of his

safety vest for reassurance and continued rowing with a sure, steady pull. Pain sparked his side, taking his mind intermittently off his fears and the soreness in his muscles. He hadn't worked a pair of oars in almost twenty-five years, not since his father was alive and used to take him on fishing trips in the Upper Peninsula. In fact, his last clear memory of the old man was of him standing astraddle the center seat of a rented boat smeared with tar, a big man with legs slightly bowed, wrestling with a huge bass off Whitefish Point and cursing a blue streak when the line snapped and the fish took off trailing his favorite lure. Soon afterward he had made the mistake of changing pinball machines in his bowling alley on Lafayette, and a neighborhood dog was discovered playing with his head in the parking lot.

Macklin rowed, growing warm finally inside the rubber insulation of the wet suit. The butt of the gun wrapped in plastic gouged at his good ribs, a comforting annoyance. Up ahead the lights of the boat seemed closer at last, down from the horizon and taking on symmetry. He could make out three distinct layers with a pale glowing crown on top. No other vessel in these waters could be mistaken for it. His heart thudded dully, pumping adrenaline like electric waves to his brain and extremities. He had an erection such as neither Donna nor Christine could ever generate.

He quickly erased those two from his mind. They only clouded his thinking. His father had told him that the reason Indians were better hunters than white men was that they thought about nothing but their quarry. Macklin was concentrating on Siegfried.

You'll be dealing with one pro, two semis if you count Blakeman and MacKenzie and their combat training, and two dangerous amateurs, Tonda Kalu and Delbert, the Beast That Blew Up Hollywood.

When he could make out the slightly lighter bulk of the boat against the black background, he shipped the oars and dug his face mask out from under the seat, spitting on the glass and spreading the saliva around with his fingers to prevent clouding, then put it on. He clamped the snorkel in his teeth and strapped on the waterproof sheath containing a knife with a broad blade and a wicked sawtooth edge near the hilt. Before lowering himself into the water he peeled off the safety vest and jammed it under the seat. It was designed to pick up light for quick rescue, but in his case it could only attract bullets. The only safety devices he could rely on were those that were ingrained.

Although the suit absorbed most of the shock of the cold water, he was completely immersed before his heart started up again. He tried a couple of side kicks to get his blood circulating, raised his head clear of the water to get a fix on the boat, then submerged again and flutter-kicked in that direction, stroking his arms close to his body in a streamlining movement that bartered minimum effort for maximum speed. Even so, in just a few hundred yards his chest was pumping fit to burst his damaged ribs. He came to the surface again and removed the snorkel to breathe air untainted by rubber, treading water.

The droplets on his mask gave him a bee's-eye view of the triple-decked boat, fully visible now, its interior lights spilling out onto the water. He could make out figures moving within. The vessel was at anchor and reluctantly giving way to the motion of the more persistent waves; tall and curved and white and suggestive of mint juleps and magnolia blossoms, it seemed more at home than Macklin on this ancient lake. The danger would begin when he entered that circle of light. From that point on he would be square in the kill zone.

He ducked his head and resumed swimming, slower now.

"What do you want?"

With his back to the starboard wall of the pilot house, Don pointed his Luger at the face of Ted Delano coming up from the captain's quarters below. Delano stopped. "Just getting some air. It's close down there."

The leader of the hijackers studied the square-jawed face. It was slick with perspiration and the young intern's dark hair was plastered to his forehead. "How's the hero?"

"Sleeping. I'm leaving the bullet in his arm for now; he's lost too much blood to risk losing more while I tried to take it out."

Don nodded and moved away from the opening, belting the pistol. Delano came up the rest of the way. His dinner jacket was on the dance deck and his dress shirt was wrinkled and clinging wetly to his drenched skin. He shivered a little in the cool air coming in over the bridge wings.

Don said, "In Westerns they just heat up a knife in the campfire and pop the bullet out, just like that."

"What they don't show you is how long the man lived until the infection killed him," said the intern, smiling faintly. "Provided the shock didn't do it first."

Not having a medical bag, he had used first aid materials from the ship's stores to cleanse the hole Don had put in the wheel man's arm and patch it up. After the first round of cursing when the alcohol had touched the torn flesh, the sailor had lapsed into unconsciousness and hadn't recovered yet. He had bled a great deal before Delano got to him. The intern's gaze flicked down to the brown stains on the floor of the pilot house. Don saw it.

"I fired too fast or I'd have put one through his pumper," he said. "I didn't figure that one for the Batman type. I wonder who put him up to it." He was looking at the first mate, sitting on the turning stool nearby.

"I'd have done it myself." Phil Holliday glared at the well-polished tips of Don's shoes, the curve of his handlebar moustache accentuating the grim set of his features.

"No, it'd be like you to use someone else's balls."

The mate tensed and started to rise. The young security guard, who had been half-dozing standing with his back to the windscreen, stepped in front of him, laying a hand on his shoulder.

Don said, "Let him up. Let's see how fast he moves. I'll just start with my hands down here." He hung them to his hips, well below the butt of the Luger in his waistband.

"That gun makes you pretty big," said Holliday.

"No bigger than I have to be, Wyatt."

"Oh, for Christ's sake." Captain Fielding was seated on the chart table with his big knotted hands on his knees and his cap hanging on the handle of the steam whistle. His white hair was thick in front but worn down to pink scalp at the temples from constant contact with the cap's sweatband. "You call him Wyatt, but who's acting like a gunslinger?"

"They're all crazy," Delano rasped. "Fay tried the same thing with the bandleader. Their own lives don't mean anything to them. They've considered themselves dead since they came on board."

The atmosphere inside the octagonal enclosure dripped silence. Except for light catnaps, and Don hadn't even had that, none of them had slept in three days. Even the lookout, barely out of his teens, showed middle-aged lines in his face. Then Don smiled behind his drooping moustache. Tension drained out the openings leading to the bridge.

"You're a tough old fart, Cap'n Eddie. Bet you were something to see on one of those big ore boats in a storm." He looked at the intern. "You stay quiet."

"It's true, isn't it? You'd just as soon blow this tub to toothpicks right now, and to hell with everyone aboard, even you."

"That's up to the Governor and the warden of Jackson prison."

"Bullshit."

"Steady, boy," said the captain.

Don glanced at the lookout. "Crank up that radio. Maybe they're having trouble getting through."

"I'd like to go back down now," Delano said. "I want to be with Carol when the boat goes up."

"What about your patient?"

"You can get me on the P.A. if you need me. If it matters."

"Stay here."

"Why?" The intern bristled. "Scared I'll spread the word and you'll have a counter-mutiny on your hands?"

Don swept the pistol out of his belt and backhanded it across Delano's face. He staggered backward and would have fallen down the short flight of steps to the captain's quarters had not Fielding sprung down from the chart table and caught him. Delano put a hand to his bleeding cheek, torn by the Luger's steel sight.

"Go back to your woman," Don spat. "Try spreading that crap down there and Sol or Fay will feed you to the fish."

"Boblo boat, this is Detroit," crackled the radio.

A foot below the surface, the light from the boat turned the water lime-green, flashed off the bodies of schools of tiny fish, and made looming dark shadows of larger creatures gliding below. That sight made Macklin feel colder than he actually was in the watertight suit, for he knew he was a shadow himself and visible from above. If any of the terrorists happened to look down . . .

The boat's keel was black and solid below the waterline. He approached it broadside. If he were in charge of the hijackers, he would post one in the bow and one in the stern on each level to keep an eye on as many passengers as possible. He hoped that Blakeman or Don or whatever he called himself was as forward-thinking as he was. When he had drawn near enough to touch the peeling hull he surfaced, hunching his shoulders against the expected hail of bullets.

There was none. A blue-painted ledge ran around the boat two feet above the water and he held on, letting his legs hang motionless for the first time since he had left the skiff. Water streamed off his rubber helmet and snorkel and mask. The noise it made seemed deafening. He propped himself on his left forearm and tore off the mask and breathing apparatus, hesitated, then lowered them into the water.

The instant they drifted out of his reach he regretted it. The glass of the mask caught the light and threw it back like an undulating beacon as it bobbed on the waves. An oval of reflected white fluttered across the underside of the second deck. He poised himself, preparing to slide back underwater at the first shout. But again there was only silence and the trickling of water running off his suit.

A very long time passed, or seemed to pass, before the motion of the waves pushed the flashing glass outside the circle of light. Macklin glanced at his watch, but moisture had seeped inside and clouded the crystal, obscuring the face. When what felt like another full minute had gone by, he reached down and slid the flipper off his right heel, then his left. Like dazed fish they spiraled down slowly through the illuminated water and disappeared into the murky depths. Peter Macklin, the barefoot killer.

The center section of the bottom deck was closed in, with curtains blinding the sliding windows. He hoisted himself the rest of the way onto the ledge and flattened out against the painted metal, as much to rest and wait for the aching in his ribs to recede as to conceal himself from anyone standing by the rail in the open sections. He unsnapped his wet shirt from the pants, drew the revolver out of the plastic bag plastered against his pelvis, rewrapped his money, and closed the snaps. If nothing else he would die wealthy. Then before inertia got to him he crept forward along the ledge, feeling his way with his toes. The boat swayed and he pressed his hand flat against the vertical surface to maintain his balance.

At the end of the closed section he brought the gun to chest level and peered past the edge, braced to pull his head back if spotted. He saw only stationary shadows in the dim overhead light.

When after several seconds none of the shadows had moved, he gripped the edge of the metal and lowered himself through the opening until he felt more cold painted steel under his feet. He was standing there in a crouch and wondering which way to go when a quiet voice spoke at his left ear.

"Hold still, frogman, or I'll fill that rubber suit with leaks."

CHAPTER 28

LOUISE GABEL, RANDALL BUR-
lingame's handsome bur-
nished secretary, had gone
home. Without her, the outer office looked and felt like an
abandoned fort. Bill Chilson walked around the barricading desk
and through the open door that was leaking light into the
darkened anteroom. He found the inner office full of smoke and
the FBI bureau chief, vestless and with his necktie loose, on the
telephone. Burlingame raised his pipe in greeting and pointed it
at the chair on Chilson's side of the desk. The Secret Service
agent sat down. The lights of downtown Detroit made a glittering
sheet of the window behind the desk.

"Play that back, will you?" Burlingame paused, then fitted
the receiver into the speaker attachment to the intercom. A
frantic, high-pitched squealing like dozens of mice caught in a
fire came out, then stopped. Burlingame's voice followed.

". . . into port and release those passengers. Then we'll
talk."

"Fuck you, Fed. I trained as an M.P. before I switched to infantry. I know that hostage negotiations crap inside out. Now, are you going to open those gates and let those political prisoners walk, or are you going to practice looking sad for the cameras when they bury what's left of these people in a shoe box?"

Chilson mouthed, "Don?" Burlingame nodded, fingering his pipe. His disembodied voice resumed.

"We know your position, Blakeman. You've seen the helicopters."

"I've seen them. I see one more I'll touch off the boat and to hell with the two hours left."

"What do you hope to gain from this? What does Siegfried hope to gain?"

"Headlines. Bulletins. Götterdämmerung in living color on the six o'clock news. We are a high-profile industry. Bigger than Revlon."

"You won't live to see yourselves."

"A lot of people like us will. The seed is planted in fire and blood. The revolution is *on*, man. Do, re, mi, fa, sol, la . . ." He trailed off. "Two hours, Burlingame. Talk to you again at five minutes to midnight. This radio gets all the public frequencies. I got eight hundred people hoping to hear it's Bastille Day in Jackson." Something clicked.

"Thanks, Carl. Get some sleep." Burlingame turned off the speaker and cradled the receiver. "Interesting paradox. A madman pretending to be mad."

"Maybe he's not mad. Just bored. It wouldn't be the first time a suicide took somebody with him just for the pure hell of it." Wiping his glasses with a handkerchief, Chilson blinked smoke out of his eyes. "The Governor's waiting for your call. He's got the papers all ready for those prisoners' release."

The FBI man nodded absently. "I thought about feeding a phony statement to the broadcast networks that we were springing those cons, but that kind of cooperation went out when Nixon's enemies list came in. They've got a hard-on for accuracy."

"You going to call the Governor?"

"I don't know."

"Have you heard from Macklin?"

"Not since early this morning."

"That's a lot of time to get dead in," Chilson said. "Or change his mind."

"You couldn't change his mind with a club."

"One middle-aged killer. Seven terrorists. Call the Governor, Red."

"Some choice. I dump a load of scum back into society or help fish ears and noses out of Lake Erie. Either way I lose my pension."

Chilson smiled. "Maybe they'll make a movie out of this and ask you to star. You could have a whole new career."

"What would be new about it?" He put down his pipe, lifted the receiver again, and got the switchboard. "This is Burlingame. Get me the Governor's mansion in Lansing. Well, look it up." He broke the connection.

"If it means anything, Red, it wasn't that bad an idea," Chilson said. "This is a different world. I'm damn glad I'm just visiting."

"You can get used to anything, like the Indian said."

The telephone rang. Burlingame lifted the handset. "Yes, put him on." Covering the mouthpiece: "In the old days you got hemlock."

"Progress," said the other. But the FBI man was already in conversation with the Governor.

"Ackler?" whispered Macklin. He remained motionless, his body turned away from the voice that had addressed him. The deck of the huge old steamer shifted gently beneath his feet. He sensed a lot of people nearby but could hear nothing of them.

"Here it's Sol." It was a young man's voice, scarcely a murmur. "You're who?"

"Macklin."

Pause. "Peter Macklin? Mike Boniface's Macklin? No. Christ, he's sixty."

"Thirty-nine."

"Well, flip the gun overboard, thirty-nine-year-old Peter Macklin. Let me hear it splash."

Macklin obeyed. The .38 made a little noise going into the water.

"Okay, turn around slow."

He turned, hands out from his body. In the shadows, Ackler's hair was his most prominent feature, blown full and sprayed to a metallic sheen so that at first glance he looked as if he were wearing a silver-plated helmet. His face was regular and ordinary and stubbled brown in contrast to the hair. He had on a sportcoat with a tiny check that looked as if he hadn't had it off for a while, over an open-necked shirt and a pair of wrinkled dark flannel trousers. The squat ugly snout of an M-16 remained steady on Macklin's midsection. By swinging it no more than three inches up and down, Ackler could squirt bullets from Macklin's hairline to his toes, the trajectory was that sloppy. At this range it was not a weakness.

The young killer kept his distance. No amateur barrel-digging-into-the-ribs for him. Well, Macklin had hardly hoped for less.

"What's a button for the wise guys doing way out here?" Ackler wanted to know.

"I was thinking of asking you the same thing," Macklin said. "Minus the cute jargon."

"Me first."

"Boniface wants out. The authorities want a hero. Boniface gave them me."

"No good. Go again."

"Okay. I just happened to be swimming by and thought I'd drop in and talk shop."

Ackler watched him. The whites of the young killer's eyes glistened in the gloom. "Who else is coming?"

"I left fifteen federal agents on the boat. They gave me a ten-minute head start."

Ackler's face aged. "I guess you kill better than you lie."

There was something in his tone. Disappointment? And why were they speaking so low, on a vessel under his friends' command? A wraith of hope stirred in Macklin's chest. He tried something.

"My turn. What's a big kid doing playing with pre-schoolers?"

A cloud scudded in front of the moon, filling in the spaces between shadows. Only Ackler's hair and white shirt and the sour gleam of the automatic rifle showed. He stepped back, placing his shoulder blades against the wall of the darkened enclosure where snacks were sold. "Step into my office."

He gestured with the gun and Macklin walked ahead of him to the lighted rear of the deck. A large group of people were there, seated and lying on the deck and standing at the rail, their clothes wrinkled, their faces gray. Some of the women had on men's suitcoats and sportcoats over shoulders left bare by their evening gowns and summer dresses, the hems of which were universally soiled. Surprise and hope rose in their eyes at the sudden appearance of the barefoot stranger in the wet suit, then fell back as the man they knew as Sol came into view behind him carrying the M-16. Macklin smelled despair.

On Ackler's orders he turned his back to the stern and draped himself, stomach down painfully, over the heavy painted mechanism of the windlass blistering four feet above the deck. In that awkward position he was expertly frisked and relieved of the knife in the waterproof sheath. Ackler tucked the blade under his belt, and before his coattail swung forward to cover it Macklin saw out of the corner of his eye the square butt of a semiautomatic pistol showing above the waistband of Ackler's pants. Next came the plastic bag containing nearly fifty thousand dollars, which the young killer riffled, whistling low, and then transferred to an inside pocket. "I heard they paid you union boys good," he said.

Macklin said nothing. He tried to keep most of his weight on his right side to keep from caving in his cracked ribs. He had lived with the pain so long now it seemed like a tiresome old friend.

"Okay, get up."

The process was more uncomfortable than staying as he was. He rolled off slowly, placing his weight on one knee and his right arm. He exaggerated the difficulty a little and let out a grunt. That wasn't hard.

"You *sound* sixty," Ackler said. He was standing with his back to the rail, the automatic rifle cradled comfortably in front of him. But ready.

"Swimming takes a lot out of me."

"Yeah. I can see."

He couldn't tell if Ackler believed him or not. "You were going to tell me what made you decide to play junior commando," he said.

"Was I?"

Macklin grunted again, leaning his hips against the winch. "I'm too old to play statues. I should be a grease spot amidships where you caught me. You would be, if the positions were reversed. You know why it's harder for a professional to kill the President than it is for an amateur?"

"The professional has to have an escape route."

"Any nut with a Saturday night buster can do the job if he isn't concerned with getting away afterwards, just like any bunch of nuts can get automatic weapons and explosives aboard an excursion boat and take it over, because they don't care if they're still around after the band goes home. So how come a paid gun with as good a future as any in this business lets himself get talked into committing suicide with music? I mean, Siegfried, for chrissake. It sounds like a commercial for breakfast cereal."

Ackler looked at him a long time before speaking. His eyelids flickered. It was as much of his human side as he'd shown so far.

"I made a mistake when I was nineteen," he said. "I was out to make a name for myself in this line. A guy I met in a bar in Scranton sent me a plane ticket from L.A. and I flew out there. I was to skag his wife and make it look like a burglary. Only I didn't think he might be getting drunk and whimpering the same thing in bars out there, and when I slipped the lock on the guy's house and went inside, two uniforms who were waiting there got me on the floor and stood on my back and read me my rights."

"Christ."

"I know. I was nineteen, what can I say? They tried to get

LOREN D. ESTLEMAN

me to make a statement but I kept my mouth shut, and the guy
that hired me pressed charges because his lawyer told him it'd
look bad if he didn't and the judge could have been good to me. I
pled guilty to breaking and entering and it was my first offense,
but I wouldn't talk about the other thing and I was from back
East. He gave me a year.

"Well, I learned from that, and I don't work for husbands or
wives or brothers-in-law that didn't get invited to Christmas
dinner. But most of the people who might hire me on the straight
are with the organization and only come to me when the available
talent is low. So when a guy who said he met a guy I knew in Q
sent me a thousand faith money and a plane ticket to Detroit I
came. That guy's up on the second deck. It's his explosives we're
sitting on."

"A thousand isn't a lot to kill yourself over," Macklin said.

They had been speaking low, and some of the passengers
present were straining to hear them. Ackler dropped his voice
further. "It was a sweet deal. I was getting another thousand a
week just for sitting around listening to this bunch of loonies
talking about optimum maneuverability and the casualty factor
and dreaming up cute names to call themselves. It was like you
said, a cereal commercial. Cap'n Crunch and his Super Secret
Assholes. This Blakeman that's in charge won't miss my cut out
of what he pulls in dealing stolen guns and tape decks, you tell
me why he has to go turn radical. Anyway, I did one job for him
back on land—"

"Jack DeGrew," put in Macklin. "Chester Crane's original
bass player."

The young killer blinked. "They know that? I thought I did
a pretty good job throwing a blanket over that one."

"You left a witness."

"Shit. The guy that was with him when I picked him up?"

"Yeah."

"I figured he'd be too stoned to remember."

"If that could happen, no musician would remember how to
make the notes."

"Yeah. Shit. Anyway, I did that job for Blakeman and went
on a couple of dry runs aboard the boat to get the lay and the rest

201

was like retirement, only the pay was better. Right up until we took her I didn't think anything would come of it. I mean, hijack a steamboat? We got Beaver Cleaver and Gidget up top and Sergeant York and the Mad Professor in the middle and Farina down there at the other end. *Mission Impossible*, right? And Blakeman threw in a month's rent on a sweet cottage on Lake Huron. Then, wham! Here I am holding Sweet Mary in my hands and I get my cue to burn the powderhead we put in for DeGrew, and just like that I got a bee in a jar and you tell me how to unscrew the top without getting stung.

"I wouldn't have done it at all if I didn't like being on the water. I wouldn't mind coming back and fishing this lake sometime."

Macklin said, "Well, there's plenty of bait aboard."

Ackler looked at him closely. "You fish?"

"I have. But what we're talking about right now is hunting."

"In tandem?"

"We're the only hunters here."

"You didn't come aboard looking to recruit me, Macklin."

"I didn't come aboard looking to get jumped. But I don't see that either of us has a lot of other choices. I can't speak for you, but I really don't think I was born to wind up feeding the carp off Sandusky."

The young killer fiddled absently with the M-16's actuating lever. "Say we bag the limit. Then what?"

"Then I guess we take up where we left off when I boarded."

After a moment Ackler straightened and, balancing the rifle along his right forearm, pulled the pistol out of his waistband and handed it to Macklin. The .45's deep blue finish looked black in the pale light.

CHAPTER 29

CHARLIE AS THE EARLI-
est grunts named
the Viet Cong for
their radio designation "Victor Charlie," was fairly far down on
the list of enemies to watch out for in the jungle. Clouds of
mosquitoes carried diseases that the bacteriologists that sometimes accompanied David Blakeman's unit hadn't had a chance to
find a name for, and the rust and mold that crept into the squishy
actions of the early M-16s almost on the heels of the cleaning rag
had left more than a few G.I.s with jammed weapons in the teeth
of a Cong charge. That, together with the flower-child mentality
of the later draftees who would rather stick a posy into their
corroded muzzles than a bayonet into a blood-crazed guerilla's
intestines, had made a lottery of the prospect of getting out of
Southeast Asia alive. That one of every two combat soldiers that
went in succeeded said something about the poor organization of
the North Vietnamese and America's chances for victory, had a

soldier and not a succession of bureaucrats been behind its involvement.

"Phil, no!"

Don, lulled into a waking sleep by the murmuring of the all-news station on the boat's radio and by the subtle motion of the deck beneath his feet, had no idea at what point he had stopped remembering Khe Sanh and started dreaming. In any case he came out of the tropical steam into the Erie cold just as Phil Holliday launched himself from the stool by the starboard entrance to the pilot house, hands grasping for the Luger under the hijacker's belt. Don drove his forearm across the bridge of the mate's nose, feeling the bone give, and they wrestled, but the blow had robbed Holliday of his momentum and when Don jammed a knee into the other's groin he gasped and started to fold. Don placed a hand against Holliday's chest and shoved. The mate sprawled to the deck. When he raised his mashed face with the blood running out of his nose into his moustache he was looking at the business end of the German automatic.

"You're going to get what every real sailor wants, Wyatt," said Don, cocking the complicated mechanism. "Burial at sea."

Captain Fielding, standing at the other end of the chart table, took a step forward. Don backed up to cover them both. "You've seen this thing spray," he warned.

Cap'n Eddie stopped. "There's no need to kill him."

"Leave him alone," said Holliday. His voice was thin coming through his smashed nose. "You kept your mouth shut before, I'd be standing there with that gun now."

"Then what? You were going to kill the rest of them with that one gun? What happens to the passengers meanwhile?"

"It'd be a better chance than we've got now."

"We're better off riding it out."

The mate snickered, or maybe he was crying. A fat red drop splatted to a deck still stained with the wheel man's blood. "You old fart, we're on the rocks now."

"Listen!"

All eyes turned to the lookout. He turned up the volume on the radio.

". . . to release the prisoners. A list of the names of the

inmates whose sentences the Governor has agreed to commute in response to the terrorists' demands will follow this." A commercial for a Cincinnati restaurant replaced the announcer's stern voice.

"Find another news station," Don barked.

The lookout manipulated the dial. Music came out of the speaker, a litany of baseball scores, more music. He stopped on an expressionless female voice. "Repeating that bulletin, the Office of the Governor of Michigan states that it has agreed to commute the sentences of ten Southern Michigan Penitentiary prisoners as demanded by the revolutionary group holding eight hundred passengers hostage aboard the hijacked Boblo boat. Efforts to locate the captured vessel. . . ."

"Well, well." Don took the Luger off cock. "Well, well."

He was reaching behind his back for the portable transceiver on the chart table when a burst of gunfire sounded below. He cursed and depressed the speaker button. "Fay, what now?"

There was no answer.

It wasn't Fay.

For all the speeches she had made during automatic weapons training about taking as many of the bastards with them as possible if something went wrong, eliminating her had proved absurdly easy. Ackler called her over to the port railing across from where Macklin had boarded, and as she approached from her post in the bow she turned her back protectively to the water. And to Macklin, invisible in his black wet suit in the darkness, standing at the rail holding the knife Ackler had returned to him behind his hip to avoid reflecting light off the shiny blade.

"This better be damn good," she snarled. "We both got hoojies need keeping an eye on."

Ackler said, "I just wanted to say good-bye."

The whites of her eyes showed in an uncomprehending glare. Then she must have heard something behind her, because she started to turn with the M-16 just as Macklin pinioned her with his left arm and drew his right fist across her throat. The razor-edged steel sheared through her vocal cords along with her jugular, silencing her screams just as a fountain of bright orange splattered the wall of the concession stand four feet away. Ackler had stepped out of the way just in time to avoid being doused and wrenched the rifle out of her convulsing grip before she could trip the trigger, breaking three of her fingers in the process. When Macklin let go she sank to her knees and then sagged sideways, twitched and lay still.

"You're good," Ackler said, then indicated the stairs at the rear of the boat.

"What about the passengers?"

"Yeah, right."

Macklin wiped off both sides of the knife carefully on the dead woman's skirt. There was a splash and he glanced up quickly to see the young killer holding only one M-16. The one he had taken from Fay was missing.

"I can't carry two and it's no good arming just anyone that happens to come along," Ackler explained. "I heard you don't like squirt guns."

Macklin nodded. His companion unstrung the portable radio from Fay's arm and sent it after the gun. Together they went to the bow, where the passengers, musicians, and a gray-haired security guard in uniform were sitting on folding chairs and squatting cross-legged on the deck. An old man with a discolored lump on his bald head exclaimed at the sight of the stranger with the man who had killed the bass player. The others stirred, then settled down as Macklin spoke.

"We're the cavalry. Stay where you are and don't move, no matter what you hear. You'll only get in the way."

"Are you a policeman?" someone asked.

"I'm as close to one as you'll see on this boat."

"There's a wounded man on the bridge."

Macklin had started to turn. He looked at the young man who had spoken. He was seated on one of the chairs, holding hands with an attractive redhead whose parted lips exposed a slight overbite. She was wearing a man's sportcoat like a cape over her bare shoulders. One of the young man's cheeks was swollen and discolored where the flesh had been broken.

"He's a crewman Don shot," he said. "I patched him up. He's resting in the captain's quarters below the pilot house."

"You're a doctor?"

"I'm interning at the U of M."

"Ted Delano, right? That's Carol Turnbull with you."

The young man pursed his lips on the verge of a question. Macklin cut him off, speaking to the woman. "Your father's worried about you." His eyes swept the group. "We'll have you all back with your families by morning."

More questions came all at once. The armed men turned their backs on them and went back the way they had come, stepping around Fay's body.

"Her father?" asked Ackler.

"Clarence Turnbull."

"Who's he?"

Macklin made the same speech to the hostages in the stern, who listened in silence with alert expressions on their drawn faces. Then the pair turned to the stairs. At the foot Ackler handed Macklin the M-16.

"Give me the knife."

Macklin surrendered the weapon. "Wait here till I call you," Ackler said, and headed upstairs without waiting for an answer.

Three minutes later, Macklin heard his name whispered from above. He made sure the safety on the automatic rifle was off and started up cautiously. Ackler was standing at the top, light glistening off the dark stuff slicking the blade in his fist. They traded weapons again and started forward, pausing at the emaciated boy lying on its face in a voluminous sportcoat. Macklin grasped a handful of hair and lifted the man's narrow features into the light.

"Delbert?"

Ackler hesitated. "Yeah. I had to think. We've been calling him Ray so long. I got him under the ribs while he was lighting my cigarette." He crushed out the butt glowing on the deck. "Anyway, that stops the clock. He was the whiz with explosives."

"Maybe."

"No maybes about it. It was his job to touch 'em off."

"I know Blakeman's file. It isn't like him to trust that kind of thing to anyone not named David Blakeman. Where are the passengers on this level?"

"Up front. Don—Blakeman, damn it—had them moved yesterday. Ray wasn't that good with people and the boss man didn't want to take a chance on someone jumping him before he could set off the charge."

"Who's up front?"

"Teddy. His Royal Excellency Captain Philip MacKenzie." He paused. "This one'll be noisy. He doesn't trust anyone."

"Okay."

They approached the lighted bow along both railings, Ackler port, Macklin starboard. A stony-faced young man with crewcut hair who wore his jacket and tie as if they were part of a uniform, sat with one hip on the rail with the hand holding his .45 pistol resting on his thigh. The passengers were sitting crowded together on the deck without an open space to be seen. The skin of the young hijacker's face was taut and white and his eyes were ringed purple. He jumped a foot when he saw Macklin striding forward holding the semiautomatic Ackler had given him and raised his own weapon just as Ackler opened up with a short burst from the shadows to his left. Flame stuttered from the muzzle. Teddy bared his teeth in a grimace and slammed into a deck support, barking his elbow and dropping his gun. He slid down into a sitting position, his legs spread and blood leaking down his left side.

A bearded black man seated with the passengers leaned forward and scooped up the abandoned .45. Both killers drew down on him. "We're friends!" shouted Macklin. "Dump it overboard."

A woman had been screaming since Teddy was shot, drowning out the words. He said it again louder.

"How come, if we're such good friends?" The man was holding the gun flat on his palm.

A black woman sitting next to him touched his arm. "Leon, do like the man says."

"I been doing like the man says my whole life." But he pitched the pistol over the rail.

"Lot of metal down there tonight," reflected Ackler.

"Fay, what now?"

It was the radio, resting on the deck beside Teddy. Ackler stretched a leg between passengers to pick it up.

Macklin said, "Leave it."

"Fay?" said the radio.

Teddy groaned. Blood came to his mouth and spilled over his chin. Ackler said, "Shit," moved the indicator on his rifle to single, and put a slug into the wounded man's brain. He arched and sagged.

The woman stopped screaming and started laughing hysterically. Someone shook her. The laughter soared and then receded into rhythmic moans.

The radio said, "Teddy?"

Macklin looked at Ackler. "You said Beaver Cleaver and Gidget are on the top deck. That's John Carlisle and his girl, Melissa What's-her-name?"

"Yeah. Larry and Doris."

"She's yours. Wait." The radio had started up again.

"Larry, go see what's going down with Teddy and the others."

"Okay."

A forward staircase trimmed in elegant brass led up to the top passenger deck. Macklin signaled to Ackler and they took up positions on either side, out of sight of anyone coming down. Ackler returned the indicator on his rifle to full automatic.

CHAPTER 30

LARRY FELT LIKE SUPERMAN.

With less than an hour to go before the deadline, he had felt safe in using the last of the cocaine Don had given him and his senses had never seemed so acute. There were a thousand smells in the lake air, each one different, and his ears were so sharp he swore he could hear the engine crew moving around in the hold. He could see in the dark and through the soles of his shoes his toes felt every lump and ripple in the metal deck as if he were barefoot. When he started down the echoing steps to the second deck, the heavy semiautomatic pistol felt as light as something carved out of driftwood in his hand. It was a shame not to be spending some of this energy on Doris.

He felt movement to his left and stopped and said, "Teddy?"

There was no answer and he felt a tingle of unease. Then a platinum head moved into his line of vision. He smiled in relief. "Sol, what—?"

Something shoved him hard from behind emptying his lungs and throwing him against the brass banister but his senses were clicking and he swung around with his momentum his shirt getting wet against his back and squeezed the trigger of the .45 blindly and nothing happened and then flame splatted in front of him and this time he didn't feel the blow the stairs came up . . .

The echo of the big pistol's report pressed Macklin's eardrums, dulling the screams and crying from the passengers while bitter gray smoke curled over the young man sprawled face down over the stairs. Ackler moved in quickly to retrieve Larry's gun, smiling tightly as he looked at it before shoving it under his belt. "Someone should've told him they don't work when they're not cocked."

"Johnny!"

It was a shriek. Macklin spun with his own .45 in time to see a slight figure with long blond hair in a pale dress standing at the top of the stairs before the night shattered into pieces of blinding light and more noise hammered at his thickened eardrums and something hot burned his right hip. He returned fire, the pistol throbbing in his hand. He was deaf now. From the corner of his eye he saw the muzzle of Ackler's M-16 flash in sputtering silence as in a film without sound, but by that time the girl was gone. They hit the stairs running.

Macklin skidded on something slippery at the top, looked down and saw the dark spots on the deck. His hearing was blinking back, on and off like bad radio reception, and shrieks and shouts from among the passengers on that level led him to the stern, where the blood trail broadened and vanished into a milling crowd of hostages. Ackler followed him. As they approached on the trot, people got out of the way, and Macklin shouted and threw himself sideways just as a fresh burst splintered the air where he'd been standing. He didn't look back to see if Ackler had been hit. His ribs were throbbing from the running and his right leg was soaked to the knee with something thick and warm.

The girl was at the rear of the boat with her skirt hiked up to her thighs and one leg hitched over the rail, trying to balance the

M-16 in one hand while with the other she sought to staunch the dark flow from just under her left breast. Her face was a smear of white against the darkness behind her. Her mouth worked. "Johnny, Johnny."

Macklin, lying on his stomach, stretched his right arm along the deck and sighted down it to the end of the pistol. He fired just as Ackler's rifle clattered behind him and to his left. The girl perched on the rail jerked several times and a black hole opened in the center of the white smear of her face and she lifted a stained palm as if to grasp at a deck support and then she was gone. Something bumped the side of the boat. Water splashed.

"Macklin!"

The shout was Ackler's. Macklin reacted without thinking, rolling inward toward the shelter of the wall of the enclosed section rising out of the center of the deck. There was a noise like a string of firecrackers going off and a dazed passenger who was standing near where he had been lying howled and grabbed his leg and fell. He rolled back and forth, grasping his knee and moaning. Macklin looked up over his left shoulder and saw a man's silhouette moving along the roof of the crew quarters near the smokestack. Twisting painfully, he rested the .45 on the corner of his shoulder and pressed the trigger. The figure ducked behind the stack.

"Is he hit?" Macklin called.

Ackler, crouched near the rail, shook his head. "I couldn't see. I saw some kind of movement near the bridge just before he fired. He's got a Luger converted to full auto. I think he's got a spare clip."

"Keep him busy."

"I'm knocking on empty now." He patted the M-16.

"You've got MacKenzie's .45."

Hugging the wall of the enclosed section and dividing his attention between the skyline and the deck in front of him, Macklin crept forward. His right leg was growing numb and he was thankful for that. He didn't have time to worry if the bullet was still in his hip or if he'd just been grazed, or if any major artery had been clipped. It was just like him to get shot by the one member of the band least likely to hit him. But he was still better off than the innocent wretch sobbing over his shattered kneecap on the deck.

He kept to the center and the minimal shadow offered by the enclosed passenger section and the quarters of the captain and first mate. The moon was high now, and while the lights in the pilot house had been extinguished, probably by Blakeman's order, pale illumination washed the painted metal at Macklin's feet. He made for the steps that led to the bridge.

Ackler fired twice, yellow and orange flame flicking out of the end of his .45 in time with two solid blams. He was saving the ammunition in his M-16, Macklin knew for whom. Without looking to see if the young killer had hit anything above, he sprinted the rest of the way and started up the metal steps on a dead run. Three hornets sped past his face, one of them knocking paint off the rail two inches in front of his hand. Before the stuttering reports of Blakeman's burst faded away, Ackler's gun spoke again once. Macklin hurdled the remaining steps and leaped through an opening into the pilot house. Another bullet struck sparks off a post supporting the roof.

"He's by the funnel!"

Macklin didn't wait to learn which of the figures standing with him in the dark had spoken. He bounded across the enclosure, colliding with and shoving someone's body out of the way, leaned out through the opening across from the one by which he had entered, and raised his gun just as a bulk vaguely man-shaped moved into view between the smokestack and the funnel curving up on the starboard side. Something glittered in the hand that wasn't holding a gun.

"You better not, Batman!" Blakeman shouted. "This is an electronic detonator. I press this button, we all go up in burning pieces."

Macklin lowered the .45.

Watching the man he had glimpsed earlier in the act of shooting Doris, Don cursed the panic that had caused him to waste ammunition on a fleeting target and the muzzle flashes that had destroyed the night vision he'd gained after killing the lights inside. But his brain was clicking as it hadn't since his last fire fight. He had no idea how many reinforcements this faceless commando had brought with him, but now that Don had found cover from whoever had been sniping at him from the passenger deck, he stroked with his thumb the single button on the simple electronic device Ray had designed and pretended it was the world.

"Put it down, Blakeman," said the man. "You don't want to die."

"The name's Don. And I've been dead since I got on board."

The man paused, and Don knew an instant of bleak fear that he wouldn't behave as predicted. He didn't care about dying, but he didn't want to do it with his back to the wall. That wasn't the reason he'd planned the thing from the first. To expire in a sheet of flame at the moment of greatest triumph; that was what it came down to. Then the man spoke.

"What do you want?"

Don grinned. He'd been imagining monsters under the bed. "Ditch the piece. Dump it overboard. Or there won't be enough left of any of us to feed the fish. Do it, man!" He brandished the detonator.

After a brief hesitation the man moved to hurl his pistol out beyond the lower decks.

A hideous bellowing wail rent the night, shearing through Don's eardrums and making the boards buzz beneath his feet. He staggered. The Luger vibrated in his hand, splattering fire. Blindly his thumb sought the detonator's button. There was a single flash from the bridge. A fist slammed into Don's chest. Both his hands sprang open, relinquishing their burdens. He knew pain and noise and falling and darkness.

Amid the white steam still leaking from the whistle mounted in front of the stack and the fading phosphorescence of Blakeman's wasted shots, Macklin watched the stricken figure drop out of sight between the two sheltered sections on the crown deck, the device he had been holding in his left hand falling over the side. There was no mistaking, and no faking, that loose rag-doll tumble.

Siegfried was done.

"You all right, mister? You're bleeding."

Macklin started at the sound of the voice at his ear. In the sudden silence after the whistle blast it sounded loud. He turned and saw moonlight on a craggy, weather-roughened face with steel-rimmed glasses on its nose. The tall old man was staring at the glistening leg of his wet suit.

"It's just flesh," Macklin said. It hurt again, too much to be anything else. "You blew the whistle?"

The old man smiled loosely, showing just his lower teeth. "This old girl practically runs herself. It's just about the only thing the captain gets to do these days."

"It sounded pretty good."

"Are you the police?"

The man who asked the question, about Macklin's age with a nose that was all over his face and dried blood in his handlebar moustache, tripped a switch, flooding the pilot house with yellow light. Macklin barked at him to turn it off. The man raised his brows at the captain, who nodded curtly. The command was obeyed and moonlight took over again. In the dark, the captain said, "Didn't you get them all?"

"No, there's one more."

CHAPTER 31

ACKLER?

MACKLIN'S voice over the public address system rang through the boat and echoed away over the water. There was no response.

He tried again. He got the first syllable out when something that sounded like a handful of pebbles rattled against the windscreen in front of him and he dropped down, shouting to the other men in the pilot house to do the same. They obeyed instantly. Even the captain hurled down his brittle old bones faster than the killer would have believed him capable of moving, just as the windscreen collapsed before the chattering of the M-16 in the bow of the crown deck. The burst ended. A triangle of swaying glass dropped with a clank.

"How'd you know?" whispered the young man in the uniform of a Boblo security guard.

"Heard the first slugs ricocheting off the glass. Those M-16s only carry a 55-grain load. They'll glance off hard surfaces at some angles. Keep down."

Huddling close to the wall, Macklin crabwalked past the port entrance to the chart table at the back of the pilot house, where he reached up and grasped a rustling handful of charts and cast them out through the opening. They fluttered for an instant, then the automatic rifle rattled again and they jerked this way and that in the air and then vanished into the darkness beyond the bridge. Ackler couldn't have many rounds left. But he still had the .45 he had won from Larry.

"Stay here," Macklin told the others. "No matter what happens, don't leave the bridge." He made his way down the short flight of steps to the captain's quarters.

A man lay groaning in the bunk. Macklin went past him without pausing and through the connecting door into the first mate's quarters. Another door led out onto the crown deck and he used that. From there he went forward.

The bow was deserted.

He heard movement below, as of the hostages on the top passenger deck stirring restlessly, and started down the forward steps. His right leg was throbbing from hip to knee, but from the dry crackling of his caked rubber pants, he determined that the bleeding had stopped, or at least slowed.

A woman below him and to his right shrieked when he was halfway down and he spun that way and drew down on a figure standing by the starboard rail, tilting something long and wicked-looking up at him. Even as he pressed the trigger he knew he was a half-second too late. His insides coiled, bracing themselves for a rain of lead.

The M-16 clicked.

Ackler cursed in a high-pitched voice and clawed the pistol out of his belt. Macklin fired. Then part of the crowd of panicking passengers shifted in front of his target. Something flashed and tumbled in the light and hit the water with a crash. The M-16, empty now and useless. Macklin glimpsed a running figure hurtling through the crowd and grasped the staircase railing and vaulted over it, landing on his feet on the deck with an impact that jarred him from wounded leg to injured ribs. Spreading his legs and double-fisting the gun police fashion, he took aim on the back of a head bobbing among the passengers amidships, then swung the muzzle skyward and took his finger off the trigger. There were too many innocents too close.

Ackler felt no such compunction. He spun, clearing a hasty space around him, and his pistol barked and something *spang*ed off the deck behind Macklin and to his left and went whistling into the night. Then Macklin lost him in the press of bodies along the rail.

Macklin kept absolutely still, straining to hear over the screams and babble. But the old boat was creaking and rumbling with the agitated movement of its charges and there was no separating whatever noises Ackler might be making.

"He's going down!" someone shouted.

Equidistant from the bow and stern, a steel ladder for the crew's use led from the crown to the lower decks outside the railings. Macklin mounted it, gripping the water-beaded side-rails, and climbed down to the next level, the rungs icy under the soles of his bare feet. He alighted silently and moved just in time to clamp a hand over the open mouth of a startled woman standing near the ladder. He placed the end of the .45 against his lips warningly before letting go. She kept silent.

Repeating the gesture from time to time for the other passengers, he strode swiftly aft and reached the stern just as Ackler was leaving the stairs. Macklin fired twice, the two shots coming so close together they sounded like one long report. Ackler grunted and fell back against the staircase railing and raised his pistol. Macklin squeezed the trigger again. Nothing happened.

He ducked back behind a beam supporting the overhead deck as lead from Ackler's pistol cracked past his left ear. Then he heard shoe leather on metal running away.

Cautiously he peered around the beam. The small cluster of passengers gathered around the foot of the stairs had opened a path that was now empty. Either Ackler was unaware of Macklin's predicament or he had been hit and panicked.

Presently Macklin spotted the dark drops spattering the deck and decided that it was the latter.

He examined his pistol. He couldn't be out of ammunition unless the gun hadn't been fully loaded to begin with. He ran back the action. The brass casing of his last cartridge had swelled, failing to eject and jamming the mechanism. He used the point of his knife to pry out the troublesome shell and racked a fresh cartridge into the chamber. He hoped the action was undamaged.

It took him ten minutes to reach the dance deck on the next level, moving cautiously and following the blood trail on the steps. From there it led meanderingly between the starboard rail and the enclosed concession stand, the wall of which at one point bore a scarlet handprint where the wounded killer had stopped to rest, and ended at an opening in the deck with steep steel steps leading down and a loose chain hammocked across it with a suspended sign reading ENGINE ROOM—KEEP OUT. There was a large patch of blood with a heelprint in it where Ackler had stooped to clear the chain. Macklin did the same and started down.

As he descended, gripping the pipe rail and crouching on each step to scan the area around and below the stairs, the temperature rose and sweat built up under his rubber wet suit and prickled along his hairline. Before him the ship's intestines opened like the gray steel belly of a mechanical whale, slabs of raw riveted metal and ducts and pipes and thick-glassed gauges describing a naturalist's concept of mechanized hell. He had been aware of the lazy throbbing of the ship's huge pistons maintaining steam since coming aboard, and now he felt as if he were entering the beating heart of a sleeping organism.

A group of men in wilted work suits, some of them bare-chested, stood near the foot of the stairs. Macklin stopped four steps from the bottom and met and held the gaze of a youngish big man with a lank moustache and dark hair plastered to his forehead. After a moment the man's eyes wandered to Macklin's left. Macklin glanced down and saw a thin arc of blood staining a flooring of steel plates in that direction. He descended the rest of the way. The floor was warm beneath his feet.

To his left, a ribbed aisle scarcely broad enough for a man to pass through led past a bank of gauges through a portal into the engine itself. Before continuing he changed hands on the gun and mopped his palm down his rubber-encased thigh, then changed hands again. The checked grip grew slippery again almost immediately. He stepped toward the portal, breathing air that was mostly water.

A bullet struck the edge of the opening to Macklin's right with a resounding clang, *boing*ing around inside the steel walls seconds after the echo of the first impact had faded. He spotted a moving shadow and returned fire. His bullet did some caroming of its own and buzzed across the portal at least twice in opposite directions. The shadow vanished.

"Ackler, you're trapped."

He had to shout to make himself heard over the champing of the engine at parade rest, and to strain his ears for the answer. There was none.

"There's no way out of here except the way we came in."

Still nothing. He put a foot through the opening, braced to withdraw it in a hurry. When no bullets greeted him he entered the rest of the way. The engine clanged and wheezed and threw waves of moist heat into his face. His body slithered and squelched inside the watertight suit.

"It's over, Ackler. There's a doctor on board. We can get you back to port alive."

"That's a point against you, Macklin. I've had all I need of prison."

There were long spaces between the words, which were barely audible over the great racket and impossible to trace. Macklin guessed from the minimal amount of blood the young killer had spilled that he was gutshot, bleeding internally. Turning his head he caught a blur of movement in the corner of his eye and whirled and squeezed off a shot. His bullet clipped a steel lever arm seesawing at the end of a plunging piston rod.

Ackler laughed shrilly, madman's laughter. Something tapped Macklin's left shoulder and he looked down at a gash of white skin showing through black rubber. The report swallowed by the noise of the machinery. He dragged his right forearm across his eyes, clearing them of sweat, glimpsed movement behind the pistons, and fired. Then a blossom of flame opened in the shadows just as the lever arm came up and sparks and bits of metal flew into Macklin's face. He shrieked, dropping his gun and clapping his hands over his eyes.

More laughter. The engine seemed to join in. Keeping his burning eyes shut tight—he was afraid to open them and still not see—Macklin felt around the floor for the gun. He found only floor. Still on all fours, he groped his way behind a shield of boiler plate just as something struck it and made it hum against his hand. He let go, his palm stinging from the vibration. Ackler laughed.

"Ever been hunted, Macklin?"

Hot lights soared and burst behind Macklin's lids, like the optical memory of fireworks after one's eyes have closed. Tentatively he opened them. At first he saw nothing and his heart turned over. Then the rough gray surface of a sheet of dull steel bloomed out of the darkness two inches in front of his face and he would have kissed it had he not known it would burn his lips. He ran a hand over his face and felt the uneven spots where the sparks had burned the skin.

There was enough left of his panic to make his voice quaver convincingly when he called out. "I can't see! Ackler, I'm blind. Help me out of here."

"Gladly."

And then it came flashing at him between the pumping rods and around the leprous support posts and under the tentacles of galvanized pipe, a platinum head atop a slim body in flannel trousers and a checked coat stained dark on the left side and a huge blue muzzle in a tight right hand pointed at him. Seated on the ribbed floor, Macklin braced his shoulders against the boiler and brought the hand he had cocked behind his head forward in a long smooth stroke that ended in a snap.

He hated throwing knives. Three out of ten that were designed for the maneuver were balanced wrong, and the skin diver's weapon, with its heavy handle and curved blade, was designed for anything but. It required compensation.

But the knife executed a credible somersault in the air and righted itself just as Ackler ran into it. Upon impact, the young killer's finger clenched reflexively on the trigger. The muzzle flamed and a light exploded in Macklin's skull with darkness hard on its heels.

CHAPTER 32

HE WAS AN ASSASSIN FOR THE KING AND HE had to make his way back to the palace to report the success of his mission before his master affixed the royal seal to the surrender pact. But his return route lay across a field of the men he had slain and every step he gained he bought by hacking with his broadsword at the half-rotted limbs that rose from the putrefying earth to snatch at his boots and drag him down among them. He swung and swung, his blade slashing through loose gray flesh and sagging sinew until the edge was thick with gore and would no longer cut, and then he used it as a bludgeon to cave in the slick skulls with gaping mouths while the bent green fingers scrabbled and grasped and pulled and his knees gave and he felt himself sinking into the bubbling decay while the corpses moaned and clawed blindly at his arms and chest and face. . . .

He shot upright with a tongueless shout, slinging pain from the top of his head down his left side and around to his right hip and looked about, blinking. He was on a bed in a room with a low rounded ceiling paneled in wood like a barrel lying on its side, naked under a thin quilt that had slid down to his lap. An overhead lamp coaxed a rosy glow out of the varnished oak and he knew in the instant of awakening that he was still on the water. A blind drawn over a window across from the bed stirred with a rhythmic swaying motion. The boat was under power.

He was drenched with sweat, whether from his nightmare or from all the activity in the humid heat of the engine room, he didn't know. Thought of the engine room brought a hand to his forehead, where his fingers traced the outline of a square cloth patch stuck with adhesive above his left eye. He remembered the muzzle flash then, the last thing he had seen before the dream.

He peeled down the quilt and looked at another bandage on his right hip. His leg had been scrubbed of blood and when he moved it he felt an agreeable pull. He was examining further when a young man in a crew uniform entered through a door at the rear of the cabin, gaped at him, then turned around and ducked back out. "He's awake! Mr. Delano! Captain!"

Macklin settled his throbbing head back onto the pillow, listening to the shouts and the answers and footsteps approaching briskly outside. The captain came in, a very tall old man who had to remove his cap and stoop to avoid bumping the ceiling, followed by the crewman and the young intern Macklin had met soon after boarding, three or four hundred years ago. He held up his hand in front of Macklin's face in what the killer at first took for a sign of benediction.

"How many fingers?" asked the young man.

"You're kidding."

"How many?"

"Two."

"Okay." He lowered the hand. "It's not scientific, but it'll do till we get your head under a fluoroscope. How do you feel?"

"Like I've been shot twice and dragged feet first up a flight of stairs."

"Five flights, actually. You're in the first mate's cabin on the crown deck. From what I pieced together of what went on all over this tub I felt you'd earned the soft berth. You're one lucky son of a bitch, you know that? Bullets bend around you. Couple of inches to the right and that crease on your hip would have been through a major artery. And Sol's hand must have jerked when that knife went into him or his bullet would have carried off the back of your head instead of taking the scenic route around the curve of your skull."

"Where is he?"

"With the rest of the dead in the crew's mess. Which I think is appropriate." Delano didn't smile. "You got him square in the heart."

The captain spoke for the first time. "We owe you, son. If you don't get some kind of medal for what you did here, I'll have one struck for you out of my own pocket. You said you're a policeman?"

Delano said, "He's a federal agent. That's how he knew my fiance was on board. Her father's a cabinet minister."

"That right, son? You're FBI?"

"I'm an assassin for the king."

"He's still fuzzy from the blood loss," murmured the intern. To Macklin: "Rest now. I've got another man with a leg wound and some hystericals. The captain's radioed for ambulances at dockside and you'll all be taken care of when we put into Sandusky."

"Radio them again," Macklin said. "Get the state police bomb squad in to defuse the boat. Some of those gelatins are tricky."

"They've already been notified."

Delano turned, and the young sailor held the door for him and the captain. "I'll take the helm, by God," Macklin heard the tall old man say as the door was pulled shut. "First time in five goddamn years."

In a cabinet with louvers in the doors to prevent mildewing, Macklin found a civilian shirt and trousers among the uniforms and pulled on a pair of deck shoes that were a size too large. But the clothes fit fairly comfortably, and after sitting on the edge of the bunk for a moment while his head spun to a rest he got up again and went out through the door leading onto the deck. The intern was just leaving the captain's cabin next door, where the wounded wheel man was recuperating, and approached the killer, shaking his head. It was still dark out and the slipstream from the bow lifted his collar.

"What are you trying to prove? Get back in bed."

"I'll just get stiffer," said Macklin. "I've got work to do when I get to shore. When will that be?"

"About an hour, according to the Captain. You can't walk around with a possible concussion."

Macklin left him standing there and went below, where the passengers, the clouds lifted from their faces, greeted him warmly and asked him questions he ignored. He strolled the decks and climbed up and down stairs, working the stiffness out of his joints and looking at the heel marks in the patches of blood where the slain terrorists had been removed, all except Doris, who had fallen overboard. In the crew's mess he looked at the bodies laid out on the long tables with their hands folded on their chests by some pious amateur mortician: Fay of the angry expression and bloodless gash describing an idiot smile from ear to ear beneath her chin, rat-faced Ray with his intestines gathered back inside the tear under his ribs, his mouth set in a sneer; Teddy, his left side crusted with blood, a blue hole in the side of his head, blood and brains messing up his military crewcut; boyish Larry, seeming to smile with a dot of red in one corner of his mouth and his eyes half-open and shining through the net of his lashes; Don, looking surprised, eyes popping, lips parted to show white teeth behind his gunslinger's moustache, the rude white X all but invisible now against his waxen cheek; Sol of the metallic hair, mussed by his none-too-gentle handling on the way up from the ship's bowels, his face peaceful despite the handle of the knife no one had wanted to remove protruding from his chest.

On a sudden thought, Macklin patted down the body, removed a long envelope from the inside pocket of the smeared and snagged sportcoat, riffled through the bills inside quickly, doubled it and stuffed it into his own hip pocket.

"Do, re, mi," he said.

The shoreline was a jumble of rotating red and blue lights and banks of hard white illumination provided by television camera crews snatching final comments from the authorities present before the boat docked. Police radios turned up to maximum volume drowned the babble of voices under garbled calls. Ambulance attendants in white uniforms smoked cigarettes and waited to wheel their stretchers up the gangplank. When all the lines were fast and the plank clattered down, a cordon of uniformed police officers formed around the end to hold back the reporters and gawkers. Macklin, standing on the dance deck now, spotted a familiar dumpy figure in a gray suit flashing his way through the blue guard with an open leather folder whose celluloid window caught the light. He bounded up the gangplank, his eyes darting among the faces gathered at the rail until they landed on Macklin's. Randall Burlingame seized the killer's arm in a grip that could split bone.

"Come on, I've got a copter standing by."

"Where are we going?" Macklin resisted the pull.

"To a certain elevator I know. Let's go before the fucking press stampedes."

"This man needs medical attention."

The FBI chief glared at Delano. "Who the hell are you?" The intern told him. His expression changed. "Carol Trumble's Delano?"

"Turnbull," he corrected.

"Whatever. She okay?"

"She's fine, but—"

Burlingame turned back toward the gangplank. "Bill! Let him through down there."

A lanky bald man in tinted glasses and a dark suit joined them from the crowd on the dock. Burlingame introduced the stranger as Bill Chilson and sent him off with Delano through the press of passengers. The intern's puzzled protests were swallowed in the confusion.

The FBI man looked Macklin up and down. "You look plenty healthy to me. Shoes are too big."

"They're dead," Macklin said.

"Who?"

"All of them. Siegfried."

"Son of a bitch. All by yourself?"

"Bomb Disposal. Coming through."

They got out of the way of a group of men in green fatigues and billed caps carrying a leaden chest three feet by two feet by its side handles like a coffin.

"Let's move," said Burlingame, after they had passed.

The two descended the gangplank. Behind them, the orchestra stood at the rail, playing "Happy Days Are Here Again" under the direction of a smiling bald man whose toupee perched jauntily atop a bump the size of the Astor ballroom.

The helicopter pilot was a black man with long sideburns, wearing a fisherman's cap and a denim jacket over a gray T-shirt with white lettering spelling out I'D RATHER FLY THAN MAKE LOVE. Macklin strapped himself in behind the pilot and Burlingame climbed into the front passenger's seat and the lazily swooping propeller blades picked up speed with a whine and the craft lifted free of the empty parking lot behind a brick factory building and tilted as it swung around in a climbing arc, its skids narrowly missing a forest of television antennas on the roof of an apartment house. The black surface of Lake Erie to the east was taking on a gray metallic sheen with the coming of dawn.

Burlingame hung an elbow over the back of his seat and raised his voice above the beating of the blades. "One out of every four people standing on that dock is a federal agent. I'm damn glad to be handing this one over to the Ohio headquarters. I have to say I never thought you'd get as far as the second deck, Macklin. Those Jackson cons were as good as sprung."

Macklin said nothing. Away from the scene of his ordeal he felt a deadly fatigue creeping into his limbs and eyelids. He sank his chin onto his chest. Evidently the FBI man noticed, because he said:

"Do you really need a doctor?"

"Just a bed."

"There'll be a room waiting for you at the hotel after the debriefing. I want to get everything that happened aboard that boat down on tape while the details are still fresh. Then Howard Klegg wants to see you. He called the office right after I heard from the Sandusky authorities. I think the old shyster has a tap on our phones. He said he wants to give you something."

"I won't be needing the room," Macklin said. "I've got something to do first."

"If you mean settling things with Maggiore, forget it. At eleven o'clock last night U.S. Treasury agents arrested him for illegally transporting firearms to South America. He'll be tied up in court for the next five years anyway. No matter how it comes out, as a power in the Detroit area he's finished."

Again Macklin made no answer, pretending to sleep. He hadn't been thinking about Maggiore.

CHAPTER 33

THE SUN WAS WELL UP AND SHINING through a thin haze of blue smog icing the buildings of downtown Detroit when Macklin caught a cab from in front of the hotel. Burlingame had told him an agent would be driving his Cougar in from Sandusky. Macklin didn't care if he did. He was carrying nearly a hundred thousand dollars in two envelopes on his person and the good will of his employer's powerful attorney. Klegg had assured him, coming just short of laying his arm across Macklin's shoulders, that he would brush aside the various gnat-bite charges the government would undoubtedly have ready for Boniface the moment he left prison, and that things would be like old times by Thanksgiving. "And while I can't speak for Michael, I wouldn't exactly fall down if you were to find yourself with some new responsibilities—say Midwest sales representative for Addison Camera?"

In the special parlance of the Boniface family, "sales representative" meant enforcer. The position would place Macklin in charge of persuading reluctant corporation presidents from St. Paul to Cincinnati to surrender controlling interest in their companies to his employer in return for not getting strung up on meat hooks for unpaid debts. It meant also a healthy percentage of every dollar he managed to squeeze out of them. The hundred thousand would be pin money. He'd told Klegg he'd have to sleep on the offer.

Burlingame had told him to expect arrest by the Southfield police for Freddo's killing, but that the victim had already been identified from a photograph as the man seen leaving the scene of the apartment house manager's murder in River Rouge; in the light of that discovery, the neighbor who had witnessed the shooting in Macklin's back yard was prepared to swear he'd seen Freddo threatening Macklin with a gun.

As the cab headed west and the cityscape rolling past the window went from vertical to horizontal, flattening into the suburbs, Macklin felt a slight autumn chill and huddled deeper into his borrowed clothing. His feet, sockless in the first mate's oversize shoes, were still cold from having gone bare so long on the clammy decks of the Boblo boat. But the feeling was as much a reaction after the triphammer activity of the past three days as anything. The driver, a sallow-faced Arab with a moustache, saw his passenger hugging himself in the rearview mirror and turned on the heater. The blower whooshed. "Winter coming, eh?" he said. "I'm sure not ready for the cold."

"No one ever is."

The driver made a few more attempts at conversation, but Macklin didn't take it up and they swung north on Greenfield in silence. After eleven blocks Macklin told him to pull over and gave him a hundred-dollar bill. The driver grumbled but made change from an almost-full money box. He drove back to the garage to end his shift.

Macklin hoped he wouldn't remember the man who had handed him the big bill and where he'd let him off. But he'd had nothing smaller. He walked north another five blocks, beginning to limp now.

The front door to the store was locked. His watch read ten of eight. The store didn't open until nine. But there was a light on in back and he grasped the handle and shook the door, rattling it loudly in its frame.

He had been doing this for perhaps thirty seconds when a broad figure emerged from the light into the shadows near the front of the store, gesturing impatiently with one arm toward the sign in the plate glass window listing the business hours.

"Open up, Umberto!" Macklin called. "It's Peter."

After a pause the figure came forward the rest of the way. The light from the display window carved shadows into the rocky hollows of the old Sicilian's face, making him look even more like an Indian than usual. He had a pearl-gray vest on over a striped silk shirt with a silver tie that shone like his hair. He unlocked and opened the door but stood in the entrance. His massive shoulders extended beyond the frame.

Macklin said, "It's done."

Pinelli hesitated. "Ackler as well?" The other nodded. "You were lucky, Pietro."

"Didn't you once tell me that sometimes luck accounts for better than half?"

"But it is not a thing to depend on. You must behave as if it does not exist until it is needed." His eyes flicked toward the bandage on his visitor's forehead. "You are in pain?"

"Yes, Umberto."

The old killer studied his face. After a beat he moved aside to admit Macklin and closed and locked the door behind him. "There is tea in the office."

The storeroom was cluttered as always. Pinelli waved a big hand in the direction of a standing bolt of fabric by way of offering a seat and removed a second cup from the drawer of his gray steel desk and lifted a white china teapot from a hotplate on a shelf of tall ledgers. Macklin remained standing, leaning against the door jamb. "None for me, thanks."

Shrugging, his host topped off his own cup with steaming yellow liquid. Macklin wondered if it was ginseng. "My heart swelled when I saw you, *figlio*." The old man blew on his tea. "The odds were great against you."

"Greater than I'd thought."

He set down the cup untasted. "And now, my friend, you will retire and come to work with me. You can afford to buy in."

"I still don't know anything about selling clothes."

"I will teach you. The eyes are your most important tools. They will tell you what is stylish and what is not. Your eyes are good, like mine. They are one reason we have lived to our respective ages."

"I don't think so, Umberto."

"It would please your wife. That is no small thing, whatever other problems you may have. The pain of my existence is that I did not listen to my Clovis when she pleaded with me to change occupations. It killed her. That is why I gave her name to this store. It is small penance and does no one good."

"I won't have a wife much longer," Macklin said. "That's done too."

"I am sorry, Pietro. Will you then marry Christine?"

Macklin paused. "I'd forgotten you knew about her."

"We confide in each other much. I myself have told you more than I have any priest."

"Not just me."

Pinelli had been standing with one foot propped up on a wooden forklift pallet. Now he lowered it to the floor and leaned back against the desk, folding his arms and bunching further the mound of muscle atop his shoulders. "I wish you would tell me of your trouble, the one that brings you here today."

"I think you know. I saw it in your face when you opened the door."

Unexpectedly, the Sicilian flashed Macklin his old wolf's grin. "I am proud. It was I who taught you to read faces, remember?"

"Stop it! That proud tutor act has been phony from the start."

"No, *amico mio*." The grin was gone. "It was not, as you say, phony. It was never that."

Macklin said, "I accused Christine of informing on me to the FBI. She denied it but I didn't believe her. I thought because Randall Burlingame knew enough to try to reach me at her number, she was the one who filled their file on me. But you

234

knew I was seeing her. And you knew about some of the hits I made, because I discussed the knottier ones with you before making them. Christine couldn't have known about them. The Feds did. Not enough to convict, not on hearsay when their informer refused to testify. But enough to hobble me if I ever came in handy.

"What did they promise you, Umberto?" he asked. "I'd always thought you were incorruptible."

The storeroom-office swelled with silence. Macklin watched Pinelli's expression, but without the element of surprise there was no reading the face of a man who had been reading faces since before he was born. The old killer unfolded his great arms, looked down at his hands. There was no shame in the gesture, only sadness.

"There are no incorruptibles, Pietro. Not one. I would not have had you know for anything. I would rather you'd died on that boat."

Macklin felt his face get haggard. Until that moment he had hoped the old man would deny it, even lie. He would then have gone away to convince himself. Now he spoke from the depths of his exhaustion.

"What could you have wanted that would make you do it? You have money."

This time it was Pinelli who looked hurt. "How could you think I would do this thing for money? How could you think that? I did it for freedom."

"You are free."

"No man is free who owes a debt. I told an untruth on my application for citizenship. It was an old arrest, for a small burglary during my youth in Messina. It was so long ago that more than once I thought of it as a childhood nightmare. I made no mention of it. Twice when I was employed here I was summoned to police headquarters for questioning. I was released both times for no evidence, but had the police known of this forgotten untruth I could have been deported. But a federal agent who knew of this questioning took my immigration file home for study. Afterwards he came to me.

"I left enemies in Messina, Pietro, enemies who remember

the old ways. I am strong but I am old and they are many. They would nail me to a tree and slice off my *virilità* and thrust it down my throat to choke me. I am not afraid to die. But I fear dying in this disgraceful way. I could take my own life, but that is the most difficult killing of all when one is still in good health and has his wits. And so once a month, sometimes twice, I meet this young man for lunch and we talk."

"You have nothing to fear from deportation, Umberto," Macklin said after a moment. "You have no *virilità* to lose."

The big man straightened. "It has come to this?"

Macklin's jaw ached. He realized he was grinning. "You're a clown. *Buffone*. You talk of honor and loyalty as if you had any and you've killed, but when a man insults you that's the greatest sin of all."

"To kill is not the sin. Not when it is in the service of one to whom you swear fealty. It matters not to whom, only that you swear and that you uphold the oath."

"Where is the honor in being another man's instrument?"

"You are an instrument too; you forget."

"Not any more. I'm leaving Boniface."

"Then you are retiring?"

"Maybe. Probably not. There won't be a great deal left of the hundred thousand after I divorce Donna. I had a dream. It does no good to be an assassin for the king and be damned for his sins. There are people out there with good reasons to kill but no talent for it. It's a big market and where I agree with those reasons I can make a living. A living from other people's dying," he added, when the thought struck him.

"A wildcat." Pinelli looked grim. "I would see you dead first."

"Just so."

The other hesitated. "This is how you would have it?"

Macklin said it was the way it was.

The wolfishness stole back over the old Sicilian's face. Macklin saw the tension go out of his muscles. "In my country, when a man knows his enemy is looking for him he puts on his finest clothes and goes into the town square to wait for him. But there are no town squares here. A man must make his own." He put a hand behind his back and brought it around holding the knife that had belonged to his great-grandfather. The hand moved quickly and the weapon flipped up and he caught it by the point, then flipped it again so that it landed point-first in the softwood floor halfway between them. Then he removed the studs from his cuffs and put them on the desk. "I am old and not so strong as once I was," he said, turning back the cuffs. "But you are wounded and tired. It should be an even contest. One of us will remain here. The other will watch the sun set tonight."

Hours later, Macklin decided that he had seen better sunsets.